Child of Three Halves

By Harlowe Frost

ISBN eBook: 978-1-959981-26-8
ISBN paperback: 978-1-959981-27-5
ISBN hard back: 978-1-959981-28-2

Editor: Weslee Imrisek
Developmental Editor: Angela Grimes
Cover Art: Getcovers.com
Formatting: Huckleberry Rahr

Books In the Kam Strega Series

Series 1: Child of Three Halves Saga

Book 1: Glass Witchling

Book 2: Child of Three Halves

Book 3: Prophecy's End

Series 2: Lucere Amon Saga

Book 1: Demon's Intrigue

Book 2: Hope of Angels and Demons

Book 3: Angel's Dream

Content Warning:

- This is a high spice book.

- There are male/female, female/female, as well as, male/male open-door scenes.

- There is bed play with toys.

- Because there are vampires, there will be mentions of blood.

- There is dubious consent and non-consent in this book.

Chapter 1

"Can she even have a baby?"

Several of the witches in the meeting turned to Casey where she sat in the coven circle to see how she reacted to Perry's query. She sat amongst the witches, but the scents of the barn distracted her from their words. The barn smelled of the herbs Hildegard, the coven leader, had hung from the rafters last year to dry and recently simmered into spells. The boiled potions saturated the air of the barn, filling Casey's nose with the scents of spice, love, and death. Part of Casey's mind was busy cataloging, trying to figure out what the coven's leader had brewed, the rest took in the ire of the witches in the room.

Licking her lips, she rubbed her hands on her skirt, and searched the eyes of the other coven members. Some were wide with wonder, others cold with calculation. She knew what they were thinking. About three and a half years ago, she'd been attacked by a vampire, and now she was both a witch and a vampire. If that hadn't happened, this would've been the year of her testing to become a full coven witch, but after her attack, the coven had voted, and Hildegard had moved her test up.

Thinking back on her transformation and testing made her think of her vampire family and Rowan the head of her clan. She suppressed a smile thinking of him. Working together to educate the general population about vampires, they hoped to counteract all the misinformation still circulating. Though the truth of their existence had been out for years, normal people were still scared. Rowan worked hard to change that. In the early part of the process, a prophecy came to her: A child of three halves, combined of the immortal and hexed, will bring the unity or destruction of the ancient clans.

The only thing vampires and witches agreed on: she ... Casey ... was to be the mother. Both vampire and witch, she brought two of the three parts. No other person, to her knowledge, held two heritages.

Casey rolled her shoulders back, gazing into Perry's eyes. "My control is much better than it was at the start. I can stay female for nine months. Besides that, I've spoken to vampires from my family who've become pregnant, and even when they morph to male, the body doesn't lose the parts to protect the baby. So, yes, I *can* have a baby."

His sneer grew as the scent of disgust wafted off him. "But what's to say the prophecy is even about you. And are you supposed to have a baby with one of us?" He threw his hands out to encompass the group of old witches surrounding him. "Or a vampire?" He spat the last words out like a curse.

Sunray smirked. "Have we even decided that with Casey being witch and vampire, the third of the prophecy isn't human?"

A general groan reverberated around the room. "No more of that." Grandpa said quietly. "We know the baby has to be of three supernatural parts and my granddaughter brings two. We've joked about werewolves, which aren't real, nor are there any other shifters about."

Sunray raised an eyebrow. "Do we *really* know that?"

"Enough!" Hildegard snapped out, knocking her walking stick on the ground, the silver point digging deep into the dirt floor, the dragon at the top appearing ready to take flight. She turned to the instigator of the topic. "Perry, are you propositioning our young Casey?"

A growl came from Grandpa Parker. Glaring across the circle, he snapped, "My granddaughter is twenty-five. Can we let her finish her finals and graduate from college before we whore her out like a broodmare?"

Spinning to glare, Perry snapped, "We have to figure this out. If she gets pregnant by one of those blood suckers, then they'll own the baby. Do we really want that?"

Next to Perry, a slightly rotund man with thick, curly brown hair, sat Tilly, a slender woman with wavy red hair. She smirked as she faced him. "Goodness, Perry, your understanding of women and children really explains your current lifestyle, doesn't it? Let me try to explain this: it's the nineteen eighties, we are progressive now! The baby will be Casey's. She will be the mom. If she has the baby with someone she cares for, she may share the raising with him, or, she may raise it where she lives—which is primarily with the vampires."

As she spoke, Perry's face began to turn redder and redder. "I know how these things work, Tilly. I'm not an idiot. But we need to control the situation. Just because you've become a blood-sucker lover, doesn't mean the rest of us are in their thrall. We need to get Casey out of that house and back with us. We need to control the situation."

Across the circle, Damion, wearing dark jeans and a t-shirt, with his dark hair cut short, and dark eyes twinkling, considered Perry. He slowly crossed his arms. "Are you planning on volunteering to be Casey's blood donor while she's living here? She needs at least two full time blood donors, and I assume, if you demand her relocation, you'll be one of them?"

Perry's eyes almost bugged out. "No!" he spat. "What do you mean? There's no way she's taking any of my blood."

Pinching the bridge of her nose, Casey bit her lip, ready for the topic to be over. *I've had enough of this!* "Look, I live in the city, I'm not moving back here. I'm not going to go out of my way to get pregnant. From what I understand, that isn't how prophecies work. It will happen when it happens. Damion's right, I need to get blood regularly, and living at Cambia House allows for that. There are trainers living at the house, which has helped me figure out how to control my new abilities. I've learned most of what I need to know about vampires, but not everything. It's good to be close if I have questions. It's also close to school. Living there is just too convenient, and I like living near the city."

Again, the walking stick thumped the floor. "There are other topics we need to discuss. Skyler's testing is coming up. We need to determine testers. Her strength is fire, but we need a variety of witches."

As people volunteered, Casey thought back over the meeting. This was the third time the topic of her possible pregnancy had come up over the years. Grandpa had warned her that Perry had been snarling about the prophecy and she should be ready. He wanted her back near the coven and away from the vampires. She had debated skipping this meeting because of school, but she needed to hear the arguments firsthand and be ready to defend herself.

"And Casey will finish off the list in mind magic."

Her head snapped up as Hildegard called her out. "What? Me?"

"Yes, Casey. It's been long enough. I know you and Skyler were friends, but you are the strongest mind witch we have—save me—and we need to get you into testing rotation."

Groaning on the inside, she just nodded with a slight smile. Dread filled her at the thought of assessing others, but she knew her responsibility as a coven witch ... as much as it made her stomach churn. Shortly after the witches to be examined were selected, the meeting ended, and everyone filed out. Casey gave her grandpa a hug. "I miss you already, Grandpa, but there is so much studying to do these next few weeks."

"Is it safe for you to drive, honey child?"

She smiled at his name for her. She leaned down to give him a kiss on his cheek. His scent of Old Spice and the garden reminded her of her childhood. "Yes, I'll be fine."

"Okay, honey. Don't let Perry get to you; it'll be fine. Now, go on and get going. I know vampires like the night, but I still worry. Call me when you get home."

Grandpa turned away as she opened the door of the green VW bug she'd named Chameleon. She held the door open for an extra few seconds to allow a white ferret to sneak in. As she pulled out, the ferret curled up on the floorboards of the passenger seat. She drove onto the interstate and began the long trek back home.

Casey glanced down at the floor of the car and smiled at the small furry animal. Normally, she'd want to pet such a cute creature, but today she resisted her urges. She wouldn't want to give the wrong impression.

Once well away from the coven barn, the ferret jumped to the passenger seat and, after a few minutes, began to shimmer. Casey kept her eyes on the road. The animal morphed and, with magic she didn't understand, became Cyran, one of the master vampires of her family.

When she became a vampire of Rowan's family, it shocked her to learn her body would suddenly present male outside her control. Her transition to vampire wasn't normal, and she didn't know that taking life's blood would trigger this aspect of her family's magic. Too young to gain this skill as a vampire, she didn't have control over her body's shifts. Now, three and a half years later, she could choose when her body wore female or male bits.

Though many people in the vampire and witch communities knew about the gender shifts, the ability to shape change to other things, like a ferret, was a hidden secret. Casey's abilities weren't at that level yet.

Completely comfortable in his skin, Cyran sat naked next to her. He smiled suggestively. "So, that meeting went well."

Used to the bodies of the people in her house, Casey watched the road closely, ignoring him, though her mouth twitched. "Are you going to stay naked the whole ride?"

"Maybe. Is it bothering you?"

She tried to force her heart rate down, knowing he could hear it. "You wish," she mumbled as he laughed, navigating a curve in the road. It was late and there weren't many other cars, but the ones approaching her seemed obsessed with leaving their high beams on. Nearly blinded, she half feared she'd run them into the shoulder or worse, a tree.

Cyran leaned back to grab a shirt and a pair of shorts from the back seat. "Are you ready for your exams?"

That got her focus straightened out as she thought of a week of testing. She shook her head. "No, that's why I'm driving now. I need to study."

A smile stretched across his face, Cyran turned to Casey and winked. "What are you going to do about Perry? Graduate, move up here, and date the guy until you get pregnant?"

She leaned over and punched him in the arm and mimed gagging.

He laughed and rubbed the spot she hit. "Just checking. The witches aren't the only ones wondering what you'll do."

"It isn't like drinking blood has left me celibate. It will happen when it happens."

"That's true, but your blood-taking and bed sport is with humans, not vampires. Unless I've missed something. Maybe you need a master vampire. You needed Lucas to open the door. Maybe the prophecy is waiting for power. How about you talk to Lucas ... hook up with him."

Though Lucas appeared to be about twenty-five, he was the oldest vampire she'd ever met. She wasn't sure how old he was, but being around him, she could feel the years on him. The prophecy that predicted a child of three halves would come from her appeared when he entered her mental glass bubble, and with magic of his own helped her open a magical door. Through the door they found a book written in a language older than time, and from what she could tell, only Lucas could read it.

Squeezing the steering wheel, Casey glared at the road. "Can we please not talk about who will knock me up?"

"Fine. How about Kailey? She becomes a vampire this summer. Thoughts?"

Relaxing with the change of topic, Casey almost danced in her seat. "I know, it will be so weird having her as a vampire. You're probably more used to having people you know make the switch."

"Yeah, but it's always weird at first. Do you think Jen will ever switch sides?"

"Like, go for girls?" It was his turn to hit her arm. She snorted. "No, she's all human all the way."

"Such a waste. She'd be a great vampire and fantastic to have around forever."

Casey grasped her chest. "Are you in love?"

"Hush! Don't use such words! Vampire love is few and far between."

She rolled her eyes at him. "You're such a dork."

"Hey, how tired are you? Need me to drive? I slept most of the day while you were socializing with the family."

"Not a bad idea. I could use a break."

Casey pulled to the side of the dark road. They switched places and she curled up, resting her head against the window.

With a chuckle, Cyran said, "You *do* know you're a vampire, Case; you're supposed to sleep during the day, live during the night!"

With a grunt, she turned to narrow her eyes at him. "I'm a student. I have finals coming up. If it's *that* important, oh, leader, I can retrain my body then."

Cyran's eyes sparkled as he rotated to face her. "I'm just saying ... three years in, you could be a better vampire."

"Bite me." It would've been more threatening without the yawn.

He chuckled. "You keep saying that, but where's the follow-through?"

Beyond being her teacher, she'd never had follow-through with Cyran because he was a vampire. Vampires needed blood, and blood from other vampires didn't fit the bill. Although it would work in a pinch, it wouldn't fulfill the need for blood in the long run. Casey took blood to fulfill the need, not for sexual pleasure, and that was what sharing blood vampire to vampire tended to do. Because of the prophecy, Casey had been avoiding romance with other vampires. *Just one less thing to worry about.*

Chapter 2

Casey sat in the front room under the large picture window where the sun streamed in and brought out the oak table's warm, rich tones. A few other people lounged over their books about the room, quietly reading. She studied social psychology, one of her more challenging classes. She found the subject fascinating and frustrating in equal parts. The professor had scheduled an exam in preparation for finals in two and a half weeks. Then came graduation.

Living in Cambia House, activities came up, so Casey had studied ahead and was prepared for a weekend study break. Despite that, she wanted to get in every second of study that she could.

"Okay, everyone, come and get the itinerary for the weekend."

Putting down her book, Casey looked up. Her friend, Jen, stood by the front door holding a clipboard, surrounded by duffle bags, vampires, and fully human blood donors. With a grumble, Casey closed up her books, rose from her seat, and joined the crowd. She wasn't really annoyed; Jen had been bouncing and bubbly about this trip for over a month. Mostly, Casey agreed and supported Jen. There was only one bit she worried about.

Jen searched the faces of her 'volunteers.' ... 'voluntolds?' "This weekend, we're camping out in the forest. You are going to learn how to survive in the wilderness ... *without your magic*. I want each of you to reach into this bag and pull out a silver bracelet. The silver will dampen your ability to use your fancy vampire tricks. The animal on the bracelet you choose matches another person's. Whoever has the matching animal will be your partner for the two-day excursion."

Kailey raised her hand and Jen pointed to her. "Are we partnering up a vampire with a donor?"

"No. All the vampires should've fed earlier today and should be good for at least three days. The bracelets will be locked on by me and I'll be the only one who can take them off."

Jaxon, who was tall with shaggy blond hair and shiny blue eyes and had been a vampire a few years longer than Casey, reached into the bag to grab a bracelet. He snapped his bracelet on and held his wrist out to Jen. "So, we're powerless until you let us go?"

She locked the bracelet on with a key. "Yep. I want you to learn how to survive if you're ever cut off from your superpowers." Her smile and exaggeration took away a bit of the sting of being shackled.

He studied the crowd. "Why is it just us newbies? Shouldn't the older vamps be here, too? I mean, I remember being human."

"I don't," Casey mumbled low. Glancing over at Jaxon's wrist she asked, "What animal did you get?"

"A donkey?"

Jen rolled her eyes. "That's a horse, you nitwit!"

Laurel, a shorter woman, and the most recent addition to Rowan's vampires, said, "I've never heard about silver, what does it do?" She reached in and grabbed a trinket. Her brown eyes, which perfectly matched her brown hair, brightened as she smiled. "Oooh, is this a unicorn?"

Jaxon poked his head over her shoulder. "I want a unicorn. I'm stuck with this ass, and she gets a unicorn?"

Casey snorted. "Silver has some quality that blocks all magic. No one's really sure why."

Laurel held her wrist out to Jen while staring at Casey. "All magic? Like, even witches?" Though Laurel asked her in particular, Casey was fairly certain Laurel didn't know *about* her. Growing up, Casey had learned to keep her secret. When she started college, she knew her admittance depended on being strictly human. Even now, after all these years, within the family, only a few vampires and human donors knew she was also a witch ... Laurel wasn't one of them.

Casey reached inside Jen's bag. Her bracelet had a dragon on it. She snorted. "Really Jen? A dragon?"

Jen grinned. "Couldn't plan it, Case."

Casey held out her arm with the bracelet for Jen to lock. Suddenly, everything she was became muffled and dampened out. *Gods above, I've never felt like this before.* Casey reeled, the room spinning around her. Arms caught her before she fell to the ground.

A voice whispered low in her ear. "You okay?"

"I ... I don't know." Gazing up, she saw Jaxon's clear blue eyes. "I guess I'm just used to the magic."

Another voice flowed over her. "Let me help." A new hand slid around her, supporting her. Jaxon moved away as Casey rested her head against the new chest. Finally, she looked up and stared into the pale green eyes of their leader. A sense of calm flowed through her seeing Rowan and feeling his strength. She leaned in and let him take more of her weight for a second before she tried to get her own feet.

Suddenly, it hit her that he stood with them, and without thinking, she blurted out, "What are you doing here?"

Rowan smiled. "I thought I'd learn how to survive in the wilderness without my powers."

She raised an eyebrow and asked, "You're going out with us?"

"Yep, just grabbed my jewelry." He raised his free arm where the silver bracelet glinted. "Apparently, I'm a lizard."

Jen came over and placed a hand on Casey's arm. "You going to be okay?"

Casey rubbed her forehead. "I've never felt like this ... is this how you live all the time? I feel so ... blind."

Rowan's arm tightened around her as Jen gave her a quirky half-smile. Jen waggled her brows. "It'll be good for you, buttercup." She turned to the group at large. "Everyone should find your animal partner. This will be the person who will help you survive over the next two nights. They'll also help with tomorrow's challenges."

He leaned down. "Think you can stand on your own?"

Casey closed her eyes and took stock. "Yeah, I think I'm good." She pushed away and tested out her balance, holding her hands out to the sides. She took a breath and was about to search for her dragon mate, but everyone had already paired off. With a sigh, she slid her focus to Rowan. She grabbed his wrist and studied his 'lizard.'

"Do you even know what a lizard is? This isn't a lizard."

"Not a lizard?" He inspected the bracelet on his wrist, frowning.

She shook her head and gazed up at him. "Not a lizard."

Rowan squinted, looking at it closer. "What is it then?"

She sighed. "A dragon."

On the drive to the park, Casey visited her mental glass bubble. All witches had one, a mental scape to protect their minds and store their magic. When she'd first become a vampire, she'd thrown her mind into her glass bubble and that had saved her from dying. With the silver, she hoped both that she could access it and that what she stored in it was safe.

Though she was on the bus, she still felt drained and dizzy without her magic. She didn't know how the vampires felt, but she felt off. Despite her queasy state, her bubble still existed in her mind. Her magic felt dark, like a house with the power turned off.

Standing in the center, she turned in a circle and saw her library with all her books, the door of prophecy, and *the* book. The book that had appeared when she and Lucas finally got the door to open. The book that held the prophecy stating she would bring the child of three halves. Several other people had tried to help her open the door, but it had finally been Lucas's presence that got the door to open and the book to appear. She assumed his age, the rumor of him being the oldest vampire alive, had convinced the door to open.

A wave of relief flooded her at the sight. Even without her magic, she had everything she needed to protect her mind.

Jaxon, sitting near her, sniffed. "Casey, did you use a new perfume? You smell great."

Laurel lifted her nose. "He's right, you smell really nice! Why gussy yourself up for a camping trip?"

Next to her, Rowan's mouth twitched, as he tried to keep a blank face. He knew why she smelled good to the other vampires on the bus. Without her magic, her shields were down, and the vampires on the trip would smell her witchy scent, which apparently attracted them.

Inwardly groaning, she lifted her hands out to the sides. "Probably too much time in the kitchen baking this week." Every vampire in the house had a job, and Casey was assigned the kitchen, especially baking.

When Rowan first invited Casey to move into Cambia House, she'd resisted. She hadn't wanted anything to do with vampires. But eventually she'd realized she needed to learn how to control what was happening to her. Jen had helped at the beginning, and her abilities as a trainer were recognized by Rowan and Cyran so that she, too, was invited to move into Cambia House to help vampires hone their skills.

Jaxon's brows knitted together, then he shrugged. "Maybe that's it."

Once they arrived and parked, they carried the bags a couple of miles up into the woods. Jen had selected a park just outside of town with old oaks, eucalyptus, and redwoods. The canopy was thick, and the sky only peaked out cerulean blue in spots. The scent of eucalyptus infused the area.

Jen read from her checklist of jobs. Some were assigned setting up the tents, others collecting wood, and the list went on. Casey and Jaxon were assigned to cook dinner. Apparently, these jobs were assigned before the bracelet pairing, based on skill sets. Rowan and two others set about building a fire. They'd selected a spot with downed trees, so they'd have a place to sit and enjoy their evening. Tonight's plan was eating and stargazing. Eventually, Jen would fill them in on the rest of the trip.

Once the logs started popping with the heat of the flames, Jaxon found the rack and got it balanced over the flames.

Casey watched Jaxon use the tongs to get the cooking surface level. She finally raised an eyebrow and whispered to her friend, "You know, Jen, with magic, dinner would be *much* better ... and faster."

Jen gazed back at her with wide eyes and said mockingly, and equally as quietly, making sure only Casey could hear her. "Can you actually cook without any special skills? Monica seems to think you can."

Casey threw a marshmallow at Jen. Monica was the house chef and had recruited Casey early on as a baker. After tasting her treats, Monica decided Casey would work in the kitchen. Though Casey could create baked goods magically, she often did it the old-fashioned way as well. It was a connection she'd kept with her deceased grandma.

Jen caught the marshmallow and popped it into her mouth.

Jaxon finally got everything set up, and they started cooking hot dogs. Getting into a groove, Casey turned to her cooking partner, avoiding sparks from the fire. "Why don't you go find good sticks for the marshmallows? That way we're set for the s'mores."

His eyes narrowed. "Are you sure you have this?"

Not sure if she should feel amused or frustrated, Casey's face scrunched up and her shoulders hit her ears as she gazed at Jaxon. "You didn't actually believe Jen, did you? I mean, I work in the kitchen. You do know I cook almost daily. Go, get the wood, let me work."

He laughed as he trotted off.

Once everyone had eaten their hot dogs and were enjoying their sticky deserts—roasted marshmallows sandwiched in gram crackers with half a chocolate bar—Jen explained what they should expect for the rest of their adventures. "Tomorrow, you and your partner will search out five plants that can help you if you are injured. They're on this list, including descriptions. Once you've found the plants, return here."

Jaxon leaned forward. "Is it a race? Are there prizes?" His brows danced as he got excited.

His partner, Jess, sitting next to him, with her blond hair up in a ponytail, knocked her shoulder into him. "Really, Jax? Are prizes all you think of?"

He faced her. "Come on, Jess, you don't? Think of it, we're great together, we could *totally* win."

"Casey knows more about herbs and plants than anyone I know, and her partner is *Rowan.* Like, really, come on. Do you think we'd win?" she said as her face dropped.

Jaxon turned to them slowly, studying the competition, then his nose scrunched up. "Yes. We can beat them. Rowan's been traveling on and off for years; they barely know each other." He started to bounce, and he turned to her. "We, love, work together all the time. We've got this."

Casey laughed. "It's either us or you? That's it? You know, there are three other teams."

Reis laughed. "I think I know as much about plants as I did about the city before moving here from the burbs."

With a punch to his arm, Kailey snarled, "You are not leaving me to lead us to victory, buster. And these two teams are not the only ones in contention. Buck up!"

Laurel snickered. "Y'all are insane. This is more than knowing the plants, it's finding them."

A low growl came from Jen. "Enough. This is about survival, not competition. Now, get some sleep. I know you all love the nights, but I'm waking you up early."

There were four big tents. Casey crawled into one and found her sleeping bag. The day had started off early in class and hadn't gotten better. She still felt dizzy and empty with the silver bracelet on. She knew silver only dampened her magic, but she'd never played around with it before now.

It was dumb of me to have never experienced this before, and smart of Jen to force it on us. I need to figure this out in case it ever happens again. Rolling to her side, she tried to get some sleep.

The next morning, after a cup of strong coffee, Casey and Rowan headed out with their list of plants. Each of the five teams were given a direction to go with the goal to have them not run into each other. Despite his love of well-tailored suits, Rowan wore jeans and a black shirt with David Bowie holding a globe. Underneath were the words: *You remind me of the babe.* Casey wore jean shorts and a pale blue button down top.

They weaved between the eucalyptus trees in search of the items on the list.

They stopped when they couldn't hear the others. Rowan faced her and leaned over the sheet of paper to look at the front with the images of the plants and their names. "Chicory, stinging nettles, comfrey, yarrow, and plantain."

After he had studied the front, he flipped the paper over to read why the plants were important. Though Casey knew for the most part, she read along with him. "If we find the chicory, maybe it'll help us wake up."

Rowan snorted, then pointed at the description of the stinging nettles. "True, and chicory can help if we have a parasite in our intestines, very important; but look here, if we are desperate for food, and willing to dare the nettles of this plant, we'll eat like kings ... or queens ... maybe just royalty."

Casey continued to read. She decided she liked the list Jen had put together. "Then we have the first aid plants. Comfrey, if we can get the roots, and mash them, will help with a sprained ankle or bruises, and yarrow will stop the bleeding of whatever caused us to sprain our ankle, if there's blood."

"And last, to save ourselves from poison, plantain." Rowan chuckled. "Our Jen has thought of all the basics. A good list indeed. Ready to go searching?"

"I am." They started off side by side. After a few minutes, she shot him a quick look. "Have you enjoyed your recent travels?"

His shoulders sagged. "Not really. I mean, the goal has been good. The coalition that we've created here has been a great start. Other cities in the U.S., and then those abroad, were curious how to start one. But spending so much time away from my power base has been draining. A week now and again at home just isn't enough."

She knelt to inspect a patch of likely-looking herbs. Nope, not what she thought she saw. "Does that mean you're back for good?"

"Yes, that's the plan. There are enough boards started now that I believe they don't need me to travel. The idea of what we want is now fully understood; it is no longer shiny and new."

"That's good. You've been missed." Casey felt her face heat, so she looked intently under a bracken fern. "I mean, Cyran does well in your absence, but ... you are the head of the family, not him."

He chuckled as they continued the search. His eyes narrowed. "Is that one of the plants?"

She reached into her pocket and pulled out the sheet with their five plants and descriptions. She held the page out to him, and he went to grab it, but a stiff wind tore the page from her, whipping it around, high and out of reach through the trees.

For a second, they both watched as the paper twirled and spun in the air before flying away. Sharing a bewildered gape, they both took off after the paper detailing their goal for the day. Like a kid's game of chase, the page fluttered through the trees on the wind currents, sliding between the branches and leaves as Casey and Rowan pounded after it.

As they ran, Casey felt like a fool. She knew all the plants on the page, but the point was using the clues. All she had to do was hold on to the damn paper.

An updraft lifted the page higher as they both reached for it—and then Casey's heart plummeted along with her body as she tumbled down a cliff. Jabs of pain vibrated through her side and back as she bounced down. Her arms wrapped around her head in protection.

A small ledge caught her as she landed in a crumpled pile a second before Rowan crumpled down next to her. Heart pounding, her body began to tremble as the pain of her fall took over. Slowly opening her eyes, she took in the area around her. Behind them was a small inlet that may be considered a cave but, staring up, she knew it was too high and sheer to climb.

As she gazed up the way they'd fallen, the page flew like a bird in the sky, out of sight. Above all, she saw was a small strip of blue of the sky, with the green leaves of the trees reaching up to grab at the few clouds. Casey felt that need, too, knowing she couldn't reach the clouds, much less the ground the trees grew from. She searched the sheer face of the cliff they'd tumbled down. She saw no jutting rocks, no handholds, nothing they could use to climb out.

They were trapped.

Chapter 3

Casey stopped trying to find an exit strategy and lamented her torn outfit and bruised body. She liked these clothes. She knew shock guided her motions, but she feared her next move. Her eyes stung a bit since Rowan hadn't made a sound.

She braced before turning to stare at Rowan crumpled next to her. He lay in a heap, not moving. Her stomach in the back of her throat, she tried to form words. "You okay?" The wispy sound of her voice surprised her.

A grunt proceeded his roll to his back. His clothes were as ruined as hers and he bled from a cut on his arm. He gazed up the cliff, then over at her sitting beside him. The sky shimmered, a small blue slit far above them. "Ouch ... you know, if we didn't have these bracelets on, this would be much simpler." His voice slid over her like a soft blanket, though his worry cut through to her center.

She gave him a half-smile. "Right, but now we get to figure it out the human way. Do you see any comfrey? It's good for bruising."

"Have you ever done *anything* the human way?" His brow rose in challenge, then he searched the shear wall and ledge, free of vegetation, and snorted. "Maybe if you'd picked a different ledge for us to land on, we'd have some useful plants from that list."

A bubble of laughter threatened her. She pursed her lips to keep from laughing. "Next time we fall down a cliff, dear leader, I'll aim better." She rubbed her temples as her head throbbed. "When was the last time *you* were human? I mean, let's not throw stones here."

He snorted and managed to get to a sitting position, legs out, leaning back on the cliff wall. He flinched at the tears in his outfit. "Fair enough."

"So, now what?"

"We wait, I guess. Someone will find us eventually."

She fidgeted with her jewelry and glanced upward. "You can't work your way around the bracelet?"

"Can you?"

Casey slumped. "I should be home studying for the exam I have this week. And finals. I mean, I prepared for this time away from my books, but this isn't the best use of my time."

He reached over, grabbed her hand, and gave it a squeeze. "Was Jess correct? Did you know all the plants that we were looking for?"

"Yeah. I've been scouring the forest with Hildegard, our coven leader, and my grandpa, for years. Before that, I helped my grandma with her garden when I was little. Between those two things, I knew all five items on the list. How about you?"

"I knew four of the five. I used to live in the country and the more you knew about the plants growing around you, the safer you were."

Casey shifted so her back was against the cliff wall, then stretched out her legs. "Tell me about your childhood," she said, darting a glance at him "... or is that some sort of house secret?"

He shook his head. "Not a secret, just not something I've told many people. I guess no one asks; they all figure it *is* a secret."

"Well, I'm asking." Casey shot a look at him from the side. *He's all alone ... and someone has to care. I care.*

He scooted over so that he sat closer to her, their shoulders touching. "Let's see if I remember back that far." He gave a small smile, staring across at the far cliff wall. "I come from a small farm town in Italy that isn't there anymore. I was the eldest child born in my family. I had four younger brothers and sisters, two of each. Life on the farm was good—until I turned fifteen. My mom died and my dad went into a depression. That's not what we called it then, but that's what it was. It fell to me and my next eldest sibling, a brother, Ermanno, to support the family."

Rowan gazed over the cliff's edge for a bit. The distance to the ground gave Casey vertigo. Rowan seemed to search the bottom for unknown answers. "Ermanno was at such a loss. No doubt, he felt the world bearing down on his young shoulders and he needed to do everything to provide for the family. He took over the running of the farm and our day-to-day life. I tried to help, but he refused. I'm surprised he didn't try to marry us all off.

"One day I went into town to trade for some ingredients we needed to bake bread. It may be hard to believe, but I can bake a mean loaf of bread."

Casey chuckled. The thought of Rowan cooking was beyond her imagination. *He's never even been in the kitchen, as far as I know. Does he know where it is?*

"I must have been about eighteen at the time. While trying to trade my sister's embroidery for coin, I ran into a man. I didn't recognize him as the leader of the local vampire house. He offered me gold, not for the decorative cloth, but to hire me. My brother, my family, we were desperate for money. I agreed. I didn't tell my brother, but I became a blood whore for the vampires. For Ashby, their leader. Times were different then. Vampires were out and known in the larger towns and cities. However, my family was provincial, off on a farm. They wouldn't have understood."

Casey sat enthralled by each word revealed to her, like a gift. She flinched at the idea of him being a blood whore but didn't know how that may have been different back then.

He rubbed his face as she assumed he thought about his past, then he reached down to clasp Casey's hand again. A warmth infused her. "I would go home at night to be with my brothers and sisters but spend my days in town with the vampires. I told my family—my brother—I had a job; that's where the money came from. It took a few years for my brother to learn what my job was. He promptly disowned me."

Casey frowned, furrowing her brow. "Weren't you the older brother? Didn't you have some say in all this?"

"No. I didn't even get to say good-bye to my sisters and youngest brother. It was another year before Ashby turned me."

Even with the silver blocking all her magic, the emotions pouring off Rowan were clear. Twisting to her knees, she leaned over and embraced him. He hugged her back, resting his head on her shoulder. "I haven't thought about them in years." His words were soft, almost lost in their embrace.

"Did you ever go back to see them?"

"I did, but they never knew. My brother grew up bitter, never marrying. He did eventually marry my sisters off; they were much happier for that. My youngest brother inherited the farm when Ermanno died. He married a lovely lass and had a litter of kids." The tenderness in his voice told her everything she needed to know about his feelings about family.

She swung back around to sit next to him. "How long did you follow them?"

"I still know where some of my family's descendants live today, but the connection to me is thin."

"Any more vampires?"

"No. One of my sister's lines became vampire hunters. I lost track of them when they moved to the new world. I ended up here, but years later. They'd married and changed names enough that it was tricky to follow. Landing here often brings a change of the name as well."

"You have family that are vampire *hunters*?"

He huffed a laugh. "I know, it's ironic."

"Have you always been called Rowan?"

"I have, but like your name, it's a fluid name. It works if I present as male or female. Not all vampires from our family can do that. I've lucked out with that."

"So, you've tricked people into thinking you're female. I've always wondered what you'd look like as a female." She gave him a wink. "How long *can* a vampire go in the sex opposite from what they were born as?"

Rowan's mouth twitched. "That, my dear, is an excellent question."

Narrowing her eyes, she tried again. "What is the longest time you know a vampire has gone?"

He bumped her shoulder. "I've never timed it. We can ask Cyran to run tests if you'd like."

"No, I was just curious." She narrowed her eyes at him, considering.

"Any more questions? Though, I do shudder to open up that Pandora's box with you." He smiled wide, chuckling. *It's nice to hear him laugh.*

Turning to face him, she glared at him, but his laugh made her smile, taking away a bit of the sting. "I wasn't going to, but now, with that, I have to, you know. Why no girlfriend, or permanent lover?"

He rested his head on the rocks behind him. "How do I know if the person is with me for my position or me?"

"Talk to them?"

He raised his eyebrows. "Is it that easy?"

She shrugged. "I dunno. I'm twenty-five. I still haven't figured any of this stuff out. I'm just trying to determine how to stay out of people's heads, graduate college, and how I'm going to be part of Skyler's testing in a few weeks."

He rotated his head towards her. "Have you done testing before?"

"Nope."

"And Skyler is?"

"We were friends ... with benefits. And when I became a vampire, she dumped me. It was one weird thing too many, I guess. I haven't seen her at any of the coven meetings since; she only goes when she knows I won't be there. Grandpa says she's been pretty scarce, off studying on her own. So, she's been avoiding me over the years. Makes a gal feel great."

Taking her hand and giving it a squeeze, Rowan asked, "And this is who the leaders chose for your first testing subject?"

"Yep."

"Sounds fun."

Casey snorted. "So not fun, but maybe it will be nice to see her again. I dunno. But I think *you* should find a companion. A confidante. You need to talk to someone. Keeping everything in can't be healthy."

His brow lifted. "Do you have someone to talk to?"

"I talk to everyone ... well, not *everyone.* But several people."

"You don't have a specific love in your life, like you're trying to find for me?"

Turning her head to him, she smiled. "Again, twenty-five, versus, like, a million years old. There's a difference."

Genuine laughter this time. "Shocking I can manage to totter out of bed at such an elderly age."

"I know! You're amazingly spry for your age."

He raised an eyebrow. "Thanks."

"Oh, before I forget. For my graduation party, can we update the waitstaff uniforms?"

Casey first met Rowan working for him as a waitress at his business club. The dress code for the waitstaff consisted of excellent skirts full of useful pockets, and Chuck Taylor shoes. That was it, nothing else over or under. The same outfit was expected for males and females alike. There were enough staff that once she started service, it didn't take long to forget she was half naked, but the initial shock had been ... a bit of a surprise.

The space was beautiful, and large enough for the graduation party that Casey suspected was doubling as a business affair, a bit of a welcome home for Rowan, but with the number of people showing up, she'd prefer a less revealing outfit for the servers ... not to mention, it was 1987, much more progressive!

His smile lit up his face. "You don't like the half-naked look?"

Casey suppressed a shiver, recalling how chilly she'd been without a shirt. "Um, no. I was thinking a skinny tube top and a similar matching skirt."

Nodding in thought, he gazed off for a few minutes. "I think that that could work. Similar idea, but a bit more coverage. Bold, yet sexy. The board should still agree."

She yawned. They'd been sitting down there a while, and her body was trying to heal. "How long do you think we'll have to wait?"

He threw his arm around her shoulders, pulling her in. She rested her head on his chest. He patted her mess of bleached curls. "Rest. I'll let you know if anything changes."

Turning into him a bit more, she swung an arm around his waist and let her mind wander, wondering what it would've been like growing up hated by your family, disowned, and unwanted.

Chapter 4

A kiss to her forehead woke Casey up. She cracked open her eyes and saw it was dark outside. Every muscle in her body cried in pain when she tried to move. Panting, she tried again. "I don't think I can move."

Rowan's arm tightened around her. "That fall was far; you may have done some damage. Even vampires can get hurt." He slid his arm away and shifted her until she lay on the hard rock ledge. Every move sent a shot of pain throughout her body. She gazed up at the narrow strip of stars and tried to disassociate from the pain. *I don't want to die.*

With a small noise of concentration, Rowan started at her head and moved down her body, thoroughly probing her. He seemed to be checking for any spots that were more tender than the others. Her shoulder and hip elicited louder moans, and he spent extra time in those spots.

He sat back on his heels and took in all of her. "We should have done a simple field evaluation prior to the nap. This is what this weekend is all about. My sincere apologies." He bowed his head.

Casey huffed out a laugh, a stab of pain twinging her side. "It isn't all your fault. I think I was in shock from the fall, and then in even more shock that you told me about your past. I didn't even think of assessing the extent of my injuries, which seems stupid. Now that I look up and realize how far we fell, I'm surprised we're not in more pain."

Rowan sat cross-legged and gently raised her. He scooted her underneath him, so her head rested in his lap as a pillow. "How bad are your injuries? *Are* you in much pain?"

Moving her shoulders, and then wiggling each part of her body, she sighed with relief. "No broken bones. I think I'm just really stiff. Nothing permanent. I don't want to move for a long time. Again, the silver isn't helping. And hey, I'm a vampire. I heal fast, right?"

He moved his hands to her shoulders and arms and began a simple massage. "That you are, but because of the silver, the healing will take more time. You'll also need more blood, which we really don't have."

Fingers probed tense muscles and her body began to unwind. *Oh, that feels good. Too good. Dammit, I shouldn't fall asleep again.* With a frustrated grunt, Casey tried to fight it as her body went limp from the massage. "Tell me more about your past. I need a distraction."

"What would you have me tell you?"

"Well, you were the oldest of your brothers and sisters, but your next eldest brother took over. How did that happen? And was it hard to give yourself over to ... um, what was his name?"

"Ashby."

"Yeah, him, as a blood whore." She shivered. "I can't believe you called yourself that."

A slight smile played over his features. "It was the title of the times. Well, that's how it would translate to the words we use today. I could soften the title, but it's how I think of it."

His hands slowed their rubbing and his fingers ended up on the tips of her collar bone. She looked up to see him staring off into space, no doubt seeing another world. The past. "Calling someone a blood whore today would be a terrible insult, but then, in the city, it was a position. It didn't hold respect, obviously. No one would want to marry me after holding such a position, but no one would spit on me as I walked the street. Well, beyond my family that is." He let out a small laugh.

Lifting his hands, he rubbed his face before returning them to her shoulders. "Ashby was good to me; he was good to all his humans. I had a room, even though I didn't sleep there. I had a wardrobe. No one loved the farmer look. I'd come in, wash off the smell of the animals, and change. Once I was dapper, I'd present myself. Many of the vampires from his family came from Africa, so my pale skin, light, reddish hair, and green eyes stood out. I became a status symbol, of sorts. I think it was why I'd been invited in, on that first day."

"Was Ashby female then, or were they more open?"

A genuine smile broke out on Rowan's face. "You know our family's ability. It didn't matter what Ashby was, Ashby was what Ashby wanted to be. Open, carefree, sensual. Ashby was known for being both during a single dalliance. I learned a lot in those first few years. Ashby wasn't the only vampire I donated too, but mainly him .... Most often when we were together, Ashby presented as male."

Casey's eyes met his. "I didn't know that about you." She wasn't sure why this surprised her. He was the head of a family of vampires that could be anyone they wanted to be, yet he always held himself apart. *Who is this man? This leader? The more I learn, the more I feel I don't know.* The cold began seeping into her back, but she focused on his story, letting it warm her soul, ignoring the aches and pains of her body.

Rowan chuckled. "Casey, dear, haven't you learned to never make assumptions? As you said, that was a million years ago, and I was a very different person then."

A thrill surged through her. "Tell me about the Rowan you were, then."

"I'm trying." He began to massage her temples. "After my brother disowned me, I was lost. Somehow, in the back of my mind, the vampires, the blood, the sex—it always seemed a bit of a dream. I thought I'd wake up, go back to the farm, marry, and live my real life. I'm not sure how I thought the pieces would fall back into place, but I never saw another path for myself. Any other life was unthinkable."

I tried to focus on his eyes, but he was again off in the past, a tear threatening to trace its way down his cheek. "When my brother kicked me out, I locked myself in my room in the vampire house for a week, crying. Finally, Ashby forced his way in and made me an offer. I took it, and some time afterwards, he made me into a vampire. I had to learn things first. The move from blood whore to vampire always involved education. However, I was a sponge. I wanted to learn it all. Not unlike a certain person I know."

Casey's hands started to shake, and a low moan escaped from deep in her throat. Closing her eyes, she felt Rowan's warm hand on her forehead. "Damn. Listen to me. Your body is healing you, but it has used up the last of your resources ... confounded jewelry. Your body is in desperate need of blood."

"I can wa ... wait. They'll notice we're gone s-s-soon. They'll look."

"I know they'll come for us, but you can't wait. It's dangerous. You need blood. Remember back when we met, we discussed that band-aid? You need one ... now."

She needed human blood, but vampire blood would work in a pinch for a short amount of time. That was what he offered. A band-aid solution.

"What about you?"

"I'm older. My need can wait. I can spare some."

Before she could argue more, his wrist was in her mouth and blood flowed in. The warm elixir of life dripping over her tongue and down into her belly gave her the shivers. His blood was so much richer than any other she'd tasted, like a fine, aged wine. Slowly, it integrated into her system, her body, her soul. She felt life and strength return to her limbs as euphoria took over. She moaned when he pulled his arm away.

It took a few pants before she straightened her mind out enough to focus on his pale green eyes. She licked her lips, breathing heavily. Finally, after a few minutes of just gaping, she said, "Wow."

The side of his mouth quirked up. "I'm glad you're feeling better, youngling. That should tide you over for a bit."

Shaking her head, she felt her mind click back on. "What about you? Can I donate a bit back? Or would that be counterproductive?"

"A bit, but it may be necessary if it takes the others too long to find us. It'd be better if we can wait." He stroked the hair from her forehead then went back to resting his hands on her shoulders. "Where was I?"

"You'd just been changed."

"That's right. By then I was twenty-six and deemed knowledgeable about what it was to be a vampire ... the basics. That first year, learning about my new power, magic, and strength—it was intense. The second year, when I could shift my sex at will, I started spying on my family's farm. It had been long enough since I'd been there, and I could go incognito. My sisters had been married off, so it was several years before I found them. By then, my father had died of a combination of old age and his depression. The only people left on the farm were my two younger brothers."

Casey frowned. "And they didn't recognize you—or they didn't see you?"

Dropping his head back to lean on the crevice wall, Rowan frowned in thought. "They didn't see me at first. Later, when they'd aged enough, I went to speak to my youngest brother, Giuseppe. I saw him enter a local tavern and followed him in ... offered to buy him a pint. He didn't recognize me. We became acquainted, after a fashion. He told me about the family after a few mugs of ale. He'd had a good life, though Ermanno had not. He never got over the feeling I had betrayed them all. The *vampires* had betrayed them all."

"Did your youngest brother sound like he wondered about you?"

His face hardened. "Yes and no, but in the end, I was too much of a disgrace."

"That is so funny. Usually, I think of daughters being a disgrace, not sons. I'm not sure why, anyone can disgrace the family. Must be all the stories I've read growing up."

"Casey, love, who ever said I was born a son?"

Chapter 5

Casey struggled to sit up and failed. Her body shook, weaker than it had ever felt in her life. Taking a deep breath, she got her hands underneath herself and tried again. Once she was up, she sat cross-legged, facing Rowan. "Say what?"

A wide smile split his face and he grabbed her hands. "I haven't told anyone that in ... gods, years. It really isn't a secret, per se, but I don't think going public with this is a good idea. At least not now."

She nodded, her mouth agape. Closing it to swallow, she finally wrapped her head around his words. "How long have you kept yourself in this form?"

His eyes danced with mirth. "A long time. When I crossed the pond, as they say, I figured it would be easier to run a house as a male. No one knew me but the few vampires who came with me. As for them, I had shifted back and forth so much the whole time they knew me, who knows if they were aware which set of parts I was born with."

"Do you ever shift back?"

He shook his head, slowly. "Not for long periods of time. I do it as needed—my body seems to crave its original form—but then I return to my preferred shape quickly."

"I'd like to see you in your other form." Casey immediately blushed, realizing how intimate her request had been. *Gods, I hope I didn't offend him ... but he'd be gorgeous!*

Rowan grinned and patted her arm. "I'm sure you would, but let's worry about surviving our current predicament."

Covering her mouth, Casey yawned. "I've already rested. Why am I tired, and you're not? You've told me stories while I've rested ... and you've given me blood."

"Because you were hurt more than me and you're younger."

Casey nodded, her face scrunched in thought. "You said one of your sisters' line became vampire hunters."

He sighed. "My goodness, your mind does jump around." His shoulders slumped and his face fell as sorrow settled over him. "Yeah. The oldest of my two younger sisters, Aurora. She married Ermanno's best friend. After I moved into the vampire house, Ermanno and his friend had so much anger."

"Do you know what happened to them?" She leaned closer, engrossed in the story.

"They were hard to follow. Getting close to the people hunting you is never wise, especially for a vampling. I know several of the family ended up on this side of the pond, like me, but I stopped tracking them."

Her eyes widened in disbelief. "I know you have a spy network, I mean, you're the head of a vampire family, *don't* you have a spy network?" His head lowered a pinch, but it was enough. "So, how do you not know where your family ended up?"

She kept secrets from her parents and often spent large chunks of time away from them, she even encouraged her dad's business trip over her graduation. Having them miss the party was easier than trying to explain to them about partying with vampires and witches. Despite the physical and information separation she had with her parents, she knew they'd always be there for her. She couldn't imagine having family alive but not knowing anything about them.

Staring at his hands, he shook his head. "None."

A lump formed in her gut at the emptiness in his voice. "Do you have any desire to find them?"

He sighed. "Not really. What help would these extended family members bring me?"

"Hello?" A small voice came from above. "Casey! Rowan! Are you alive?"

Casey leapt to her feet, then nearly fell as her healing body tried to collapse, dizzy with injuries and loss of magic. Rowan's hand on her hips kept her upright. "Jen! Jen! We're down here! Jen!"

A head of red curls popped over the rim of the cliff. "Are you down there?!"

Casey blinked away the tears stinging her eyes. "Jen! Oh, my gods! Jen! I hate these stupid bracelets!"

"Yep, it's you!"

Jen lowered a rope to the ledge with the key to the bracelets tied on the end. With a long sigh, Rowan unlocked the dragons from their wrists.

She looked at them. "Why couldn't we have snapped the silver?"

He shook his head. "A magical compulsion. It stopped us from even thinking about it. It's worked into any silver that's placed on vampires."

Casey growled at the jewelry before she slipped the silver into her back pocket. She clung to Rowan as he misted them to the top of the cliff. The world spun as if she were at a club and the trees were dancing to heavy punk rock. A hand under her arm kept her from falling ... again. It had been a while since a teleportation had shaken her so much.

She tightened her fists, the bite of her nails focused her, and she caught her balance. A few steading breaths and she finally threw off the effects of the jump.

Rowan turned to Jen. "She needs blood. Her body's healing but the fall did a lot of damage."

Jen visually searched them both for injury. "What about you, sir?"

"I should be fine."

Casey grumbled, "He needs blood too. He gave me some when I started shaking. We both need blood, and probably a private tent ... though I'm too tired for anything but blood and sleep."

Jen snorted. "Damn, you *must* be tired."

Casey began the long hike back to camp; they weren't close. She made it all of three steps before she got dizzy again and began to sway. Rowan collected her, and with another mist, they arrived in the middle of camp without further mishap. Jen would have to find her way back alone.

"Hey!" Jaxon shouted. Casey's head lolled to the side, and she saw him straighten up from leaning over the fire pit, small flames starting to catch as a log popped. "That's not fair! Why do you get your magic back? I thought this was about survival without magic?"

Jess hit his shoulder with a twig she'd brought over. "Look at Case. She looks like hell. They both do."

The words flowed over her as she watched their byplay. She tried to turn back to Rowan and got as far as the sky. The leaves overhead turned into a tent. Rowan's voice rose in command. "Kailey, Reis, in here now. She needs blood, and one won't be enough—unless you want to meet your maker."

She felt a soft bed, like feathers, as she slowly began to slip off to sleep, all her muscles slack with fatigue. She began to dream she was floating on a cloud through a blue sky with birds around her. A sudden shake, and she gazed into eyes like the night sky, mesmerized. A waterfall of dark hair surrounded an oval face. She felt a small smile tug at her lips.

Kailey's forehead touched hers. "Stay with me this time, hon. My neck is coming down to you. Take a drink, love."

Warm skin rubbed against her mouth and the scent of life penetrated her nose. Sharp teeth descended, forcing her to either lower her jaw or pierce her own lower lip. With a moan, she opened her mouth wider, biting down on the offered meal. Warm, metallic-flavored blood pulsed into her mouth and down her throat. As it slid down to her stomach, her body greedily incorporated it into her system in a process that left her sizzling with lust.

She heard Kailey's heart slow; with a flick of her tongue, she stopped the flow and flopped down. *Not enough.* However, she'd taken as much as the donor could afford to give. She'd learned the lesson of listening to the donor's heart ... the hard way. She'd killed a person once, and she didn't plan on doing it again.

Kailey shifted and kissed her deeply, investigating Casey's mouth thoroughly. Her hands explored the rest of Casey's body.

For a moment, Casey gave in to the lust, desire flooding her system. As her teeth scraped Kailey's tongue, Casey pushed on the woman's shoulders. "It wasn't enough. I need more."

Sitting back, Kailey looked down, lips swollen, and eyes dilated with need. *Damn, the woman has skills.* She'd somehow gotten Casey's shirt unbuttoned. Without Kailey's warmth pressed against her, the cooler air made Casey extremely aware of her exposed, braless chest.

Kailey's hot gaze raked over her. "Well, damn. I guess Rowan was right. Next time ... maybe. I don't know how many more donations I'm giving before my own change." She bent to give Casey a chaste kiss, then jumped up to leave the tent.

Casey still struggled to breathe as she watched the sway of her hips as they exited the tent. Strength returned to her body, but with everything that had happened, she still felt weak. Casey closed her eyes and relaxed back into the sleeping bag, no longer the feather bed her mind had imagined. She moaned at the rocks poking into her shoulder.

A weight straddled her hips, and a warm breath caressed her ear. "Are you ready for round two?" Reis's voice flowed over her like a warm caress.

When the neck pressed against her mouth, Casey didn't hesitate to bite down. This deep into the drinking, her hormones were on fire. Her back arched as a low whimper escaped her. Reis chuckled as his hands cupped her breasts and his thumbs rubbed her nipples.

Once she knew she'd taken enough blood, she licked his wound closed. Pulling back, she gazed past his curly blond hair to his clear blue eyes, so light they were almost gray, and smiled.

His open face smiled wide back at her. "I was told you were to rest after your ordeal ... nothing more than blood."

Raising her hips, she rubbed against him. She lifted a brow. "Is that so?"

"It is indeed." He scooted down, taking her shorts and panties with him. "So, if we're going to do this, you're going to have to be quiet. No sounds."

She bit her lip, then smiled at him before asking, "Are you challenging me?"

He gazed back, eyes sparkling. "I believe I am."

She slipped out of her shirt, then helped him out of his. Built of muscle, bronze and beautiful, she ran her hands over his torso and his excitement infused the tent. He reached down and slid a finger into her. "You're wet and ready."

"I may be wet, but I'm not ready." Her eyes dropped. "Though you look ready."

His eyes danced and his brows waggled up and down. His hand moved up to play with her clit. With a gasp, she fell back and licked her lips, her focus on that talented thumb. A whirlwind of sensation grew in her, swirling out as she began to breathe harder and faster. Heat gathered within her as his insistent play continued. She bit her lip to try to stop the small sounds she was making.

Reis leaned down and licked her nipple then sucked it into his mouth. Arching up, she tried to encourage more. Blue eyes bright, he pinned her with a stare and reminded her, "No sound, love." Then he scraped his teeth over her nipple, using his free hand to gently massage the other.

Casey tried to control the grunts and moans she made, but oh, gods, *what is he doing now?* He moved up to catch her mouth in a deep kiss, more delicate than Kailey's. He pulled back as she started to moan. "None of that, Case. Quiet."

Centering himself, he pushed in, keeping his thumb on her clit, the other hand bracing himself. A pool of sensation in her gut built as he found a rhythm, pumping in and out. She got closer and closer to climax with each deep thrust. When she was about to break, he removed his hand, and her eyes flew to his.

"Remember, no sound." Then he moved his hand up to her breasts and began to rub, then squeeze, and then pinch her nipples, roughly.

The sensation shot to the pool in her center, then vibrated out through to the rest of her body, sending tingles everywhere. She felt a scream building up, threatening to expose their play. Eyes wide, she slapped her hands over her mouth to seal it inside. His eyes narrowed as he pressed tighter, pumped faster, then moved a hand down to tease her between her legs.

In desperation, her hips flew up to meet his, whimpers trying to pass by her hands. Each time a sound did escape her, he punished her by reaching up and pinching her nipple, hard. The sensation electrified her body straight to her core. She bit her lip, eyes wide as small fireworks of pleasure exploded within her. Closing her eyes, she thrashed as he played her body like a musical instrument. He rubbed against her as heat built within her.

Too much! Her core exploded, her head snapped back, and she held the scream in, both hands still covering her mouth. He leaned down and sucked her nipple into his mouth, scraping his teeth over her sensitive skin as she tried not to make a sound, his suction extending the waves of pleasure, pulling them deeper and longer as he used her breast to muffle his own passionate outcry.

Afterwards, he rolled off her and pulled her in to rest on his shoulder. She felt boneless as the two of them laughed silently at their mischievous tryst.

Chapter 6

Casey circled the parking lot for a second time, searching for an open parking space. She wanted to bang her head against the steering wheel in frustration as she navigated through the forest of vehicles. Ready to give up, she saw a Buick pull out and another car turn the corner from the other side, but she slammed her foot down on the gas, sliding her small VW into the spot ahead of the snarling face of the perfectly coiffed mom. As the other car passed, a crying kid in the back screamed as the mom continued on her own quest to secure a parking spot.

Grasping the wheel, breathing deeply to release the stress of finding the spot, Casey watched the families out enjoying the beautiful weather on the playground. Mostly, she saw mothers with their kids running off their late-morning energy on and around playground equipment. Casey's face softened as her gaze settled on one mom with a baby boy, maybe a year old, still in diapers. The boy couldn't quite walk. She lifted her son and dropped him at the top of the metal slide and smiled wide enough that Casey saw her teeth as the baby squealed to the bottom.

Maybe that will be me one day. I'll have a bouncing baby boy I can bring to the park and play with. She shook her head and tried to focus on why she'd come. With a sigh, she gathered everything from the car, her walking stick and robe, and then she lumbered out in search for a path to the right, west of the park. *Of course I found a parking spot all the way on the east side.* She stared up at the sky and snorted at her luck. The lot of cars was lined by a small path that she used for her search.

She skirted the playground and flinched at all the high-pitched yells. Casey finally found the trail Tilly had told her about. Today she planned to meet two of the local coven witches, Tilly and Damion. The dirt path wound through trees and descended a mild slope towards a small pond. At the bottom, she found an old and crumbling picnic table by the pond. Next to it stood Tilly and Damion, deep in conversation. They both turned and smiled as she navigated towards them.

Tilly's face lit up. "Hiya, Case! You made it. We should've told you to park at the house and walk. The park is crazy this time of day. I know carrying everything is a pain, but I think this is the only safe place outside our backyard to do this."

After the insanity of the parking lot and playground, Casey let the serenity of the pond and quiet of the field fill her. She gazed around. "It's so peaceful here compared to up top. How is that even possible? And why not at the house? I'd think doing a spell would be done at Witch House, not out here in public."

After becoming a vampire, it was decided several witches would relocate to help in town. They started out living in Cambia House, but soon found their own abode ... Witch House. There was a room there for Casey, though she didn't stay there enough. When she was there, they could perform five-witch-circle spells ... a small circle.

Damion chuckled. "Zen. He's in the backyard, meditating. He can't handle moving his time here, too uptight, though he claims it's the random squeals from the kids that disrupt his calm, and, of course, he's claimed the backyard. We decided we'd shift, and figured you'd be willing to move with us."

Of course it was Zen. She shook her head at the peculiarities of the man, then nodded. "Okay, tell me exactly how this works. This is a new one for me. And are we sure the mobs of insanity won't come down here?"

With a smile, Tilly spread her hands and spun. "Look at this place. No one comes down here, no entertainment for the kiddos. The only kids who may explore, escaping their parents, are at school." Dropping her hands, her face became serious. "You'll need to throw your third eye up to the sky, and your dragon, Zoryda, will catch it. She'll fly it over the city, letting you suss out if there are hidden witches. This isn't a perfect system, but it will give us an idea of what's out there."

Her stomach cramped in dread. Casey gaped at the witch. "My what now? I *throw* my third eye to the sky? That's a thing?" Her mouth dropped as her eyebrows came together.

Damion chuckled. "It's a thing. We've been doing a lot of studying, and when you don't have a full coven, or even a five-witch-circle to perform the searching spell, this works if you have a flying familiar ... which you do. Tilly will set wards blocking off the path, ensuring our privacy. I'll monitor you during your divided consciousness. You've taught me a lot of mental magic, so I'll be partially in your mind, helping to keep you whole."

Heart beating fast, Casey nodded. "Okay, right, sure. Sounds rad." *More like, sounds insane!* She reined in her tongue to keep herself from babbling. "Let's just do this. Tilly, talk me through the spell."

It took about fifteen minutes, but by then Casey felt prepared to commence the search. They each donned their white ceremonial robes. This was more to focus their minds than part of the spell. A spell this tricky needed routine, and Casey was glad they had the routine of their customs. Tilly placed five white candles in a rough circle, lighting them with a soft word. They stood while facing each other in the corners of an equilateral triangle. Casey placed her left hand on Tilly's shoulder, Tilly's hand went on Damion's, and Damion's onto Casey's.

They each crossed their walking sticks in the center, holding them at an angle, the silver-tipped bottoms anchored near their feet. Damion's tiger lay curled in a ball, as if asleep, and Tilly's panther sat on its haunches, alert and watching. On top of Casey's walking stick, Zoryda crouched in the same position she'd adopted when she'd last landed: wings tucked against her sides with her snout pointed straight ahead. *The three appear to be a strange family, happily getting along.*

The witches began chanting the incantation. Casey let her head fall back and gazed up into the sky. Closing her physical eyes, she opened her third eye, noting the open sky appeared the same to her third eye as to her plain sight. *Focus, Casey!* She tried to let her physical form go as she tensed her gut and rolled up through her body. She imagined her awareness leaping into the clouds. A moment of dizzy nausea overtook her, and her vision began to darken. Then, she landed on Zoryda's back, the dragon's wings beating hard. She could see how fast they flew but couldn't feel either the dragon or the wind. The visual without sensation caused a gut retching disorientation.

For a moment, Casey worried about passing out. She gazed down and realized Zoryda circled the park, but she could see through her friend's body. *Clever girl; Zoryda must've set an invisibility shield over herself.* It took a few moments for Casey to adjust to the separation of mind and body. Searching the park, she stared at the playground full of families, and then the small pond. The families appeared as blotches of darkness and the three bodies by the pond glowed with a witchy light, like a holiday display, each color representing their specialty.

Though Tilly could conjure better than Casey, her specialty was in ice magic, and she glowed in silver, with only a pinch of the conjuration red. Damon swirled with purple and green, mind and healing magic. She glowed purple with her own mind magic, though some red showed for conjuration, and a bit of gold for air magic, both of which surprised her. A full circle would glow like a rainbow.

Casey took a moment to orient herself and then connected to Zoryda's mind and indicated her readiness to move on.

Zoryda took off to circle the city. Casey's head pounded, her stomach churned, but she focused on locating glowing spots. She would know when the spell finished. It wasn't an exact science, but they'd soon have an idea of how many witchlings lived within the city limits. Gazing down at the husks of the building, the glowing areas were vague. Casey counted as Zoryda flew, her head spinning. *For all I know, I'm counting the same bright patches more than once.* Unsure how much longer she could fly as a phantom with her mini-dragon, she felt her physical arm anchored to Tilly begin to shake with the strain.

A warm voice spoke to her mind. "Casey, you need to come back. Even if you aren't done surveying the city, you're done with this spell." Damion, using his mind magic, had been monitoring her, and decided to call her back.

Her muscles cramped, and the nausea returned. Zoryda's wing beats increased as her flying sped up. Casey felt disjoined with the motion and wondered what would happen if she fell from the dragon's back.

Vision going dark, she couldn't see beyond Zoryda's back. She felt herself slide, the wings bouncing her. *Gods above, can I get off this ride?* Bile rose in her throat. *What happens when a third eye leaves a body? Why didn't I ask before?*

Unable to hang on, she slid off and landed in her body. Her muscles slack and stomach churning, she fell to the ground on her butt. She twisted, placed both hands on the ground beneath her, and threw up.

Damion knelt beside her and rubbed her back. "Turn off the third eye, Case."

She did, and though she felt less dizzy, she didn't feel any better. Tilly handed her a bottle of water. Taking a few sips and spitting them out to rinse out her mouth, she finally gulped down a full mouthful. Damion helped her up.

Tilly's cool hands felt her head. "How do you feel?"

With a groan, Casey hugged herself. "That really sucked. Please tell me that's not the only way to find witches?"

Taking an arm, Damion led her to the picnic table. Casey carefully lowered herself onto a bench. Tilly sat next to her, sliding an arm around her back. "No, there's another way. We'd hoped this would work well. Obviously, we were wrong. We won't use it again."

A sound of approval and pain bubbling up from her throat, Casey just sat, waiting for her body to return to equilibrium.

Damion squatted in front of her. "Did it work? Did we at least get some useful information for the hell we put you through?"

Casey quirked a smile and nodded. "As Zoryda flew in circles. I saw a few bright spots. I tried to count. It's something between four and ten, but I don't know if I recounted the same spots. It was too hard to focus that way."

Tilly's excitement flowed over her, and Casey braced, not knowing how much more sensation she could endure. Damion took her hands and pulled her up. "Why don't I help you to your car? Do you need a ride home, or are you good to drive on your own?"

The park threatened to spin around her, and her hands wouldn't stop shaking, but she shook her head. "I can drive, I'll be fine. Thanks." She let him help her to the car and was glad they couldn't smell the lie as well as she could. Relieved the drive between the park and Cambia House didn't take long, Casey was still shocked when she arrived in one piece.

Chapter 7

Emerging from the steam of her shower, Casey dried off, and wrapped herself in a fuzzy blue towel. It had been a long week since her fall down the cliff and her bruises were gone. The benefits of vampire healing. Wiping the condensation from the mirror, she gazed at herself, checking the circles under her eyes.

She had one more week of classes before finals. The last week had been full of staying up late, studying. She and Jen had locked themselves in the study rooms with their books, and she'd conjured food and drink when they got hungry. They'd only been out for bathroom breaks, classes, and sleep.

Smiling at her reflection, excitement bubbled up from her belly. Tonight, she was going out to dinner with Jen and Ginger, to catch up. *It has been too long! Ever since Ginger graduated last year and got a job, she's been in her own world.* Casey frowned at herself. She knew it was half her own fault. At times it felt easier to be friends with Ginger from afar.

Leaving the bathroom to cross the hall to her room, mind on what she'd wear that Ginger would approve of, she ran into Cyran. He took her in from head to toe and she couldn't help returning the favor. *Gods, he looks amazing in his jeans and dark blue shirt. Why is he my trainer? I must look like a half-drowned rat. Save me, please!*

A smile widened across his face. "Now that school is almost out and your training is near an end, would you be up for a date?"

Her mouth suddenly dry and mind short-circuiting at how close his words mirrored her own thoughts, she just gaped at him. "Are you kidding?"

"Not at all, vampling." His voice, low and sultry, felt like a   caress. Holding the towel tightly around herself, she glared at him. "Oh, come on. I'm not a vampling anymore."

He winked at her. "We'll see ... Tuesday night?"

Her jaw dropped. "What now?"

"A date. You're finally not a student. So, what do you say?"

Mind whirling with the night's plans, she nodded at him with a small smile, figuring he had to be joking. She slipped around Cyran and entered her room, leaving him in the hall alone. She couldn't think about him right now. School, Ginger, finals—she'd worry about Cyran later.

Tonight was girls' night out. Styling her hair in their signature curls, she did her makeup, a dark eye-shadow and red lipstick, adding a beauty mark above her lip. Smiling at the result, she slipped on a white, long sleeve crop top that left her shoulders bare and a tiered black mini skirt. Black fish-net stockings and ankle boots finished off her outfit.

As she laced up and tightened the boots, Jen knocked and entered. Her friend's red curls hung down over her shoulders. She wore a red halter-top under a fitted men's pin-striped suit jacket and black leather pants. "Ready to go? Ginger said she'd meet us at the Italian restaurant downtown."

"All set." Zoryda, Casey's dragon, flew down and circled her before landing on her shoulder and wrapping a tail around her neck. Purring in her ear, she rubbed her cheek, before flying back up to the ceiling. Casey laughed. "I guess Zoryda approves of our night as well. But she needs exercise. Tomorrow morning I'll take her out to the woods, so she gets some decent flight time."

"Sounds like a plan. I'll set an alarm and head out with you. It's been a while for me as well."

They decided to walk the few blocks to the restaurant. The darkened entrance set the mood, and a hostess in a black skirt and white button down stood at a glass podium watching them enter. "Can I help you?"

Jen approached. "We're here to meet Ginger Rotta."

The woman flipped her blond hair back and gave them a winning smile. "She's here, follow me." She led them around a corner to a room lined with booths, which smelled of marinara sauce and meatballs. When the undercurrent of garlic hit, Casey began to salivate. A few private nooks, closed off with green velvet curtains gave the restaurant a warm, intimate feel. Finally, the hostess deposited them at a corner table where Ginger and a bottle of wine waited. After a moment to read the menu and order, the three sat back, and enjoyed a glass of wine.

Ginger looked them over. "It's so nice seeing you two. I've missed you, working in the governor's office. I miss being a student."

With the weight of finals coming up, Casey snorted and put down her glass. "How is it working in the big leagues downtown?"

"Crazy!" She took a deep sniff of her wine before giving it a spin. She stared back and forth between Casey and Jen with a lazy smile. "The people around here are getting more and more used to the vampires and witches. The coalition is working *so hard* for their integration, you know." Her voice dropped a bit.

Sensing Ginger's discomfort with the paranormal groups, Casey picked up the dessert menu tent sitting at the end of the table and read over what the restaurant offered. Ginger had always been one of Casey's best friends, but she had also been a bit anti-vampire and anti-witch. Casey hadn't told her she was anything more than a regular human, at least not permanently. There had been a moment she'd come clean her freshman year, but Ginger hadn't handled the news well, and despite promising herself she'd never do it, Casey had hidden the conversation from Ginger's memory. Jen had made the decision to keep Casey's secret too. She suppressed a sigh. *It's so much easier to keep her ignorant. She just wouldn't understand.*

Jen sat back, her eyes narrowing. "Are you happy about this? You've always seemed less than happy about the mixing and mingling of vampires, witches, and humans."

Ginger's lips pursed before she relaxed. "I don't know. I still don't like the idea of beings that think of me as food."

"Do you really think that?" Jen asked with a frown. "You've been with the governor for a year and working with the coalition for much of that time. Haven't you learned anything about the vampires? And what about witches? They don't feed off humans."

Brows knitting, Ginger's head tilted. "What do you mean?"

"Well, don't all the vampires have a house with blood donors? Isn't it a big part of their message, that they specifically *don't* go out after random people?" Jen spoke patiently, as if to a child.

Casey took a sip of her wine. *They don't when they're properly trained. Gods, what would Ginger think if she knew everything about my past? Is there more wine?* Casey picked up the bottle to fill her glass and it was empty.

Glaring at Jen, Ginger threw her hands out to the side. "And you believe them?"

Jen drooped a bit. "I do ... but I guess you don't."

The food arrived, a welcome interruption to the start of an unwelcome argument. Looking down at her pasta and meatballs, Casey gazed at Jen's lasagna, and wondered if she'd ordered wrong. Then again, Ginger's chicken linguine also looked great.

Ginger picked up her fork, but before she took a bite, she pointed it at Jen. "How many vampires do you even know? Have you even spoken with one? Do you *really* know how they live? How they interact?"

The food smelled divine, but Casey wouldn't be able to enjoy it if this fight continued. It was too much; she had to bite the bullet and face the consequences like an adult. Ginger had been her friend for four years. Either she accepted her, or she didn't. It was time to end the lies ... Ginger deserved the truth, and so did Jen ... and so did she.

Putting down her fork, Casey faced her friends. "All those years ago, when you got me that job my freshmen year ... I was attacked, Ginger. I was turned. I wanted to tell you but was afraid of losing you as a friend. Living with Jen ... well, she figured it out. So, yeah, she knows. And no, as far as I know, she's never been anyone's meal."

Smiling at her finally fessing up, Jen lifted her wine glass in salute. "Never been bit, never will. But I'm proud of you for finally opening up, friend."

Ginger froze mid-bite. Her eyes widened. "All these years ... you? You're one of *them?* A vampire? And you've never told me? And you live in the dorms?" Her voice rose in pitch with each successive sentence.

Casey could smell Ginger's hurt and anger. She flushed, spreading her hands in a placating manner. "No. I moved into one of the vampire houses. I needed to learn about being a vampire. The changes in my body. How to be safe around other people. They really are all about education ... at least most of them are."

Ginger's hurt smell deepened. "I can't believe you never told me. Why didn't you tell me?"

"I tried. Once. You told me about your disdain for vampires. I didn't think it was worth ending our friendship over ... and it was right at the start. I was scared."

"Don't you think it was a decision I should have been allowed to make?"

It was like a punch to the gut. *Did I make the right decision all those years ago? Should I have let her walk away? Given time, would she have come around? What have I done to our relationship?* "Do you regret our friendship?"

"How much of a friendship is it if you don't trust me enough with the truth, Casey? Heavens above, you've been lying to me for over three years. You throw our great friendship at me, but you're the one who's been living the double life."

Casey tried to keep a blank face. This reaction was the reason so many in her world kept secrets, both vampires and witches alike. The blame, the hate, the accusations. If Ginger's reaction was this bad for a double life, then what would she do if she knew about Casey's 'third' life?

Finally, Ginger turned back to Jen. "So, you've known all these years then?" Jen nodded, face blank. "And you didn't think it was appropriate to let me know?"

"Not really. I grew up with a father who was pretty closed-minded about these things. I swore, once I learned about Casey, I was going to figure things out for myself. She didn't change from the person she was before the attack ... and don't get that bit wrong. Most vampires take years to learn before they are made. Her transformation was ... unorthodox, to say the least."

Brows lowering, Ginger finished her bite of linguine before asking, "Why was that?"

Casey bit her lip. "That is a long story, and complicated. If you want, I'll explain it all to you, but not tonight. I just don't have the energy. Needless to say, it hasn't happened again, and it won't."

Ginger rolled her eyes. "More secrets, Case?"

If I could only tell you my secrets, Ginge, but my life has been keeping them, and you aren't ready. I fear you never will be ... but give me time, I'll try.

Suddenly not as hungry, Casey gazed at her plate, playing with the remainder of her meatball.

Jen put down her water glass with some force. "Can we just go back to catching up and being friends? I'm not sure when this fun girl's night went off the rails, but this isn't the night I had planned. We are under enough stress with finals in a week. We really wanted a 'fun Ginger' night, not all this tension."

Ginger sat gazing at the two of them. Her voice sounding small and plaintive, she said, "I don't know. Do I even know the two of you anymore?"

Jen pursed her lips. "Considering you work with the governor's office to help bridge the human, vampire, witch relations, I would think this would be the perfect opportunity for you to practice what you preach ... or is your job just that, talk and no action?"

Ginger slumped in her chair. "It isn't just my job, but it's hard. I've always been for humans. The idea of sharing spaces is ... different. I'll have to think on it."

Sitting there, wine glass empty, Casey realized what she'd done. Since coming to college, she'd had two best friends, and she'd probably just ended one of those friendships. More than that, Ginger was feeling alienated from both of them. Casey could feel her loneliness. She wanted to reach out and give her a hug but knew her friend ... her ex-friend? would recoil. It had always been the way.

Dread bubbling up and tears burning her eyes, she picked up the dessert menu again. Anything to break the tension. "So, does that mean we are or aren't getting dessert?"

Chapter 8

Casey sat in her favorite study room within Cambia House preparing for finals. She chose the head of the table, facing the door, the CEO of her own domain. The wooden table took up most of the room, and could fit ten comfortably, more if people scrunched in cozily. Halfway down the left side of the table one of the house phones took up residence.

Peace settled in her as she read through books and records, scribbling condensed notes, and tried to predict what would be asked in a week on the final. She knew everything, she was prepared, she just liked to be overprepared. It had always been her way.

The room's silence let her think about how she and Jen had left Ginger. It hadn't been as enemies as she'd feared, but they hadn't gotten dessert, which had been a first. Maybe in a few weeks they could reestablish a connection.

Biting her lip, she closed her eyes and thought about the next few weeks and all she had planned, when the door to the study room opened. Snapping her eyes open, she saw Riley saunter in, dragging a finger along the table as she gazed at the artwork on the walls.

Casey had met Riley at a bar several years back, a punk rocker all in black, dark and dangerous. She'd followed her back to Cambia House to be one of her blood donors, and bed mates. The woman excited Casey like no one else with her black spiky mohawk and ripped black clothing. She oozed danger everywhere she went.

Placing her pencil down, Casey tilted her head. "Hiya, Riley. I'm studying. Do you need something?"

Reaching Casey, Riley stood over her. "You know, you've really stopped practicing your witch skills. You've been training with Cyran to master all of the vampire things, and school, obviously, but you don't ever work on your witch skills, or combining things."

Brows coming together, Casey tried to follow Riley's logic. Casey's hands slid out to her sides, palms up, in confusion. "I'm not following what you're saying. I'm really busy. Can this wait a week?"

Placing her hands on the arm of Casey's chair, Riley leaning in. "No, I don't think so. You need to practice everything, love."

Leaning back with a sigh, Casey gazed up at the black-haired vixen. "Okay, I need to get back to studying. What are you thinking?"

With a small smile, Riley dipped in closer, giving Casey a quick kiss. "I want you to shift your bits to male bits. Then I'm going to duck under the table and you're going to make us both invisible. Then I'm going to ... well, you'll figure that out quickly enough. You'll continue to study, if you can, but whatever you do, you'll have to remain quiet the whole time. We will be in hiding, after all."

A bolt of excitement shot through Casey at the idea but clamped down on it. She rolled her eyes. "Again, with the silence."

"Oh? Do tell." Riley sat on the end of the table, her black micro skirt riding up to reveal her black panties.

Casey let out a small moan and placed her hands on Riley's knees, deciding to ignore the question. "How is this helping me to prepare for finals?"

Tracing her finger along Casey's jaw, Riley's focus bored into Casey. "You need to learn to relax. You know the school stuff. It's the combining of everything while staying silent I'm not sure you have down, love. I'm worried about your safety, not your smarts."

Casey's heart pounded faster, and she licked her lips. There was a logic behind Riley's madness ... and she was right, Casey had been skipping out on practicing her witch skills. Letting her hands ride up a bit, she gazed up into Riley's warm eyes. "Do I have a choice in this? You know I'm not much of an exhibitionist. We could just go up to your room."

Riley's smile widened. "If you're asking if I'll leave before I'm done playing, the answer is no. The point is, can you trust your magic in an extreme situation? Maybe no one will come in, everyone knows you're studying ... but maybe not. Who knows? That's the fun part!"

Breathing in, Casey pushed out a bit of her will, and sent a window shield around the two of them. Though she could see Riley still, she knew they were invisible to anyone else. Riley ducked under the table. "Casey, scoot to the front of the chair and shift."

With a laugh, Casey did as told. Riley was correct. In reality, if Casey had to sit for finals tomorrow, she'd pass admirably. She did need to practice her window shield while distracted. And if anyone could be distracting, it was this demon girl.

A voice floated up from under the table. "Lift up. You'll be more comfortable without your skivvies on."

Once her panties were off, and she only wore a skirt, Casey pushed out a bit of her power and shifted to present as male. Over the years she'd gotten better, and the shift felt less odd.

Grabbing a book, Casey began perusing the main chapters. Riley's cold fingers wrapped around her cock in a shock that made Casey almost leap from the seat with a squeal. Then she began pumping her hand up and down the shaft. Shivers of delight followed the motion. As good as it felt, Casey kept the shield up, and her mind half on her studies.

From below the table, Riley said, "Just to remind you, from here on out, it's radio silence. We're under an invisibility shield, so no talking because you haven't added anything for noise. So, anything I do to you, you stay quiet ... outside of moving your papers around. If I feel you've broken the rules, there will be a punishment. Understand?"

The cool hand squeezed tighter, and Casey nodded, then lowered her hand to signal her understanding. Her breathing began to get rough. Riley's hand began to move again. "Excellent, love. You stayed quiet. You *may* pass yet."

Then Riley's hot moist mouth descended on the tip of Casey's cock and every muscle in her body tensed in anticipation.

It took Casey a few seconds before she could convince her mind to stay on her studies, but when she looked down, the black squiggles on the paper looked like weird hieroglyphics and there was no way she could decipher them.

She searched the room, but nothing would help her focus. Her hands shook as waves of pleasure came up from her core. Riley continued to suck and squeeze, using hand and mouth on her cock.

About to make a noise and accept the punishment, the click of the door stopped her voice, and she watched in horror as the door slowly swung open. Riley squeezed her dick harder and didn't relent.

Body spasming with the spikes of sensation, her mind ready to explode, Casey watched as Kailey inched into the room. Her hair was up in a side ponytail, ears covered with headphones, and a yellow Walkman sat attached to the waistband of her teal and pink track suit. Kailey's head bounced back and forth as she sang, "Liv-ing in a material world, teri-*al!*"

Closing the door behind herself, she moved to the chair near the phone and flopped down. "Boys may come, and boys may go, and *that's all right you see!*"Kailey rocked back and forth in the seat, dancing. Picking up the receiver, she pressed seven buttons on the phone. "Experience has made me rich, and now they're *after me!*"

Casey could hear the ringing over the phone. On the second ring, someone picked up. Kailey's hand hit a button on her Walkman, probably turning off the music. "Hiya, handsome."

Just making out the person on the other end, Casey heard, "Are you alone?" She thought she may recognize the voice but wasn't sure.

Kailey smacked some gum in her mouth and twirled her finger through her ponytail. "You know I am."

Riley squeezed hard, and trailed teeth over her cock, bringing Casey quickly back to what she was doing to her. Riley's other hand began playing with Casey's family jewels, and Casey found it difficult to hold still.

Kailey put her elbows on the table. "You know it ... yep! Next week Saturday is their graduation, you know that."

A suck, and Riley's hand moved towards her ass. And oh, gods, what was she doing? Pleasure pulsated through Casey's body. She missed the next few things Kailey said on the phone, something about Wednesday ... or Monday? Oh, gods, she was about to blow.

"Right, love, talk to you soon." Kailey hung up and gazed in their direction, but a bit to the right and above them. With a shrug, she spun and left the room, not shutting the door.

With a wave of her hand, Casey shut and locked the door. Then she slumped. "Thank gods she's gone!"

Riley pulled back moments before Casey was done. "I said no sounds, now I'll have to punish you." She placed both hands on Casey's thighs. "Ah, I know. Now, be a dear and unlock the door; that isn't part of the challenge. Once you're done—I can tell you're close—I'll let you know your punishment."

Flicking her wrist again, the door unlocked.

Riley grabbed Casey's cock and sucked it in, performing her own version of magic. Casey exploded in seconds, her whole body shaking with the pressure of the orgasm.

Leaning back in the chair, arms hanging out to the sides, panting, she held onto the window shield with every ounce of her being. She'd somehow managed to keep quiet, though she wasn't sure how. Just as she was about to move, the door opened again. Jen poked her head in. "Damn it, I could've sworn she'd be in here. Her books are here. Maybe she headed up to her room for something."

Once the door shut again, Casey groaned. Riley spoke from below the table. "You have two choices in your punishment, witchling. I can continue doing what I'm doing, and you can study. Or you can return the favor to me, door open, me on the table. You get to choose, I'm feeling generous."

Chapter 9

Sunday morning Casey woke early. She dressed in jean shorts, a light green T-shirt, and hiking boots. She grabbed her walking stick, Zoryda happily sleeping atop it, her wings curled over her nose, and then headed for the door. Humming a Cindy Lauper song, Casey strode down the hallway to the stairs.

At the bottom of the stairs, Monica, the house chef, stood waiting for her with hands on her hips. "You are supposed to work this morning, yes?"

Casey paused, hand on the railing, feeling like her grandmother was admonishing her for dragging dirt across the living room floor. "I thought I had today off?"

"No, you work today."

"Can I work the lunch shift, then?"

Monica's eyes narrowed. "I don't like how you play fast and loose with the rules. Fine. But be here by ten thirty."

Casey really wanted coffee. *But that's a bad idea. If I don't leave now, I'll never get out.* She slipped out the front door and made it to her car before she realized she had forgotten the keys. Crossing her arms over the top of the green VW, she dropped her head down, wanting to growl.

Screw it, if someone sees, someone sees.

She reached out to her room with her mind, found the keys, and used a small push of power to conjure them. They landed next to her head on the roof of the car.

A burst of laughter came from behind her. "Wow, good thing they didn't land *in* the Jolly Rancher; that would have sucked! Two inches below where they landed and pure disaster."

Gazing at Jen, Casey tried to keep a straight face. "First of all, Chameleon. Second, the car isn't locked; not that big a deal. And third ... why are you here?"

"Okay, we've gone over this: your car doesn't blend ... like, anywhere. Jolly Rancher is a much better name." Grinning, Jen held out a steaming mug. "I brought you coffee, but you have to tell me how much you love me first. And I thought you'd like company."

Grabbing the black salvation, Casey drank greedily. "Gods, I love you! You came last time. How much sleep are you willing to lose for my mornings with this beast? Not that I don't love having you join me."

Watching with amusement, Jen said, "Slow down. You'll run out, and then what'll you do?"

Cup empty, Casey reached into the kitchen's vat of coffee and, using her witch's magic, refilled her mug. She looked at Jen and raised her eyebrows.

Jen snorted. "Oh, yeah, that."

They got into the car and drove to the local hiking trails. Casey parked in the small parking lot at the base of the trails and the two set off. As soon as they rounded the first corner, Zoryda shook out her wings, her blue and green scales glinting in the sun, and took off, flying and stretching out. She crooned in pleasure.

Jen smiled up happily at her. She was always up for a good walk. "I know Zoryda needed a good fly—being cooped up in your room must be rough—but was there any other reason you brought us to the hiking trails versus the park?"

Casey thumped the end of her walking stick into the ground. "I need to move. I get Zoryda out here every few days. But you're right, I should try to get her out more often. We're here because I needed to think about the coven meeting and the prophecy. It was given to me over three years ago, and I know now that I'm graduating the pressure will grow for me to get pregnant."

"Wait, more action than you're getting right now?" Casey punched Jen's arm and Jen laughed. "Well, at least your punch has improved over the years."

Casey chuckled. "The thing is, I've mostly only been active, so to speak, in connection with blood. It is such a turn-on, drinking blood. Don't get me wrong, I wasn't *that* innocent before getting attacked, like," she cut her eyes to Jen, "nothing like *you* but ..."

Jen hit her back, laughing. "I was only 'innocent,' as you put it, because of my dad. After my mom died, he was horrible. You met him that one time when we went back there for a visit. You saw how strict he was. You were one of the first and only friends I'd ever introduced to him, and I only did that because if I hadn't, he threatened to come to campus."

"Yeah, I'm glad you survived your dad ... so strict ... so cold. You could've ended up like him, then we wouldn't have been so close. The stories of your mom ... she sounded like she was wonderful. Like my grandma, warm and snuggly. Maybe they're both up there looking down at us with cookies and hot chocolate."

"Maybe." Jen's voice got soft as she kept shooting looks up at the sky.

They spent a few minutes with their own thoughts. *Jen has been 'studying' a lot lately. We used to have a couple nights out together to hang out or study, but that time has dwindled more and more.* A smile crept up Casey's face. She regarded her friend. "Are you saying that you're getting down and dirty at Cambia House?"

Jen blushed to match her red curls. "I don't want to talk about it."

"Is it one of the humans or a vampire?"

"Casey, I'm serious ... not now. Let's just focus on you for now. The prophecy. So, witches and vampires are completely off your dance card?"

With a final look at Jen to try to suss out her secrets, Casey shrugged. "Here's the thing. They are, to an extent. I'm not going to stop a situation if it comes up, but I won't seek it out. The witches who want to get me pregnant are frustrating me. A prophecy is supposed to happen in its own time, not be forced. At least the vampires are just letting things happen."

Jen snorted. "And that one guy, Perry, acting as if any baby of yours belongs to the coven. What an ass."

"Totally!" They continued to talk about witches, vampires, and school. Every now and then Zoryda flew amongst the leaves nearby, her jewel-like scales glittering. The path they were on grew steeper as they went up into the hills, thick trees all around them. The smell of nature—eucalyptus, flowers, moss—it all brought Casey back to her roots. Eventually, they arrived at an overlook.

Sitting on a small wall that protected hikers from tumbling off the steep cliff, Casey stared over the city below them. The spring air cooled her down after her hike. "I need to spend some time in my mind bubble." She finally turned from the mesmerizing view of the city to face Jen. "It's been a while since I've checked all my wards and done any research. You can do more of the hike—this path goes up another mile—or you can stay. Up to you."

Jen sat. "I think I'll sit and enjoy the view while you do your thing. Are we near any kitchens?"

Closing her eyes, Casey found a restaurant, pulled a few staples, and created six snickerdoodles for them—the buttery cinnamon cookie, one of Jen's favorites. The two slowly ate the sugary concoctions, Jen moaning as she finished her third, licking her fingers clean. Once done, Casey entered her bubble.

During her tenure in college, she'd built mental wards to help protect against the emotion vampires. There were several different families of vampires. The emotion vampires fed on the feelings of humans. They could also use their power to manipulate people. After being turned, the first vampire Casey had met was Jude. She'd trusted him, believed him when he promised to answer questions and help her. She never thought he'd use his own abilities to manipulate her.

That was the thing, emotion vampires' ability to manipulate others was so subtle, not even Casey, with her mind magic, realized it was happening until almost too late. Eventually, she'd taught herself and other witches how to ward against the vampires' attack.

It had been a couple of years since she'd seen Jude or any others from his family. Besides Jude, she'd met Candy, his neighbor. She really didn't know any of the others.

Jude attacked by sending in a constant barrage of tiny suggestions. His style was sneaky and pervasive. With practice, Casey became pretty good at blocking his suggestions. Candy had a more elaborate recipe she delivered in a single, powerful blast. When Casey knew it was coming, she could block it, but sometimes, even with the foreknowledge, she missed a few of Candy's ingredients.

In the beginning, Casey had spent a lot of time asking Jude questions, yet still knew little about their family, these emotion vampires. Jude was the older of the two vampires, with more experience, but Candy didn't seem young, either. His attacks were stealthy, at least that's how she felt about them. Gods, she knew nothing. She should ask Cyran to teach more about this family ... or maybe Rowan.

Without more contact, she couldn't reinforce the wards. She hoped what she did would make them stronger. With a sigh, she went to the book of prophecy, lying near the library within the mental bubble, but the language was an ancient dialect. Lucas, the oldest vampire she knew, had been teaching her, however with everything else, she still didn't know enough to translate more than a word or two. The language felt older than time itself.

Her library ... maybe she could find something to help if she ever found herself bound by silver again. She searched the books for anything that looked promising. There wasn't much. She found one book, old and musty. Most of the advice focused on not getting mixed up in it. She debated trying the door again, but usually the door remained locked when she came here alone.

Next, she reviewed videos on testing. She'd recently updated her mental video collection to VHS ... nothing like updating the glass bubble to the latest and greatest! She had her own memories and the stories her grandpa, Tilly, and Damion shared with her after she'd become a coven witch. The memory of earning her walking stick made her laugh, both her grandpa and Hildegard calling her out for cheating on her conjuration. She'd improved over the years. As she reviewed the others, she focused on how different coven witches tested mind magic. She wasn't sure if the coven's teachings were good enough, but feared what would happen if she were the person to question the way it had always been.

After slipping out of the bubble, the two headed back down the hill. Casey turned to Jen. "Once you graduate, are you staying at Cambia House, or will you get a job in a school district?"

"I've applied for positions at several schools. The interviews start in a few weeks. I love what I'm doing now with you and the other vampires, but I think I want to give working as a gym teacher a go."

Casey's chest tightened up at those words. "That's good. I know it's what you've always wanted, and most of us know what we need to at this point, but, gods, what will I do without my best friend?"

Jen's brow shot up. "Best friend?"

Narrowing her eyes, Casey smiled. "You know you're my best friend."

"Kailey will be heartbroken ... as will Ginger."

"Ginger probably already is. Gods, can you imagine if she found out I'm a witch as well? I don't know if she'll forgive the vampire side, but both together? Never."

Jen grimaced. "I know. I was a bit surprised. I mean, I know she's hurt because of the secrecy, but there's a phobia there as well. I'm not sure how she got the job as speech writer for the governor, except that she's really good at what she does."

As they neared the car, Casey gave a whistle, and her dragon dove down, reattaching herself to the walking stick with a small glow of pale blue light.

Jen's eyes shone. "That will never get old. I can't imagine not being in love with all of this."

"So, why don't *you* want to become a vampire?"

Jen glanced aside. "I just ... I have enough problems with my dad, and he's the only family I have left. My mom's parents died before I was born, and my dad won't tell me what happened to his parents. I have no idea about any of my ancestry. It's crazy."

Casey pursed her lips in thought. "We could ask Rowan and his staff to look into it. You never know what they'll find. Maybe they can learn more about your family tree ... find out you have some long-lost great-aunt or uncle ... or something."

"Maybe." She shrugged. "We can ask. I just don't want to be a bother, especially if I end up leaving."

Casey hugged her, pressing her cheek against Jen's. "Even if you leave, you'll always be part of the family."

Chapter 10

One week and college will be over. The reality of leaving college to become a 'real person' ... 'real vampire'? ... 'real witch' excited Casey and terrified her ... but she could put off thinking about it for a few more days.

The foyer sounded empty as she closed the front door of Cambia House and debated all the studying she may or may not need to do for finals. She was ready but still wanted to study. The exams loomed over her like the cliff she and Rowan couldn't climb. Adjusting her bag, she headed for the stairs. *I wonder if I could just hide in my room until my exams ... no one would notice my absence.*

"I placed a dress on your bed for our date tonight, beautiful." The resonant baritone flowed over her like silk.

Foot on the first step, and hand on the rail, she slowly turned to see Cyran's smirking face as he leaned against the entrance to the front room.

Racking her brain, trying to think past her organization for finals, she stared at him. "Our date?" She had a vague memory of him demanding they go out tonight, but she hadn't really agreed and nothing else had been said about it.

"You did agree to the date. The reservation has been made for eight o'clock; you have four hours before we leave." He winked, turned, and disappeared into the room behind him.

She paused for the space of a heartbeat before continuing up the stairs. *Right, hot vampire, date tonight ... I can focus ... did I agree?* Casey slowly ascended the stairs, imagining what it would be like spending the evening with Cyran.

Barely glancing at the outfit on her bed, she set a timer and got to work. *Two hours of studying before I can let myself drift off to this evening again ... I can do this.*

Just before her alarm went off, she gave in to the inevitable and headed off to shower. After her shower, hair, and makeup, she finally confronted the outfit. Her eyes widened and she bit her lip. *How the hell am I supposed to wear this thing without it falling off?* She slipped it on and realized that she couldn't wear a bra with it and had to try again. The top, a fitted suit jacket with shoulders that reached about an inch past her real shoulders, came together at her bellybutton. The black and white diamond fabric top attached to a skirt that barely went low enough to cover her ... assets. The only relief from the diamond pattern was a thick black belt that would – hopefully – hold the top closed. *And Cyran thinks I should go out in public like this?*

At the belt, the jacket gaped open about an inch and a half apart, and it didn't get better as it traveled up, over her chest, to her shoulders. The jacket part was tight enough she hoped it wouldn't flap open, actually exposing her parts to the world. She tried tugging the jacket closed to cover her breasts, but to no avail. The center line of her body was exposed for any and all to see. She had sheer nylons on and slipped on black heels to finish off the look. She'd almost be as tall as Cyran with the shoes.

She took one last look in the mirror and thought about how many people she'd see in the house. *Is there a way to make it out without seeing anyone?*

She left her room and shut the door, running into Rowan, who looked her up and down, a small smile on his face and a twinkle in his pale green eyes. "Where are you off dressed like that?"

Casey flushed to her bellybutton, and knowing he could track the coloring, she shrugged. "No idea. Apparently, I agreed to a date with Cyran."

Rowan nodded and his face went blank. "He's clever. I can see that happening."

Eyes narrowing, she pointed at him. "Are you laughing at me?"

His lips quivered and his eyes danced. "Nope, not at all. I'm sure you'll have a lovely evening."

She grumbled and aimed for the stairs. Just before she got there, she heard someone heading up. Riley climbed up the last few steps, and, like Rowan, took her in. The devil from her birthday peeked through as a smile grew on her face. "Oh, yeah. We'll have fun with *that* one. Where did the dress come from?"

"Cyran. It's a long story. Later." As she slipped past, Riley growled and slapped her ass.

At the bottom of the stairs, Cyran stood in a crisp black suit with a white shirt and a vest that matched her outfit. Slowly letting his eyes drift over her body, he offered her his arm. "Casey, you look gorgeous, as always. Shall we?"

She blushed and gently placed a hand on his arm. They headed out to his black Chevrolet Corvette Roadster. The convertible top was up. *Good, considering the amount of time I spent on my look. However, maybe next time we could go out with it down.*

He opened her door, like a gentleman and, after she was securely seated, circled to the driver's side and slid in himself. He drove them downtown to a new restaurant.

Casey gazed at the establishment—and the line of people waiting to get in—she wondered at the popularity of a place she'd never even heard of. "What is this place?"

"It's a new concept restaurant. It's been open for a few weeks. It's for vampires only."

She couldn't imagine such exclusivity. It didn't seem right, somehow. Wasn't Rowan fighting for a coalition to bring everyone together? And here was a restaurant all about separation. She frowned. "So, humans or witches would be turned away?"

He scrunched up his face, slowly waving his head left and right as he thought. "I think they have separate rooms for nonvampires, but the main focus *is* vampires."

She felt appeased that everyone had a place in this new, trendy, hot spot. They parked and walked arm in arm to the front door. Cyran didn't seem to notice or care about the line. The people waiting presented mixed reactions. The majority of the people in line were vampires and seemed to take it as a given Cyran wouldn't wait. However, the others didn't see him as a VIP. Scowls and angry mutterings followed them as they skipped to the head of the line.

At the door, the bouncer opened up to admit them. Hearing the grumbles, the bouncer growled, "He has a reservation."

Someone down the line yelled, "I was told you didn't take reservations."

The door shut before Casey could hear anything more. Inwardly, she winced.

A man in a full tux led them to a booth in the back with low, romantic lighting and handed both of them a leather-bound menu with a capital V in the top left corner in a circle. Opening it up, she found it was divided into five courses: appetizer, mezzanine, main course, dessert, mezzanine fin. She read through the three sections she'd seen on other menus; the two that didn't seem to fit, she ignored at first. Once she acquainted herself with the choices, she closed the menu and faced her date.

"What's up with the mezzanine courses?"

With a smile, he folded his own menu and placed his hands on the table. "You'll see; have you selected what you want?"

She bit her lip. "I'm debating between the cassoulet and hachis parmentier."

Nodding, he gave her a warm smile. "What about your appetizer?"

"Mussels or soup. I love a good French onion soup. Or foie gras."

Eyes sparkling, his smile widened. "We could share foie gras and mussels."

She couldn't help herself and answered his smile with one of her own. She bounced in her seat. Her hand slapped across the front of her outfit as she realized she wasn't wearing a bounce-proof top. He laughed at her antics. "So worth it," he mumbled. "That leaves dessert. We can share that as well. Do you have a list of those?"

"Honestly, they all look divine: mousse, soufflé, opera cake, the floating islands, macaron cookies, pot de crème. Gods, they all sound amazing." *I'm going to swoon.*

"With you, a few bites, a recipe, and then we get these desserts back at the house, right?"

She bit her lower lip, thinking. "There's a good chance if I like the dessert, yeah. That's how the crème brûlée happened."

He smiled at her. "I'm ready, if you are." At her nod, he signaled the waiter. A man in a black suit and a turquoise button-down shirt came over. Across his waist he had a cummerbund in a turquoise a shade lighter than his shirt. His tie matched his cummerbund.

After he ordered, she gaped. "You ordered one of each of the desserts!"

Cyran reached across the table and took her hands. He raised one to kiss. "Selfish reasons, trust me. Now, how are you doing? I'm asking as a friend, not your trainer. I know how the training is going. You're right on track with that."

"Am I?"

"You are, and if you're really worried, we'll discuss that at home. Too many ears here."

She searched the room and all its dark corners. The tables were filling, but she couldn't hear anyone else despite their proximity. It felt very private. "Dangerous." Her voice was low and as she thought about how easily secrets could be stolen in a place like his.

"What's dangerous?"

"How relaxed I feel now, secure. With the wrong people, secrets would be spilled. This is a very dangerous place you've brought me."

He chuckled. Their appetizers arrived and they made quick work of the food. It was every bit as delectable as she'd hoped. As they finished up, she asked, "What about you? How are things on your end? Do you feel all the information that's been released to the public has helped relations?"

"I do. I think what Rowan is doing is brilliant. I know the road seems choppy now but change always brings out fears. In the end, it will be for the best."

The waiter came to clear their plates. "Your entrée will be ready in forty-five minutes. Enjoy the mezzanine."

Cyran stood and extended his hand out to her. Casey rose from her seat and asked, "Will you tell me what this is now?"

He smiled mysteriously. "Nope."

They weaved their way through the tables before reaching the edge of the dining room with the low lights and happy couples. Navy blue velvet curtains hung there in place of a wall, through which they found a set of stairs that led to a mezzanine full of people. Some wore thin studded collars; the rest appeared to be patrons of the restaurant. A man in a suit walked up to one of the collared workers, stroked her arm, and gently brought her wrist to his mouth. And then, right there in the middle of the crowd, he began to drink. Not much, just a few sips, before licking the wound shut.

The woman smiled, then made her way to a second set of stairs where she descended, and a new collared woman came up to replace her on the mezzanine.

Gaping, Casey turned to Cyran. "Is this what I think it is? A ... a blood course?"

Cyran rubbed her back and leaned over and kissed her neck before whispering in her ear. "You don't have to partake, but yes." As they descended the stairs, he reached down to take her hand and led her to the mid-level floor.

At first, Casey just watched, uncertain. Cyran stayed by her side, waiting for her to take the lead through this course. *Oh, well. I'm here. No reason not to take in the full experience.* One of the collared donors—a blond with brown eyes—approached and met her gaze. Licking her lips, Casey lightly reached out a hand. The blond moved closer with a sultry smile. Once the blond took her hand, Cyran released her waist to find his own donor on the mezzanine.

The hand was warm, and the smile amused as Casey held the gaze of the collared donor and lifted the wrist to her mouth. A rapid pulse beat against her lips through the skin. Her donor's tongue shot out in anticipation, eyes dancing, excited. Casey's teeth descended and she bit down. The warm blood flooded her mouth and the eyes she held dilated in pleasure. A heady scent emanated from their bodies. The blood flowed down her throat, electrifying her.

After three pulls, Casey licked the puncture wound closed. "Thank you," she whispered.

With a small nod, the donor left, and Casey was alone in the crowd, a small buzz traveling through her body. Alcohol did little to loosen up a vampire, to make them feel passionate ... but blood. Young for a vampire, drinking blood made her flesh sing with primal need. As she stood there, watching her first donor walk down the stairs, a second approached, and Casey's heart beat faster as she took the offered hand without even thinking.

By the time Cyran returned to bring her back to their table, she'd taken sips from three different donors. Casey's body vibrated with desire. When the main course arrived, she placated her need with delicious food. And then the desserts arrived. *My stomach is going to explode after trying so many desserts. Revenge of the sugars!* She stifled a giggle. Just when she imagined heading home, she remembered the mezzanine fin course.

"Did you really order two stops for blood?"

Reaching across the table, Cyran slid her hands in his. He rubbed his thumbs along the back of her knuckles. "Yes, but the second one is a bit different. Remember, this is a concept restaurant for vampires. Not your usual dining venue."

Heat building in her gut, she licked her lips. Her body tense with the unknown, but languid with the evening, she realized she'd trusted him as a trainer for three years. Why stop now? Smiling nervously, she asked, "What is so different about this last course?"

"Oh, you'll see, but, since this is the last course, make sure to grab all your stuff as we leave."

Something in his eyes made her wonder if her trust was misplaced.

Chapter 11

The waiter came over one last time. "We'll have your leftover desserts ready for you on your exit. The bill will be sent to your house, as requested. Will you be letting others know of your opinion?"

Cyran's face shifted to his 'public' face. "Of course. You can let your owners know I'll call them tomorrow to arrange our house's final review for the local media."

The waiter plastered on a smile and gave a slight bow. "Excellent."

Standing, Cyran took her hand and led her to the opposite side of the dining room from the mezzanine. "Aren't we going back to the mezzanine?"

"There are two mezzanines; this is the mezzanine fin. Follow me, Case." He led her through another set of curtains. They entered a long hallway with doors. Above each door shone either a red or a green light. Cyran led her to a door with a green light. Inside was a small room with a bed, a bath with steaming, bubbly water, a loveseat, and two of the collared donors. On the wall hung a cherrywood cabinet. With a click, the door closed behind them.

Cyran turned to her and captured her other hand. "Now, this is up to you, but this is how I'd like to end the night. I won't force this. I mean it ... it's up to you."

She gazed into dark eyes framed by naturally bronze skin, and her body again vibrated with need. Casey lifted up and rubbed her lips against his, breathing out a soft, "Yes."

He leaned down and let his tongue trace her lips, deepening the kiss when she didn't pull away.

He rubbed his hands up her arms to her neck. She slipped her hands under his coat to his waist, humming into his mouth. She rubbed up his back as their bodies came together.

Pulling back, he searched her eyes. "Before I tear off that lovely dress, let's take what I've paid for, then decide what we want to do."

She stepped back and regarded the pair of donors who stood patiently watching them. "Are they here for a quick sip, or more? Is this just a restaurant with rooms, or a brothel?"

"It's what we want it to be. The staff have all applied knowing the job. Personally, I'd like you all to myself. I've been dreaming of this from the first night I met you, but you've eluded me for years. You've finally graduated from being my student and I'd like to celebrate. Kailey has been rubbing her freedom with you in my face since day one."

Chuckling, she bit her lower lip. "I'd like that too."

His eyes widened. "Wait, you've wanted me as well?"

Her face burned, and she knew he could track her blush down her neck and torso. "I think I'll go with pleading the fifth on that one."

They broke apart and moved to the donors. Each took a wrist and drank deeply before excusing the extra people in the room. Casey shut the door behind them. As the door clicked, hands wrapped around her, slipping under the coat that didn't close in front. One warm hand cupped her breast as he began to kiss her neck.

She leaned back, tilting her head to give him more access, as he squeezed her close. Her heart pounded with excitement. His other hand began undoing the clasps on the dress. She spun, breath choppy. He pushed the cloth from her shoulders and the dress puddled at her feet. She worked on getting his suit off, piece by piece. Slipping out of her hose and shoes, they moved over to the jetted tub.

Casey slid into the heat of the tub and moaned as the jets tickled and stimulated her skin. Cyran slipped in at the other end and faced her. With a raised eyebrow, he lifted a hand and cocked a finger. Giggling, she launched herself through the bubbling water until she straddled him. With a smile, he raised his knees to hold her in place. He scooted back a bit and suddenly one of the jets shot straight up into her most private area. She squealed and tried to move, but he held her in place.

Yelping, she wiggled, and he laughed. His voice wrapped around her. "Oh, no, this is too fun. You're mine tonight, love."

He slid his hands up her back and pulled her forward into a kiss. As she shifted, the jet moved up her body to even more sensitive areas. She gasped into his mouth, and he chuckled. From the heat of the tub, the sensual kissing, and the pressure of the jets, a pool of need intensified in her loins.

With a groan, she rubbed her hand down his taut stomach, grasping his cock. As she moved her hand, his tongue plunged deeper into her mouth, and he grew bigger in her grasp. The heat of the water pounded on her body, stoking the flames of lust inside her.

With a primitive sound deep in the back of her throat, she slid up him, then down, before he could stop her. His hands glided up to her chest as she rode him in the warm waves of the tub. Sparks of desire ignited as he played with her nipples. She began to make sounds of eagerness with every roll of her hips. She increased her speed, and lightning traveled from her belly down her legs and arms, sending spasms of ecstasy throughout her system.

She leaned down as she rode him. He bit her lip and then kissed over to her ear, nibbling on the lobe. Casey ground against him—harder and faster—and he tongued her ear and played with her breast. He slid his other hand between them, slowly. Lower, lower ... she wanted to scream. After an eternity, his thumb rubbed her clit, sending her over the edge in an explosion of sensations, and she collapsed on his chest. His thumb continued. *Too much! Too much!* Every nerve fired as she rode wave after wave of pleasure. *Oh, gods, it's* almost *too much!*

He played her body as she lay on his chest making sounds he controlled. He laughed low in his enjoyment. Finally relenting, he wrapped his arms around her, and she snuggled in.

"I hope you don't think we're done, love. After three years, that was just our appetizer, the first course." With a smile, she rubbed against him, cuddling deeper into his firmly muscled warmth and practically purred. The warm jetted water spun around them like a tropical dream.

He lifted her up to a sitting position and tapped her nose before she could fall asleep. "Oh, no, we are out of this bath and into the bed."

With a pout, she got up and grabbed a towel to dry off. Following her, Cyran quickly dried himself before moving to her and throwing her on the bed. "Will you obey me, or should I find something to tie you down?"

She sat up, half laughing, and let her eyes drink in the beauty of his body. The idea of letting him call the shots excited her, but she wanted to get the basics figured out. "Are you kidding?"

Standing over her, he looked down at her like a god made of gleaming bronze. "Ropes then?"

Amused, she narrowed her eyes at him as she lay back down. In her years of training with him, she'd learned one thing: he never bluffed.

His gaze lingered over her body from head to foot and a small smile played across his face. "I don't know if I'm happy or upset you aren't forcing me to find ropes ... maybe next time."

She glared at him but thought about the idea and decided she'd enjoy it with him. Sniffing the air above her, she smiled knowingly.

Cyran walked around the bed, his smile growing. "Okay, hands behind your head then." When he got to her feet, he lifted on foot and started at her arches, kissing up her leg, slow and deliberate. Every few kisses, he took a nip, scraping his teeth over her skin. At first, his actions tickled more than anything, but as he moved up her body, she began to warm.

"Okay, love, I want you to part your legs for me, and then, using one of your hands, stimulate your clit, and with the other, play with your nipples."

She bit back a moan of anticipation, not wanting to give away how excited she was getting. "Do I have any say in this?"

He bit down on her inner thigh, breaking skin and taking a bit of blood. Her head fell back in a soundless scream as the sensations shot through her body like electrical currents. "Do as I say, vampling."

She slowly brought her hands down, placing one on one of her small breasts, dropping the other all the way down to the apex of her legs. Slowly, she rubbed both in circular motions.

Cyran murmured, "I want you to squeeze and pinch. Make yourself squirm while I kiss and lick you."

Her breath got rough as she followed his directions. She continued as Cyran licked circles on her thigh, higher and higher. His tongue, her finger, her hand ... her breathing grew choppy as he made his way up. Suddenly, his tongue penetrated her; she howled as the pool of heat boiled over.

He rubbed her lower hand and said, "This one goes back behind your head." She followed his direction as his mouth replaced her hand. One of his fingers entered her, then two, then three. *Gods, the sensation!* She broke. Lava burst from her center, melting her body while stars exploded in her vision.

Suddenly, he was above her, kissing her. She wrapped her legs around him and he slid into her. He began to pump, his talented fingers on her clit, rubbing her breasts, seemingly everywhere, ensuring she reached another climax. Again, he brought her to the breaking point, and this time they came together, soaring high.

Once she could reason again, she found him collapsed atop her like a heavy blanket, her legs and arms still holding him tight. She nuzzled into his neck for a quick kiss but didn't release her hold. His weight felt good.

With a contented sigh, he said, "Next time, we both get blood ... from each other. It makes it better."

Happiness bubbling inside, she breathed in his scent and let it settle into her. She asked, "Next time?"

He growled low into her ear. "Oh, yeah. There will definitely be a next time."

Chapter 12

Casey stared up at the ceiling where Zoryda curled in a rafter, in shock she'd made it to the last day of finals. So far so good. Sitting up in bed, Casey felt a mixture of thrill and trepidation. Two more exams and she'd be done.

She dressed in a skirt and a button-down top, then headed to breakfast, grabbing coffee, eggs, and sausage. Since it was too early for most of the house to be up, it surprised her when Cyran slid in across from her. "Morning, sexy."

A heat rose from her belly. "Hiya. What're you doing up at this horrible hour?"

"I heard it was the last day of college for you. I thought you'd like company."

Her face warmed further, and the heat spread to the rest of her body. "You've been popping up everywhere, being super sweet since our date last week."

His brow went up. "Not that many things."

Casey counted on her fingers. "Chocolate on my pillow, a rose in my car, and the drive through the mountains with the convertible top down. Those things aren't nothing."

He took her hands, eyes intent on her. "You obviously haven't been treated well enough in your life if those small things make you blush. Now, after today you're done with classes, then Saturday you graduate officially, cross the stage and everything. Then what?"

Casey knew what he wanted to know. When he wasn't training new vamplings, he oversaw house security. "I see you're still recruiting for house security."

A thrill went through her as he gave her a half-smile and a wink. He squeezed her hands. "Always, you know me. But seriously, with your degree in criminal psychology, you'd be a perfect fit ... a shoo-in for my staff." His eyebrows danced. "If you know what I mean."

She laughed. The offer intrigued her. She did know, in both ways he meant it. *But, like Jen, I feel I need to open my wings and fly. Get away from here for a bit.* Casey looked away. "I plan on applying for jobs outside of the house. I think I need some diversity in my life. If that doesn't work ..." She shrugged.

He gave her hands a squeeze before letting them go. He placed a hand over his chest and said in an overly dramatic way, "I'm heartbroken, but that makes sense. You'll be of more use to me once you've had some experience anyway."

A laugh escaped her as she renewed her attack on the sausage. "I'm so glad this is all working towards your end goal."

Cyran grinned. "Exactly. Speaking of, would you care to go out with me on a celebratory dinner date tonight?"

"Where exactly would we go?"

His smile grew. "Oh, I think you know my restaurant of choice. If you'd prefer somewhere else, I'm open to suggestions."

She sat back, belly tense in anticipation. "There were definitely items on that menu I still want to try."

"All five courses?"

She blushed. "Maybe."

They both ate for a bit in silence, enjoying each other's company. Once done, Casey said, "I have a strange request."

"Hmm."

She bit her lip and looked down. "Jen's mom died when she was eight and she's a bit estranged from her dad. She doesn't know if she has any other relatives. Could you use your people to see if you can trace her family line back?"

"A puzzle? I like it." He waggled his brows. "Things have been slow. Sure, I'll see what we can figure out about Miss Clark and her family. Did you know that her father is scheduled to come to the graduation party Saturday night?"

Dread flowed through her. "He's coming? Here?"

"As head of security, I have the full list of attendees, and he's on it. Of course he is. Why wouldn't he be?" Cyran answered his own question. "His daughter is graduating."

"Because ... well, he hasn't visited her for four years. They don't really talk. He doesn't really seem to like her that much. And he's coming to the party?"

"He sure is." After a beat, Cyran seemed to catch on to Casey's dread. His head tilted, concern pouring from him.

Tension flowing through her body, Casey began ordering her thoughts. "Does Jen know?"

"Do I know what?" Jen plopped down with her own tray of food beside Casey. "And are you still planning on walking in today?"

"I am. Are you going to walk with me?" Happiness flowed from her. "You bet I am."

Cyran watched them, shaking his head. "It's a few miles, why?"

Casey smiled at him. "It will be a nice way to relax before the big tests."

Jen took a drink of her orange juice. "Speak for yourself, I only have one exam today ... then freedom! But, back to what I walked in on ... do I know what?"

Casey's nose scrunched as she rotated in her seat to face her friend. "Your dad is coming to graduation."

"Oh, I know that. He told me when I left for college if I managed to make it all the way to the end, he'd watch me cross the stage in amazement."

Cyran's brows shot up. "Pleasant."

Jen nodded. "Yeah, he and I never really healed after Mom's death."

Casey grabbed her friend's hand. "Did you know he's also coming to the party afterwards?"

Jen's eyes widened a bit. "Like, *our* party, with vampires and scantily dressed waitstaff? *That* party?"

Casey huffed out a laugh. "Yeah, that one."

"Whoa. Well, that will be interesting. Any other big news I should know about before our walk?"

Cyran rubbed the back of his neck. "Nothing much, though the coalition council is starting to worry about counter attacks by human-only groups. There's one forming who are calling themselves 'hope,' spelled H-O-A-P. Humans Only, Anti-Paranormal. I'm not sure what they're planning, but we knew as soon as we started banding together, the segregationists would pop up."

Casey slumped. "Well, on *that* bit of good news ... Jen, can we head off? Let's wrap up one thing before we open up a new can of worms."

They gathered their bags and Cyran grabbed her for a quick kiss before saying, "For luck."

Casey and Jen walked to the college, enjoying the cool morning air. Avoiding topics of school, graduation, coalitions, or Jen's father, they fantasized about their dream jobs.

"So Jen, anyone new in your life you're not telling me about?" Casey's best friend had always been a private person, but they were besties, and Casey was nosey.

Jen rubbed her hands together. "Nope, I'm not going to tell you."

Shaking her head, Casey adjusted her bag on her back. She'd get the name of Jen's boy one way or another. "Sure you will. I know there's someone in the house. If you *don't* tell me, I'll just start asking everyone, blood donor and vampire alike. You know I will. You're my friend, I have to protect you."

Jen made a sound like a wounded animal before stopping and letting her head drop back. "Case, can't you just drop this?"

Once Casey realized Jen had stopped, she turned and began bouncing in place. She rocked her shoulders back and forth, dancing. "I don't think I can, Jen. I may fail my finals, focused only on you."

With a growl, Jen glared. "Fine, it's Jaxon. Are you happy?"

Throwing a fist in the air with a hoot, Casey spun, and started towards campus. "Very!" *Jaxon and Jen, now* that *is a cute couple. I'll have to kill him if he hurts her, but he has seemed happier as of late.*

When they got to campus, Jen wrapped her in a hug. "See you back at Cambia house when you're done. I know you'll kill it."

Casey shivered in her skirt, a cool breeze playing in her hair. "Two more exams and freedom. I'm done. Success! I can't believe how close we are to sitting back, lounging, and pure bliss."

Laughing, Jen headed off to her final.

Casey entered the lecture hall, and, in a flash, she realized it was the same room she'd first changed back from male bits to female three years ago. She almost giggled but caught herself.

Ginger was with me then. Casey frowned, wondering if she'd ever be able to rekindle that friendship. Would Ginger ever come around to trusting her and being okay with her vampirism? Skyler hadn't. Sadness washed through her thinking about friends lost, and how many more she'd lose. *That's two friends lost ... how many more?*

She grabbed a sandwich from the cafeteria between finals. The first had been stressful, but she felt good about the outcome. Sitting outside the building, she wished she wore more than a button-down sleeveless top and tiered miniskirt. The air hadn't warmed up all day, and she shivered.

As she entered the building for her second final, the air conditioning was on for the heat they'd had the day before, and she feared freezing. *How can I fill in an exam booklet if my fingers are frozen?*

Trying to ignore her icy fingers, she focused on the questions and worked through the exam. She moved as quickly as she could, and a tiny thrill shot through her as she handed in the final blue book. *I just finished my last task as a college student ... I've done it!*

Once outside, she found the temperature as chilly as inside. Head down, rubbing her arms to try to generate heat, she started to walk fast to make it home quickly. She debated misting, but rejected the idea since she still hadn't mastered the skill. As she weighed her options, she ran into a solid, warm body.

"Lovely Casey, we have some things we need to discuss."

Chapter 13

She felt the world dissolve around her before she could react. When her vision solidified, a cold band snapped around her neck as a voice whispered, "Now, that's better, isn't it."

Jerking her focus up, she gazed into the eyes of Jude. The queasy nausea in her belly, and her loss of balance, let her know that the band around her neck was silver and she was trapped.

Her sudden lack of magic made her collapse. Jude caught her and carried her through his apartment to the bed. "Wasn't it nice of me to wait until after finals to bring you here? Now we have all this time to talk."

Terror gripped her in greasy tentacles as she realized how quickly he'd trapped her. The silver sapped away the control from her body. Bile pooled in the back of her throat as the fear threatened to lock her muscles. She shook as she tried to adjust. *Think, Casey. You have to be smarter than him! Think! I have to escape.* "What do you want with me, Jude?"

He stood over her, and she couldn't help but notice how sexy he still was as his eyes raked her body. A small smile played over his face as she trembled out of control in his bed. "Isn't it obvious? I want ... we want, what everyone wants. The prophecy baby."

We? Her mind went blank, and she searched the room for other presences. "What?!"

"If the emotion vampires, can get this baby, we can control the outcome. We do *not* like the direction Rowan is taking things. *We* want to control things. So, we will keep you."

Chills ran through her already frozen body. "You plan on keeping me until I have a baby?"

With exaggerated slowness, he sat next to her and rested a hand on her shin. He gazed down at her face. "If that's what it takes."

"That's absurd. You can't keep me prisoner for nine months." She fisted her hands and tried to move her arms.

His mouth quirked to the side. "I don't know *how* you survived college, kitten. More than nine months. You aren't pregnant yet."

He stood and began securing her arms and legs to the head and footboard of the bed. Since she was still incapacitated from the silver, he easily overcame her struggles. She yanked at the constraints, heart racing, but with the collar on, she was as weak as a human and her attempts were a joke. Tears burned at the corners of her eyes, terror turning to frustration. "What are you doing?"

His brows rose. "This seems terribly obvious to me, kitten. I want to get you pregnant. The process is simple. You do know where babies come from, don't you?"

She pulled a few more times, but the bonds held.

He gently stroked the hair from her forehead. "You can struggle, I won't stop you, but you're only hurting yourself. I tested these out myself at full power, and I couldn't break through."

"You're just going to leave me here, tied down until you impregnate me?" Her fear had shifted to ire, and she glared at him.

Jude smiled. "I mean, we'll have some fun. I remember us having fun in the past." He let his finger trace down her arm. "Don't you?"

Knowing it was a losing battle, Casey relaxed into the bed and tried to ignore him. She would need her strength later. She may be losing this battle, but she wouldn't lose the war.

With a smirk, as if he could read her thoughts, he began unbuttoning her shirt. "Thanks for wearing such a manageable outfit. So much easier. Oh, and no bra today. Better and better." He untied her feet, one by one, and got her skirt and panties off. She tried to fight him, but his strength was greater than hers. Finally, she bit the inside of her cheek to ignore him. "Nice of you not to fight." His mockery of her struggles hit home. "I had scissors available if you misbehaved."

Casey closed her eyes and fled to her glass bubble. But without her magic, she could feel everything he did. As his hand ran up her leg—even sitting in her bubble—she saw as well as felt the power he sent into her. 'Obey', 'Enjoy', 'Want', 'Lust', 'Crave'. She had no protection. She bit her lip as his commands washed over her, through her, into her.

As long as she stayed in her mental bubble, her mind was safe, but her body ... oh her body wanted him. Opening her eyes, her vision doubled. He slowly ran a finger up from the sole of her foot and the path burned like fire. The higher up it went, the more her back arched into his touch. When it reached the apex of her legs, he dipped down, and his finger entered her like a tongue of hot fire. She screamed out at the sensation ... it pulsed throughout her body, enflaming her.

Inside her bubble, she sat helpless, trying to ignore her body's betrayal.

Pulling out, he whispered in her ear, pushing his wet finger into her mouth so she could taste herself on him. "You are so wet for me right now; can you taste your desire? I could take you and you'd probably just beg for me to keep taking you, over and over. What a lovely wanton of a woman you are, Casey Strega. I hope you don't get pregnant right away. I have so many plans."

Cloth rustled and floorboards creaked as he moved around the room. She slid her eyes to the side and saw him stripping off his clothes and then rummaging in a drawer. He took something out and moved over to her. "I know that you don't want to give me the time of day, so I figure, making you scream in pleasure will be my special gift to you." Playing between her legs, he placed something cool on her with a cord draped over her belly.

Wiggling a bit in uncertainty, she asked, "What is that?"

He placed a controller next to her and hit a button. A small vibration began right on her clit. She jerked her hips up as a squeal erupted out of her. He placed a hand over her abdomen to hold it in place. Her eyes grew wider as the feelings of heat built and waves of small pleasures rolled through her, radiating throughout her body. It wasn't quite enough to satisfy, but, gods. Her breathing grew rough. She wanted to ignore him, but he was making that more and more difficult.

Leaning over, he bit and then sucked on her ear. "This is just the start, kitten."

Climbing up, he straddled her, ensuring the small vibrator stayed in place. Then he leaned down to suck in one of her nipples while turning the small device up to a higher level. She bucked up in surprise, the dual sensations, along with his suggestions, making her forget why she didn't want to be here.

As his teeth grazed her nipple, she arched, pushing against his mouth and moaned, "More."

"What do you want? Do you want this?" He turned the small machine up another notch. "This is as high as it goes."

Casey cried out as her core exploded. Her chest heaved as she tried to lift her hips, but with Jude sitting on them, there was no way. She whimpered with need.

He hummed. "What could you want? Could it be this?" Shifting, he plunged his cock hard into her, burying himself deep inside her. One hand continued what his mouth had begun with her breast, and the machine continued its torture. Her eyes rolled back, and she slammed her hips up to meet him. Two more pumps and she broke, the heat within taking her under in a wave that had her intermittently screaming and moaning.

Though the vibrations were too much as soon as she orgasmed, its stimulation turning to pain, Jude left it going until she lay limp, twitching. He smiled down at her and said, "You continue to behave, and this will be a spectacular imprisonment."

His eyes raked her, strapped down on his bed. "I'm going to head off to shower. When I'm done, it will be your turn. I, of course, will be watching your every move. Then you'll have some dinner, and then, right back here for an encore performance. Any questions, kitten?"

Casey rolled her head, so she didn't have to look at him. As much as her body enjoyed his ability to play it, now she just felt numb. She had to get away from here, away from him, and his ability to manipulate her. In her bubble she still had access to her books. She decided to go through them more slowly to see if there was anything, *anything* at all that would help.

About an hour later, he came for her and brought her into the bathroom. She walked sedately behind him, knowing this wasn't the time to fight. She was collared and he'd attached a leash to her.

He sat in a chair outside the open door, holding the end of the leash. She found a clean towel next to the sink for drying off. She used his products to wash her hair and body. Nothing could wash away the stain on her soul from what he'd done, not yet ... but he'd pay, she promised herself, he'd pay. Setting her jaw, she put on her game-face. She could do this; she was her grandpa's granddaughter.

After the shower, even her shirt was gone. The small act of cruelty almost broke her ... he treated her more and more like an animal. *I am no animal! I will survive this; I will survive him!* Searching the small room, her game-face broke for a moment, and she glared at him. "Do I get anything to wear?"

Lifting a single shoulder, he leaned back lazily. "I don't see the point." "You said dinner. Do I have to eat naked?"

The corner of his mouth rose, and he licked his lips. "I would quite enjoy eating you," he said, and she felt the blush rise up from her chest. "I mean, eating while you were naked. Would you feel better if I were naked as well?"

"No! Gods, no. Leave your clothes on." *Slow down. You're speaking too fast and protesting too vehemently.*

He just chuckled. "Leave the towel in the bathroom. Dinner should be ready."

It dawned on her. *He must not have stayed outside the bathroom the entire time I was inside. There really wasn't any reason for him to. Where would I go with only a towel and no magic?* With a final drying swipe around her body, she dropped the towel to follow him, closing her eyes for a moment to swallow any insecurities she had about traipsing about naked.

She sat at the dining room table, and Jude served up tacos. She tilted her head, considering him. "Do you make anything else besides tacos?"

"Yes, but I happen to make excellent tacos, and it *is* Tuesday. Try a fish taco, they're the best."

Already clutching a taco by her mouth when he said that, she paused. Holding his attention, she slowly opened her mouth, slipped out her tongue to guide the taco in, and took a bite. *Maybe if he sees me as only sexual, he'll get sloppy, forget I have a brain ... help my escape plans.* After she swallowed, she said, "The steak tacos are fine." She dropped her gaze as she finished it off.

He chuckled and grabbed a few tacos for himself.

When she went for her second taco, he grabbed her hand and moved it to the fish taco. "Trust me. You'll love it."

After eating it, she gave a half-shrug and moved to the next variety.

By the end of dinner, she'd tried one of each. They were all good. *But that doesn't matter; I don't want to be stuck with Jude in his apartment.* Her dinner date was supposed to be Cyran at the new vampire restaurant. Now, a naked dinner with him could be interesting. *Don't get distracted. Cyran isn't here. Jude is, and he is dangerous!*

After dinner, there was a stop at the bathroom, then back to bed. This time, Jude forced Casey to drink a bit of his blood. Jude, being an emotion vampire, didn't drink blood. However, exchanging blood made any vampire horny. Casey tried to resist—closing her mouth, turning away and tucking her chin into her shoulder—but he laughed off her efforts. He clasped her chin and dug his fingers into the base of her jaw until the pain coerced her to open her mouth. With a quick bite, his arm bled, and he forced that into her mouth. The blood flowed in, and oh, gods ...

Again, Casey tried not to think about how much she enjoyed his touch as he had his way with her body. But not her mind—and not her soul.

He connected a tether from her collar to the far wall and released her arms and legs. "Now we can cuddle, my kitten." She turned her back to him and curled into a tight ball, hoping sleep would come to her quickly.

The next morning, Jude walked her to the living room and connected the collar to a cable that stretched from the couch to the bathroom. It looked like a runner used for dogs. He had work to do, and this gave her the freedom to sit on the couch with the remote control or use the facilities. She checked her range, and though she could reach the other doors, the bathroom was the only one unlocked.

He'd pumped into her three times so far. He explained that he planned on keeping her naked until she was pregnant.

Once he was busy working, in the dining room, doing something on a computer set up on a table against the wall, she went back to her mental library. Book after book, she reviewed her options. Nothing, nothing, nothing!

She had to find something. *Why is there so little lore on silver? You'd think this would be well studied: the one real damper on magic.* Maybe it was, just not in the books she had. She should've called her grandpa after the outing with Jen.

She began grabbing books at random, frustrated at her lack of success so far. She sat perched on the edge of the wood table in her mental bubble to read through the book.

I wish I had someone here to bounce ideas off of. She drummed her fingers on the table as she paged through the book. By some miracle, she found a section on silver in the book. Maybe there was something to the random grab!

"Whoa!" she mumbled to herself out loud, eyes widening. "It says here, basic family powers still function in the presence of silver. The powers are not so much magic as an intrinsic part of the vampire's being."

Casey raised her head and stared at the massive bookcase. *Does that mean, when we were stuck on that ledge—if he'd tried—Rowan could have shifted to a small animal and escaped?* This was definitely something they all had to learn and practice. But Casey didn't know how to shift into a small animal, so she was still stuck. However, she didn't have to stay female. A smile spread slowly across her face.

What would Jude do if he was presented with a male?

Chapter 14

"Well, this is interesting." He pursed his lips together. "How long can you maintain the male form?"

Smiling wide, Casey felt elated. "As long as I want."

He approached, gazing down at her new form. "Gods, you're gorgeous in either form. This will work out perfectly. To the bed."

Her shoulders dropped almost as far as her mouth. "What?"

He slapped her shoulder. "You heard me, to the bed. You're still two parts of the prophecy, we'll just have to," he rolled his hands in front of himself. "Figure things out. Roll with the punches so to speak. I think I can still carry you."

Dumbfounded, she sat there and stared at him. Jude moved to lift her; she stood before he had the chance. Gazing down at her, he tipped her chin up and almost purred. "So beautiful," and then he kissed her. In her shock, she missed his power rushing in and was swamped, mind and body. "Let's move this to the bedroom, no?"

Her body hardened for him. She looked up into his gorgeous dark eyes and let him lead her through the door. Once on the bed, she didn't notice when he used the restraints.

He trailed a finger over her taut chest and asked, "Would it be too much to ask for the female form to come back?"

Part of her mind screamed, 'no', while another part wanted to please him, a moan escaping her at his touch. In a fury, she searched for the reason for the 'no,' and tumbled into her glass bubble. Enough of her mind cleared for her to remember why she needed to keep this form. She pulled on her arms and realized he'd strapped her down while she'd been drunk on his manipulative suggestion. She licked her lips. "You called me beautiful. Why do you want anything else?"

Moving to the end of the bed, he grabbed her newest member, already stiff with want. "Well, according to this, you're already happy to see me." He began pumping, then dipped his head down to suck, taking her in all the way. She groaned from the feeling of his mouth on her cock, sucking hard, playing his tongue over her. A hand dipped down to play with her balls. She threw her head back and gasped as what he did flowed sharply through her body.

Just as her body arched to a climax, he stopped. Standing up, he stared down at her. She panted, needing, wanting. "Please," she begged.

"Oh, this?" He waved his hand at her. "I won't finish you off in this form, only the other one. But I'll play. You *are* lovely and fun to play with. But never fear, I'm not so awful as to leave you hanging; I'm off to get a friend." And then he left her, throbbing and in need, tied to a bed so there was nothing she could do to assuage her desire.

It felt like he was gone for hours. In reality, it had probably been minutes, but her body throbbed with lust. Casey squirmed, but nothing she did helped. The door closed and she tried to put on a poker face, but feared she failed as Candy walked in, as naked as the two of them. Despite knowing the woman was a viper, Casey had always been attracted to her. More gorgeous and lush than a cover model, the woman gazed down at Casey like a starving woman at a feast.

"Why, Jude, what did you bring me as a gift?"

The pressure on her cock got even tighter, if that was possible. Candy was beautiful, perfect, luscious, and Casey felt when her blast of power hit her, washing through her. Unprepared, Casey hadn't retreated back into her mental bubble. Suddenly, all Casey wanted to do was please this perfection in female form. A golden-haired goddess. She would do anything the goddess asked—fetch her the moon and stars—if only she would alleviate the pressure inside Casey. She moaned in want.

Candy's focus moved to Jude as Casey tried to breathe. "What did you do to the poor child?" Sashaying to the end of the bed, she climbed up and simply slid over Casey's throbbing dick. Casey exploded, nearly passing out with the intensity of it.

Candy smiled down. "Well, that was effective, but not much fun. Let's see what more we can do." Sliding off Casey, she knelt next to her. "Hmm, no longer as happy to see me. Maybe I can do something about that."

Straddling Casey, Candy presented the moist, pink folds of her secret self to Casey's face. While Casey stared at the sculpted globes of her ass, Candy bent down and took all of Casey's cock into her mouth. All reason fled from her.

Jude put his hand on Casey's chest and began rubbing and pinching. Then he said, "Wouldn't it be nice for you to return the favor? Candy's being *so* nice to you."

Casey tried to shift her position, but there was nowhere to go. Jude licked her ear, sending shivers down her body, meeting up with the shocks coming from Candy. "Go on, Casey, just one lick."

Staring up, Casey licked her lips. She tilted her chin and her lips touched Candy in her most private place. Candy did something with her mouth and Jude gave a squeeze with his hands. Commands from both of them slammed into her and Casey was overwhelmed with euphoria.

With a groan, her tongue shot out, again and again, as the sensations flowed through her. *Oh, gods, I'm burning inside! If this could just last ... forever ...* Since she'd met Candy, she'd fantasized about such a scenario. *As long as I'm in this predicament, I might as well indulge myself.* For a moment she wondered if this was her or the manipulations, but then a wave of pleasure washed through her, and she didn't care ... it felt too good. She wanted this.

I'm taking a little control of the situation, even if it feels like I'm giving in. This orgasm is mine! She opened up her mouth, licking and sucking every inch of what Candy offered. She tasted herself, as well as Candy's essence. She toyed with her using her lips and tongue until Candy cried out on Casey's cock. The feeling of Candy's orgasm while Casey was hard in her mouth nearly unhinged her reason.

Candy flipped around to ride Casey, taking Casey's tongue in her mouth. Jude continued to play where he could. Again, Casey broke, losing her seed inside Candy, her heart beating faster than she'd ever experienced. *Oh, gods, will the orgasm ever stop?*

Finally, Candy stopped kissing her, and patted her cheek. "Good enough for now." The waves of sensations began to recede, and Casey trembled at the power of this beautiful goddess sitting atop her.

The next morning Casey woke up shivering. She'd maintained the male form, but she wasn't sure that her solution had merit. With both Jude and Candy holding the leash, she had no control over what they did to her body. She felt defeated at how horribly her plan failed.

Jude walked in with a mug of coffee. "Well, kitten, I'd love a morning romp, but alas, I'm in a hurry. Shower quickly and I'll attach you to your daily tether. If you prefer that form, then Candy will happily be the mother of the baby the two of you have. She had so much fun last night."

She groaned at the memory of how willing she'd been as he moved over to unleash her from the wall. In the shower, Casey debated, and decided she really didn't want to give a baby to this clan, especially by impregnating Candy. As the warm water washed away the previous evening's play, her body shifted back.

Clean and dry, she moved into the kitchen where she found a breakfast sandwich and coffee waiting for her. Jude came in. "Ah, breasts, lovely. I'm thrilled you decided to return to me. I do enjoy playing with this form more."

He approached, reaching out to her. She recoiled from him, shrinking into herself. After two days, she just wanted to be away from his touch. He smiled. "None of that, kitten. Don't make me tie you up for the day."

He means it. She glared at him as he lifted her onto the dining room table. Smiling, he positioned her where he wanted her. "Do you know how hard it was to watch you with Candy last night?" He unzipped his pants, pushed her back, and lifted her hips up. "All I wanted was this." He began licking her between her legs, sucking and nibbling. He used his fingers as well. "Gods, you get wet quick, love."

Her heart beat fast. *Resist, resist,* her mind screamed but with all of his suggestions pouring in, the pool of heat in her loins grew into an ocean. Even with her mind in her bubble, her body reacted to his suggestions. Each lick of his tongue, each thrust of his fingers drove her to crave more. Grabbing the side of the table, she bit her lip to stop any sounds from escaping.

She hung mostly off the table. His hooded bedroom eyes smoldered as he positioned her body so it aligned with his, and then he slowly pushed into her, inch by inch. "Now, kitten. I will stop here, head off to work and finish tonight. Or, if you ask nicely, I'll finish right now. But if you choose for me to stop, I'm tying you to the bed so you can't please yourself."

She knew her eyes were desperate as her mouth opened. She tried to close it but couldn't. He started to pull out with a smirk. Panicked, her arms began to shake, and small noises came from her.

Leaning forward, pushing in a tiny bit, he asked, "What was that, kitten? I didn't quite make out what you said." His hand gently relaxed on her lower stomach, thumb resting on her clit.

With a twitch of that thumb, she groaned. Squeezing her eyes, she pushed out the word, "Please."

"Please what? Fuck you? Or leave?"

She bit her lip, breath rough with need. She didn't want to ask him for anything, but gods above, could she let him tie her up all day in this state of need? "Please, fuck me." The words were scarcely out when he slammed into her, playing her body like a master with his favorite instrument, increasing her desire with every rub, every stroke of his hand, every plunge of his cock inside her. Her need grew with each thrust, with each circle of his thumb, until she shattered there on the table, screaming out with the pleasure and frustration of being so easily manipulated by Jude.

Once done, he tucked his limp member inside his pants, smiling down at her. "I like knowing you are filled with me, kitten." He carried her to the couch and left her there, his seed dripping down her leg, and went off to work. Again, her tether was short, and her options limited.

She sat on the couch, paging listlessly through a magazine when a buzzing started in her head. Jumping to her feet, she looked around. Zoryda appeared in front of her with a pop of misplaced air. She leapt up, amazed. A wave of relief and gratitude filled her. "Zoryda! How did you find me?"

Her dragon flew to her and with a snap of her jaw removed the collar encircling her neck. With the sudden influx of magic, Casey collapsed onto the couch. Her dragon landed on her shoulder and wrapped her tail around her neck, mirroring the spot the silver collar had been. For the first time in ages, Casey felt stable, whole, and centered.

Standing again, she went to Jude's room and found her clothes. She dressed quickly, closed her eyes, imagined

Cambia House, and misted away. She landed in her room, where she could be away from people.

Her dragon rubbed her cheek and flew to the rafters. Before she could get to her door, it slammed open and Cyran ran in, enfolding her in a hug. "You're back!"

He had to catch her as her legs gave out, her whole body shaking. "I am. Jude captured me. He put a silver collar around my neck."

Snarling, Cyran hugged her tighter "That ass! He's dead!"

Sinking deeper into his embrace, Casey tried to keep a level head. Grandpa had taught her how to have separate head spaces. She would separate herself from the situation for now. She needed to tell her house leaders what happened. "Let's have a meeting and figure this out."

"Let me just hold you for a few minutes first. I was more worried than I want to admit."

With a shiver, she let the fear she'd been trying to hide go and sank into him. A tear burned down her cheek as she swallowed her embarrassment at letting Jude and Candy get away with so much. Cyran held her, rubbing her back, letting her know she was safe.

Eventually, they made a report to Rowan, who called in the other heads of the coalition's vampire houses, Lucas and Cynthia. Casey informed them of the capture, their desired outcome, and how they went about trying to achieve their goals. After her report, she and Cyran retired to her room to rest in each other's arms for the remainder of the night. She could tell it hurt his feelings when she recoiled from his touch, but he didn't leave her side, seeming to understand she didn't want to be alone.

Chapter 15

Friday morning, Casey woke up with Cyran spooning her. His arms wrapped around her, and one hand was cupping her breast. About to lean back into him, her stomach cramped, and she curled into a ball.

Pulling away, Cyran rubbed her back. "What do you need?"

"Blood ... too long." She started to shake. "But I don't want the feelings. Too soon after ... can you stay with me?"

He left the room and she felt bereft. Pulling up the blankets, she breathed through the feeling of her body's needs. She knew if she waited too long, she'd develop blood lust and become a danger, but after being captured by Jude for a few days, she didn't want anything more than the gentle safety of Cyran's arms around her.

After a few minutes, he returned with Reis, who sat in the chair and offered his arm. Cyran slipped in behind her again, wrapping Casey in the safety of his arms. She tensed for a moment, but then remembered it was Cyran and she was safe.

After she drank as much blood as Reis could safely give, she licked his wounds closed and turned away. She tucked her head in Cyran's chest as her heart raced, almost afraid of the feelings of desire coursing through her body.

She heard Reis stand. "She needs more. Should I send someone else in?"

Cyran held her as she shook. "She does, but it can wait a few hours. She's had a rough few days and needs to feel safe."

"I can send in Tonya. She's not a morning person so for her, morning donations are always a quick feeding and then she's back to bed."

Casey nodded and heard Reis move off. After Tonya left, Casey began to feel better with the blood surging through her body. She pulled back and looked up into Cyran's almost black eyes as guilt took over. "I'm sorry. You probably have things to do. It's a workday. The party is tomorrow. Babysitting me wasn't what you planned to do, was it?"

He kissed her forehead. "No, it wasn't, but we're a family and your sense of security *is* my priority. You took a hard blow to your inner self, and I'll stay here if it means you can start to build yourself back up." Her stomach growled. "Well, maybe here should include the cafeteria," he added.

They got up and dressed. In the cafeteria, they were joined by Jen and Rowan. Jen slid in and wrapped an arm around Casey, giving her a half-hug. "I heard you ... um ... were back."

She knew the story would get out; everyone would hear eventually. She ducked her head and cupped her hands around a mug of coffee. "How much were you told?"

"Most of it. They didn't think you'd mind or would want to have to tell the story again. I was the only one told though, no one else. It sounds awful, and I really want to find and kill that asshole." Jen dropped her head to rest on Casey's shoulder. "Tell me what I can do to help you."

Casey leaned her cheek over onto Jen's curls. "I need to get out of my head. Maybe do another one of our hikes, or some of that meditation you always go on and on about. I'm kind of freaking out."

Jen gave her a squeeze. "I'm totally up for any or all of the above, but you just got back, freaking out is expected.

How about we slip on our suits and go sit in the hot tub together and just talk, or listen to music? Maybe that will help clear out your mind."

Casey shut her eyes and thought. "Yeah, that sounds really good. I've taken up too much of Cyran's time. You, on the other hand, have nothing but time."

Jen laughed.

Casey spent the rest of the day hiding first in the hot tub with Jen, then in her room alone, relaxing and reading. She knew she'd need blood again but needed to separate herself from the sensuality of feeding for a bit. She did end up calling Grandpa when she returned to her room after her day with Jen.

The cord attached to her phone in her room was tangled and Casey took a minute to let the receiver hang, twisting and turning to unwind. If not done periodically, she was glued to the base of the phone. Once done, she hung up the phone and picked it up again before dialing Grandpa.

A gruff voice answered. "Daana residence."

Smiling as just the sound of his voice relaxed her, she sat in her desk chair. "Hiya, Grandpa. How are you doing?"

"Child, why are you calling? I'm going to see you tomorrow at your graduation. Is there something I need to know about? Bring?" The relaxation fled as she thought about what she had to say.

"No, Grandpa, I just ... after finals, Jude found me and snapped a silver collar on me."

He gasped. "Well, that explains the tingles playing up and down my spine this week. How are you, kiddo?"

She closed her eyes and tried to stop the tears. A few pacifying breaths and she was ready to control her voice. "I'm surviving. I just wanted to ask about the silver. After a couple of days, when I hadn't returned to Cambia House, Zoryda found me. Showed up at Jude's place and she snapped the silver off me. Did you know familiars could do that? Is there any other way around it?"

He huffed out a sound of contentment. "That dragon is a keeper. We really need to start explaining silver earlier in the new witch training. Once you have your familiar, you should be told. Quickly followed by how to call your familiar from a distance."

"Wait, that can be done?"

"Of course, honey child. They have their own tricks; it's part of what makes them so special."

Biting back her annoyance, Casey bit her lip. "Can you explain to me how to do this trick of calling her from a distance?"

"Yes, yes, yes. You bring her into your bubble, then create a bridge, one that is a permanent connection from her to you. Then, just like you called me now, you can call her from your bubble when you need her."

With a few choice words mumbled too low for him to hear, she rubbed her forehead in annoyance. Then she thought about the directions. "That seems ... easy. Too easy."

Chuckling, Grandpa began making noises like he'd moved into the kitchen. "Not all things in the witch's world have to be hard, honey child." The two spoke for a few more minutes, but he could tell she wanted to go try out her new lesson with her dragon. "Go, honey child, figure this out, and Hilde and I will see you tomorrow."

Off the phone, Casey called Zoryda down from the rafters. She spent a minute scratching and playing with her familiar before pulling her mind into her bubble with her. There, they could communicate.

In her bubble, they built a mental bridge. In the future, she would always have a way to call her familiar, even when trapped with silver. She now had two inherent abilities not linked to magic, immune to silver's effect on her.

Her grandma always told her every day was a good day to learn something new.

By dinner, she felt centered and herself, more protected. She decided to go to bed early because graduates had to be at the field house for graduation prep at eight-thirty in the morning with the ceremony beginning at nine-thirty. By eleven a.m., she'd officially be a graduate. When Cyran asked if she wanted company, she declined. She just wanted to be alone.

The next morning, she showered and curled her hair as big as it'd go. She wore a red velvet dress that fell to mid-thigh. It had a matching inch-and-a-half wide red leather belt and long sleeves, so she knew she wouldn't be chilly. The squared off neckline almost made the arms of the dress look separate from the rest of the ensemble. She wore nude stockings and black flats. She didn't trust how much she'd have to walk to wearing heels.

Heading out, she ran into Jen who wore a similar dress to hers, a bit longer, with a high neckline, and sleeveless. It had a similar belt, but all in black. They'd bought the velvet dresses together, so they matched in style. Heading down for breakfast, they grabbed a sandwich and coffee.

After eating, they were about to head out, when Rowan stopped them. "And where do you two think you're off to?"

Casey's brow shot up. "You know exactly where we're going."

"Right, but how do you expect to arrive? You're not taking that wreck of a car you own. I'm surprised it even runs."

Casey squawked. "Chameleon's a great car! what're you talking about?"

Rowan stared at her blankly. "I've arranged a house car to take you there and back. You both look too divine to arrive in any other vehicle anyway."

Casey opened her mouth to argue, then shut it, mentally debating her best interest.

Jen laughed. "Good gods, you dumbfounded her to the point of shutting her up. I had no idea it was possible."

"For that, it was all worth it." Rowan's eyes sparkled. "There will also be security assigned to both of you in case Jude decides to show up again."

Turning to the door, she mumbled to herself, "I think I hate you both."

Jen followed close behind her. "Oh, but you don't."

Parked in front of the house was a stretch limousine, long, black, and sleek. Casey reached for the door, but Reis, dressed in a black tux, placed his hand on her wrist. She flinched at the contact. He wasn't Jude, he was a friend. His face tightened in confusion but then he smiled at her, letting his hand drop from her wrist. "Hasn't anyone taught you anything? Let me." With his other hand he opened the door, letting the two slide into the limo themselves.

The back had bench seats facing each other. Casey took the one facing the way they'd drive. There were spots cups could fit, with tumblers holding drinks for each of them. Jen got in and sat facing her. She grabbed a drink and took a sip. Her face lit up. "This is amazing."

"If you get drunk, I am *not* carrying you."

Jen stuck out her tongue. "One sip will not get me drunk."

Casey's brow went up. "But two might."

The drive was quick, and Reis dropped them off near the front door. They piled out, then slipped into the graduation caps and gowns. Casey wanted to scream from all the excitement she felt. Reis gave Jen a hug and kiss on the cheek and smiled at Casey. "Have fun. A bunch of us from the house will be there watching. But don't worry, your ride will be ready when you want to head home."

They headed into the ocean of black gowns, making their way into the building. Soon they had to separate into their different degree programs and sit alphabetically. Shortly after everyone was set, the audience began to fill in. A buzz took over the graduates, as they turned and found their people. Some waved with a squeal of excitement, some slumped when they couldn't find family or friends.

At ten-thirty, the professors and instructors marched in, walking between the students to sit on either side of the stage. Some of them wore simple caps and gowns, not much different than the graduates sitting and waiting for their diplomas. Some wore elaborate gowns depicting PhDs with stripes on their arms, and puffy hats. Each wore the color of the college or university where they graduated. They looked like jewels. Casey recognized some of her professors, but many were strangers.

Once they'd sat, the ceremony began. The Chancellor spoke, then the provost, keynote speaker, valedictorian, and finally, the naming of the graduates began. This was it, she'd finally walk the stage, get the piece of paper that stated she'd completed all the work necessary to earn a bachelor's degree in criminal psychology.

The degree programs were called up in sections, so Casey got to watch and cheer Jen on as she collected her degree. The smile on her face as the announcer read,

"Jennifer Clark!" and the cheers from all the people from Cambia House thrilled her. Jen practically floated across the stage.

One of the runners finally motioned that Casey's row could stand. She followed the others around the back of the seated graduates, a sea of black, lining up, awaiting their turn. There was a ramp to get on stage since there was a graduate in a wheelchair, and they wanted everyone to cross the stage this year. Casey held a card with her name on it to give to the announcer. As she neared his podium, she thought her excitement would explode out of her.

Hands shaking, she handed the card to the man at the microphone. She walked to the line she was to wait at until her name was called. This way there would only be one person on the stage with all of the officials at a time. Then she heard it, "Casey Strega!"

Muscles bunching, she had to stop herself from running. Controlling herself, she walked up to the line of people, shaking each hand until the final person, the Chancellor. He had both his hands out, one for shaking, the other holding a roll of paper—her diploma.

As she reached him, a voice in the balcony yelled, "Since when did this hellhole start giving out diplomas to vampires?"

Chapter 16

Casey returned to her row between the two strangers whose last names were alphabetically close to hers. The girl to her left tapped her arm. "I don't care what that asshole yelled, I'm not a vampire." Her hand shook as it rested on Casey's elbow.

Her heart pounded. How could this person have been so lucky in his nastiness to have gotten two hits in one? Casey knew the taunt had been aimed at her and tried to keep herself calm as she watched the remaining students walk the stage.

She turned to the girl next to her and tilted her head. "What does it matter? You went to classes, did the homework, took the exams, and passed. You've earned that degree you're holding. Don't let some ass in the balcony take anything away from today. We earned it."

She visibly relaxed. "You're right. You wouldn't care if I were a vampire?"

"No. If you did the work, then you've earned the degree."

"Cool. I have a friend who lives in one of the houses as a blood donor. She's debating getting her degree or just asking to become one ... you know, a vampire. She knows the family takes care of their own, but she wants to get a degree, too. I figured they yelled because they've seen me around the vampires."

"Naw, they could've been yelling it at me, too. Two-for-one special."

She laughed, shoulders dropping as she relaxed. "Thanks."

It didn't take much longer for the ceremony to end and the professors to walk out. Once they were gone, the graduates were allowed to file out and find their people. Casey found Jen, but she was with her dad, who planned on taking Jen out for lunch.

"Hello, Mr. Clark. Nice to see you again."

"Casey, glad to see you graduated as well. No wonder there's going to be such a big party tonight."

Casey plastered on a smile and turned back to Jen. She gave her friend a hug. Jen leaned in. "Hey, don't worry about the scene, there were so many graduates, you were just one of many."

"Don't worry, I'm fine. I'm more worried about you and your dad. Will you be okay?"

"Yeah, it'll be fine. See you in a few hours. Party, five o'clock sharp." Her voice was tight, but she'd lived with her dad for years and knew how to handle the man.

Casey turned and found her grandpa and Hildegard. "Grandpa!" She launched herself into his arms for a hug.

"I'm so proud of you, honey child. Hilde and I just arrived. We need to check in on the others in town, but we'll see you at that party of yours. You'll have time for us then?"

"Of course!"

Hildegard's eyes narrowed. "That's good. We need to talk about your duties."

Nodding fast, Casey gave her a guarded smile. "Of course. I'll have time to give both of you."

She spun on her heel and ran into Reis, who had his arm out, and a smile. "Can I escort you to your coach, m'lady?"

With a laugh, she hooked her arm in his, and they headed out to find the limo. Once back at the house, she found the cafeteria decked out in balloons and streamers. A large sign hung proclaiming, "Congratulations, grads, class of 1987!" Finding her seat, the servers placed dishes of shrimp scampi and lobster at each seat.

Joined by Cyran and Riley, Riley waggled her brows. "Now that you're done with college, no more hours of studying, right? Maybe a few nights out? You were way more fun as a freshman and sophomore. I miss hitting the bars with you."

Casey placed a hand on her knee. "Yes, no more studying and I refuse to read for at least a month. My brain is officially on vacation."

Cyran's eyes softened. "Your brain may be on vacation, but there is more training. You get a week or two off, but then you're mine. Speaking of two weeks off, where are your grandpa and that coven leader of yours?"

"Oh, they're staying at the witch house, and decided to have lunch there. They'll see me at the party tonight, and we'll spend time together this week. They knew today would be hectic."

After lunch, Casey made her way over to the venue for the graduation party. Rowan asked Micha and Reis, two of the house security, to accompany her. Though her and Jen's graduation was the excuse for the celebration, more was going on behind the scenes and anyone who was anyone in town would be there. Vampires, witches, and officials.

She checked over the room, making sure the tables were set up. She climbed up the stairs to check on the posting station for the waitstaff. Through a door she never used when she *was* waitstaff, she moved down a set of stairs into the kitchens. They were setting up tables and trays of appetizers.

The main chef came up to her. "Up to your liking?"

"It looks great! What are the options for tonight?"

He checked over the tables, pointing as he listed things off. "Bacon-wrapped scallops, deviled eggs, moon milk, franks in a wrap, salmon pate on a cracker, meatballs, and cheese and berry tart. There is another table in the back with more desserts."

"I got everything but the moon milk. Is it a drink?"

"Ah, there is wine, soda, and coffee for the drinks. The moon milk is more of an appetizer, a mix of cherry, walnuts, turmeric, lavender, and coconut milk, mixed with ground nutmeg and maple syrup and rolled oats. It should be fun."

Brows furrowed, Casey tried to imagine such a crazy concoction. "Where did you get such a crazy appetizer idea?"

"I'd have to check the paperwork. Most of the ideas came from your house, but the governor's people put in one or two requests as well. They are crazy over there. Do you want me to check?"

"No, that's fine. Thanks, though."

Wiggling his brows, he leaned over to grab a cup. "Would you like to try one?"

Casey debated, but decided it was too crazy not to try. Taking one, she tried a few bites. "It's good, but I think I'll stick to the other appetizers tonight. Thanks!"

Heading back out, she saw Ginger in the main hall, standing in a pink pants-suit, carrying a big purse over her shoulder. Casey approached slowly, a debate flitting through her mind about avoiding her friend. Ginger appeared almost confused, as if she weren't certain why she was there.

Ginger took notice when Casey was halfway down the stairs and, leaning on a table, watched her approach. Casey decided there was nothing to do but bite the bullet. "Hiya, Ginge, what brings you here?"

Ginger seemed to hug her purse closer as she chewed on the inside of her cheek. "I didn't know you'd be here. I was doing a last check of security for the governor's office. But I'm glad you're here. Is Jen here, too?"

"No, she's having lunch with her dad. They're spending the afternoon together as well."

Cringing, Ginger's whole body recoiled at the thought. "Good god, what did she do to deserve that?"

Casey laughed. "Right! I guess he always threatened to attend graduation if she managed to get here."

"Almost seems like a reason to fail."

"Except she's too much of a perfectionist."

A smile crossed Ginger's face but didn't quite make it to her eyes. "Look, Case, I'm sorry I acted like a jerk the other night. I was hurt you'd kept a secret from me, but I guess I get it. That creep at your graduation tells a story, doesn't he?"

"You were there?"

"Of course I was there. Just because we were fighting doesn't mean I'd miss such a big day in your life."

A warm happiness filled Casey as they stood in the large hall that would later be filled with so many dignitaries of the city. Casey's eyes narrowed. "So, why is the governor's speech writer checking out tonight's event's security? Aren't there other people for that?"

"Well, I'm low man on the totem pole, and I used to work here. They thought I'd be able to check more of the place out. You know, be an insider."

"I guess that makes sense. Well, feel free to do your work. I need to head back and get ready for tonight."

Ginger's eyes traced over Casey's outfit. "More so than what you're wearing? You look great."

"Oh, yeah, I'm not changing, I just want to get more food, sit and relax, then come with everyone else. I may try to meet up with Jen so we can show up together."

Ginger took a half-step forward, balling her fists, then relaxing her hand, stuck it out, as if to shake. "Before you go, friends again?"

Mouth quirking up in a smile, and ignoring the hand, Casey pulled her in for a quick hug. "Of course we're friends again, Ginge, we always were."

Chapter 17

Jen walked into Cambia House at a quarter to five, shutting the door behind her and slamming her back against the now closed door. "Please tell me there is something I can drink ... like, here and now."

Casey had been coming down the stairs and, with a laugh, jogged to the kitchen and poured a small glass of vodka on the rocks. Handing it to her friend, Jen slammed it all back in a single gulp. Jen's full body shook. She handed the glass back and, in a low, guttural voice, demanded, "More!"

They both walked into the kitchen where Casey poured a splash more into the glass. "Jen, you never drink. If I give you much more than that, you won't make it to our party."

"I have to wash away my afternoon with Daddy Dearest. He spoke about me moving home and paying rent. About the chores I would be doing, cleaning, and cooking, *and* getting a job. He wants me to do everything so he can sit in front of the damn TV and watch sports while he drinks beers."

"Lovely. What happened to his job?"

"Oh, he still has it, he just figures if I came home, he could quit and have a live-in cook, maid, and caretaker." She growled. "There is no way!" She practically yelled, "*No way!*" Her hands waved in the air for emphasis.

Monica saw how upset Jen was and, filling the glass almost to the top, pushed them out of her kitchen. Jen started to drink down her glass and Casey removed it. That much alcohol would knock her friend out for the night. Casey took a sip and let the fire burn down to her belly.

She pulled Jen to a couch in the hall. They sat. "He's gone. It's just the two of us, and you don't have to move anywhere near him."

Jen smiled and her eyes started to glaze over. "Good, cuz I don' lie him one bit!" She slurred as she spoke, and she pointed at Casey to emphasize her words.

Shaking her head, Casey returned to the kitchen and grabbed some bread and cheese. Making a quick sandwich, she brought it to Jen, who perked up and started devouring it. As she finished it off, the hallway filled with everyone who wanted to join them at the party.

Jaxon sat down on Jen's other side, and she gazed at him. "My dad's an ass. Did you know that?"

His face became serious. "I'd heard."

"You may see him tonight. I just wanted you," she hiccupped. "What was I saying?"

Jaxon leaned forward. "How much did she drink?"

"Not a lot, but Monica filled a glass, and she started guzzling before I got it away from her. Drunk is better than livid?"

Jen rested her head on his arm. His eyes narrowed. "I'm not so sure about that."

Casey shrugged. "Well, we're here now."

Rowan finally came down in a pale blue suit, looking immaculate. He could've stepped out of a TV show or a magazine ad. "Okay everyone, let's head off. There should be enough cars to take everyone."

When they got to the venue, Jen and Casey were the last to walk through the doors, and they entered a room full of people applauding them. Since her earlier check, more streamers and balloons had been added as well as a huge 'Congratulations' sign that included both their names.

Casey found Grandpa, and they, along with Hildegard, started critiquing the food. Most of it was delicious. Hildegard grabbed a moon milk, but Casey refused. "I tried one earlier. Not my style."

"It's lovely child. Maybe more of a breakfast thing than for an event like this."

Grandpa gave her a squeeze. "I am just so proud of you. Except for the fool who heckled you, it was a beautiful ceremony. You survived with double the trouble most of us faced."

"Thanks, Gramps. I'm just glad I have the paper and can move on to the next challenge life throws me."

He ate a bacon-wrapped scallop. "Have you started applying to places?"

Casey saw a server with a salmon pate cracker and grabbed one before answering. "I have. Mostly around here, but I may branch out."

"What about ..." He waved his hand vaguely around.

She lifted a shoulder. "If I get a job far enough away from the house, I'll figure it out."

"Very good. Now, tell me about the waitstaff. Couldn't they be allowed to wear clothing?"

She watched as the staff, men and women who wore colorful tube tops that covered their chests, barely, and bottoms, also barely covering them, as they ran up and down the stairs. She bit her lip. "All their private parts are covered. That's better than it was."

He harrumphed.

A low voice cut in. "Excuse me, but can I intrude on your conversation?" Scooting over, Lucas, with his dark bronze skin, and almond eyes, joined their standing table. He smiled at Grandpa and Hildegard. "I'm Lucas, head of one of the vampire families here in town."

Her grandpa took Lucas's hand. "I'm Casey's grandpa, you can call me Parker, and this is Hildegard."

Hildegard eyed the vampire. "You were the one who helped our young witch to open the door and is teaching her the old language."

His smile was beautiful, and he held out a hand to her. "Guilty."

Hildegard took his hand and shook it, then gave him a small smile. "You, too, have a bit of witch in you. Were you part of a coven before you were made a vampire, boy?"

Lucas's eyes danced. "It has been years, centuries, since I was called boy ... and I think I like it. No, I was never deemed strong enough to be part of a coven, though I have stood part of a larger circle. I can't stand in a cardinal position, only in a minor spot ... but it has been many moons since I've been invited to use my magic in that way. I'm not even strong enough to hold the scent that drives vampires wild, as your Casey here does."

Grandpa nodded. "How often are you two training?"

Lucas's eyes slid to Casey before returning to her grandpa. "We *were* meeting sporadically when she had time. Now that college is done, I believe we can set up a weekly meeting, if not twice a week." A waitstaff member walked by and he snagged some appetizers. "Have you tried the scallops or the salmon? Or the tarts? The food tonight is delicious."

Hildegard grabbed another moon milk. "I like these milk things."

Lucas scrunched up his nose. "There's a weird smell to them, and I don't love nuts in my cereals."

Cyran came over, placing a moon milk cup on the table. "Care to dance?"

Smiling, Casey agreed, letting him lead her to the dance floor. They moved to both fast and slow songs. Cyran leaned in, his breath tickling her ear. "Are you having fun?"

"I am! So many people, it's great. I never thought to see my grandpa at one of these things, not to mention the coven leader. It's crazy. Are you having fun, or is it all work?"

"It isn't all work, but there has been some. This part's nice." A loud crash on the other end of the room had his head popping up. Casey turned to look but couldn't see anything through the throngs of people. "Speak of the devil. I hate to leave you, but that's my cue to leave. I'll be back soon."

Stepping away from her, he took off at a quick walk, touching his ear as he spoke into a wire to other security people. She was about to leave the dance floor when a hand on her shoulder stopped her. "Care to dance?"

Gazing up, she looked into the pale green eyes of her fearless leader. Smiling, she stepped into his embrace.

The dance was slow enough for them to talk. She asked, "How are things going on your end tonight?"

He chuckled. "Better than Cyran. He has to put out all the fires."

Raising her brow at him, she gave him a small smile. "Smart."

"Being able to delegate is one of my favorite parts of power."

His honesty surprised her. "Can I ask you a personal question?"

A smile tugged his mouth up and her heart beat faster. "I fear your personal questions, Miss Strega, but go ahead."

"What are we, as a house, going to do about Jude?"

His body tightened, but he didn't miss a step. "I hoped to hold this conversation off until next week. I want to pull Velvet in. I don't think you've met the head of Jude's family, have you? And Cynthia and Lucas. This needs to be a discussion with all the heads. You'd be there, of course, and let the decision be made that way. What he did goes beyond a single vampire, a single house, a single feud. Would that be acceptable?"

Her jaw tightened as she thought about the meeting. She tried not to get mad or jump to conclusions. Would he get off because of the level of involvement, or would a bigger punishment befall him? What would she do if they decided to let him go? Would the witches help her?

Rowan leaned down. "What's going on in that head of yours?"

"I'm just wondering ..."

Next to them, Jess, Jaxon's partner on their camping trip, grabbed her stomach, her face turning blue, before she toppled to the floor.

Across the room, people began to scream.

Chapter 18

The knife of premonition slicing down her spine, Casey spun out towards the room and froze, torn between running to the woman who screamed, and Jess who had fallen next to her. Heart pounding, she watched as Rowan knelt. Her eyes widened as she watched others fall around the room. Vaguely, she noticed her grandpa and Hildegard evaluating the room as well.

Three men in the back of the hall wearing black pants and black shirts ran through the room and out the main door screaming, "Hope will overcome! Die, sun haters! Hope will overcome! Die, sun haters!" They wore bandanas over their faces and hats on their heads with the letters: H.O.A.P.

Once they'd exited, Casey saw security follow after them. With what felt like a shot to her adrenaline and a bit of her wits being turned back on, she shook herself and dropped to her knees next to Rowan. "How is she?"

His hands on her forehead and wrist, he whispered, "Dead."

A shock of dread washed through her. "What?"

His gaze on Jess's face, Rowan shook his head. "I'm not sure how, this shouldn't be possible." With a sigh, his shoulders drooped before he collected himself to stand. He searched the room; he seemed to be taking stock of the chaos. "But she's dead." Lowering a hand, he helped Casey up.

Rowan cleared his throat and raised his voice to be heard throughout the hall. "I need everyone's attention." The music stopped, but there was too much noise for everyone to hear him. Clearing his throat he tried again, louder. "I need everyone's attention." This time, he projected loud enough that everyone either heard him, or was signaled by someone near them to pay attention.

Rowan took a few steps forward to get to a more central location. "We need medical professionals to check each person who fell and someone to check the food. The doors need to be locked and everyone checked to determine how a vampire was killed while she was dancing."

From the back of the room Cynthia stepped forward, fire in her eyes. "Oh, there's more than one vampire, Rowan. From what we can determine, at least four vampires are dead and equal numbers are sick. I have some people working with Cyran's to lock down all exits. No one will get out without being searched." Once done talking, she continued to cut through the crowd until she met Rowan near the center of the room.

Lucas, coming from the table with Casey's grandpa and Hildegard, headed out to meet them as well.

Not knowing where to go, Casey walked to her grandpa. Her hands shook as he enfolded her in a hug. Once they separated, she realized Hildegard had a frustrated look on her face. "I'm sorry you are being detained, coven leader."

Hildegard's eyes narrowed. "Do you have access to your magic?"

Finding a local convenience store, she pulled in a bottle of soda. Opening it, she took a drink. "Yeah, why?"

Rubbing her chin in irritation, Hildegard said, "Because, my magic is gone." Her head snapped to Casey's grandpa. "How about you, Parker?"

Her grandpa pulled in his own soda. "I seem to be good. So, let's think about that. What did you have that we didn't?"

Her mouth pursed together. "I only had a few of the appetizers. Our lunch was large."

Grandpa opened his bottle of soda and took a drink. "True. I had just about everything. The kitchen here is good."

Casey watched them, thinking about the possible options. "Was there anything you didn't have, Grandpa?"

His face lit up. "Yes, honey child, a few items I avoided. The salmon, never my favorite. That weird concoction that you told us you didn't like, the moon milk, for another."

Casey shook her head. "I had the salmon and tried the moon milk about an hour before the party. That doesn't track ... any other appetizer?"

Hildegard though. "I had the cheese and fruit tart, and your grandpa didn't. He said the blue cheese didn't agree with him."

Nodding, Casey took mental notes to bring to Cyran. "Yeah, I'd have to agree with him. I avoided that one, too. It isn't definitive, but I think that's a good place to start. Well, I for one think that this party was a bust. This whole week's been a bust. Hildegard, what could kill a vampire?"

A hand on her arm stopped her before she got going on a full tirade. She met the gaze of the coven leader. "Is there a private place we can go? Away from prying eyes?"

Casey's hand waved around the room. "There are the alcoves."

With a nod, Hildegard and Grandpa meandered over to the one in the corner.

Casey aimed for the three leaders in the center of the room. They were in deep conversation about what was going on. As she got closer, they quieted down. Lucas was the first to invite her in. "Yes, child, how can we help you?"

"It seems that ... well ... Hildegard can't use her magic. She hoped to get out of view of others to see if we, Grandpa and I, could help her."

Cynthia's head tilted. "The witch lost her magic, the vampires died. That can only mean one thing: silver. Do you know what she ate tonight?"

"Yes and no, ma'am. My grandpa and I are fine. Grandpa thinks the only two things she ate that he didn't were the moon milk and cheese and fruit tart, but he may have forgotten something they ate. The thing is, I had the moon milk and am fine."

They all seemed to sigh, and Cynthia smiled at Casey. "Well, that at least gives us a place to start. If you can get your grandpa and Hildegard into the end alcove, I'll take them where they want to go, unless you want to go with them?" Cynthia's offer to take the witches away calmed something deep in Casey. Some vampires could carry others when they misted. Casey wasn't strong enough for that yet.

Shoulders dropping with her relief, she gave Cynthia a smile. "They're already there. As for me, I think I'll stay."

Rowan frowned. "Even if she wanted to go, it would be noticed. Eventually someone would ask about the guest of honor. Then they'd want to know why special preferences were being given to her. Both she and Jen are here until the end. She can help with the sick. Maybe figure out a way to call out the silver?"

Lucas's brows shot up. "Do you think it would work?"

With a shrug, Rowan said, "No idea. The poison is working on the sick. But a few are about to die. If she can help them, wouldn't it be worth it?"

I've spent my life pretending to be human ... but lives are at stake ... Casey looked up at him, heart dropping to her stomach. "Then everyone would know ... about me." Her voice came out softer than she'd expected ... she sounded scared to her own ears.

There was a slight nod to his head. "The choice is yours."

If I do this, I'll be telling the world I'm a witch. If I don't, people will die because I'm afraid. Who do I want to be in this world? Can I face myself if I don't do this?

She ran over to Grandpa to let him know what was going on. He gave the same answer as Rowan. "I'll support you no matter what, child. You know that. Saving lives is worth exposure."

Biting her lip, Casey debated her options. She'd lived her life hiding who she was. In the end, there wasn't a choice ...

The first vampire Casey was brought to was Laurel, one of the Cambia House vamplings. She lay on the ground and appeared dead. Placing a hand on her head and stomach, palm up, Casey searched Laurel's body for silver. At first, she didn't find any, but then, on a second pass, she found what she sought. Her magic recoiled and her head began to throb, but with a push of power a bit of white powder landed in her hand.

With a gasp Casey nearly collapsed, the silver burning her skin, and Laurel, almost at the same moment, gulped in air.

Trembling, Casey grabbed a towel and wiped her hand clean. Feeling less wobbly, but still woozy, her head began to pound. Staring up at Rowan and Lucas, she trembled.

"That ... hurts. I can maybe do that a few more times. Make it count."

The two leaders bent down, lifting her up to move her to the next of the worst. She repeated the summoning. Again, she almost collapsed. With the second pull, her head nearly split with the pain.

She was brought to a third vampire; another one she didn't know. Shaking, she pulled out the silver. Her body quivered and her muscles felt like Jell-o. Her vision nearly gone, she feared she would throw up from the pain in her head. It was too much. Tears streamed from her eyes. Staring at the floor, she tried to form words, and only hoped she was heard. "I don't think I can do more."

Rowan knelt beside her, then pulled her into a hug. "That's okay. You've done enough. They were the closest to death. The others can wait."

"How many others?" Her voice sounded so distant to her, a cry in the dark.

"A dozen or so. Some older vamps who can survive."

Casey nodded, her vision blurry from the pain. After a few minutes, she pushed away to get to her feet. She needed to find a dark place to be. Watching the ground, she saw that the sick were being lined up, both those whose silver had been removed, and the ones still fighting off death. Gazing at the faces, there, she saw Cyran at the end of the line.

With a wail, her legs gave out, and she crumpled back to the ground. *How can he be here like this?*

Then a pounding of feet stormed up behind her. "Good god, Casey, two secrets? How many more are you keeping from me?"

As the throbbing in her head evolved into nausea, she saw the anger on Ginger's face and realized this time her friendship would probably not survive the deceptions.

Chapter 19

"What the hell, Ginger! People are dying and you're really choosing now to yell at her? Why can't you just be happy she's figured out a way to save some people?"

Casey fell back on her hip as Jen stormed over to defend her. The room spun and she didn't think she could move, but Jen's voice was like a breath of fresh air.

Ginger's head snapped from Casey to the newcomer, and her voice came out like venom. "Of course you're defending her! I bet you knew about this as well. Perfect Jen knows about everything."

"That isn't even the point, is it?" Jen's shoulders dropped as she gazed at their friend and her voice lowered. "There's a tragedy happening here, and you're focused on nothing but you. Look around you, people are dying, Ginge, dying. There's an infirmary being set up. Shouldn't you be worried about that?"

Shaking her head, Ginger's eyes widened as she took in the scene around her. Hands shaking, she licked her lips and shook her head again, as if trying to clear something from her mind. Casey could hear her heart start to race as her focus moved to the bodies lying prone on the ground. "What the hell happened?" Her brow dropped and she began to smell confused.

Not really caring because of the pain coursing through her body, Casey rubbed her temples, then got to her hands and knees, and began the crawl over to Cyran, ignoring whatever else her friends were talking about. She had bigger things to worry about. Placing her hand on his head, she found he was burning up. She leaned down, kissing his forehead, then placed her hand on his chest.

Her body began to shake as she closed her eyes, trying to find the silver in his body. The nausea had her doubling over with her cheek landing on his stomach. Sucking in air, she focused on Cyran and the silver coursing through his body. She had to help him; they needed him to figure this out. The shaking got worse as she searched him for the poisonous metal.

Before she could pull the silver out, hands under her arms pulled her up. She let out a yowl of pain and frustration as, eyes still closed to block out the light, she felt herself placed in a lap and arms were wrapped around her. Trembling, she forced words out. "Let go, I have to help him. We need him."

A warm hand rubbed her back as Rowan's minty scent began to calm her. "We need you, too. He's old and will survive. I don't know that you will. You aren't strong enough to do this right now, Casey. You can do it later."

Tears burned down her face as she leaned into Rowan's strength. "He'll survive?"

Squeezing tighter, he kissed the top of her head. "Yes, I believe he will."

Her body trembled as she let him care for her. "How many died?"

"Seven. Two of ours, two of Lucas's and three of Cynthia's." Her face wet, she slid her arms around him, holding on like a lifeline. "We've been checking the guests and the waitstaff but haven't found anything. With the uniform change you requested there are no longer pockets for them to carry anything. So, security continues to search for silver."

Feeling weak, Casey stared into his eyes. "Who? Who besides Jess?"

Sadness flowed from him. "Quest."

An image of the tall vampire with thick black hair who usually stood sentry at the door. On their first meeting, before she'd ever entered Cambia House, he'd called her sister. He'd treated her as a sister ever since, joking and playing with her in a friendly manner. It felt like a knife in the heart to lose such a friendly person.

Letting her feelings flow, she began to feel grounded. Casey took a breath of Rowan's minty scent, and finally opened her eyes, letting the light pierce her head. The pain was there, but she felt better. "What about the food?"

"Lucas and I were about to head to the kitchen when I saw what you were trying to do. Can I trust you not to do that again?"

With a huff, she laughed. "Yeah, I can resist the pain." Bracing herself, she pushed away from his stability and stood. She gazed over at her friends, still talking, then across the room at all the people now tense and looking worried. At the far end she saw Cynthia. "I'm going to go see how my grandpa and Hildegard are."

With a nod and a rub to her arm, Rowan headed towards Lucas. She weaved her way through the crowd. Casey reached Cynthia, avoiding interacting with anyone else. She tapped the woman's shoulder and asked, "How is my grandpa?"

Cynthia turned with a smile. "He's fine. When we landed, he ran a hand over Hildegard and felt the silver. It didn't take him long to pull it out of her. They both wanted to return, but I thought it best to wait until the crowd thinned. We can work on the sick in private once we know everything that's going on."

Biting her lip in frustration, Casey could only agree. If the two coven leaders were here, the sick would be healed, but more witch secrets would be revealed to the public ... but Cynthia and Rowan were right, they had time. "Thank you for helping them."

"Of course, child. I was told you helped the worst of the vampires here, including one of mine. For that, I thank you. Rowan tells me we'll get together Monday to discuss with Velvet her vampire. We *will* make this right for you. That boy has played free in this city for too long."

Overwhelmed, Casey just nodded.

Cynthia rubbed Casey's shoulders. "Go, sit. You look ready to fall. Tonight will end soon enough, and the sick will heal. As they say, this too shall pass."

Casey wanted to collapse there, but she went to the corner of the dance floor, away from anyone and, back against the wall, slid to the floor. She wished she could disappear as she watched the action around her.

A few security members moved people to the door where wands were waved. The wands were held by Tilly, Zen, Sadie, and Damion—the local witches. She realized they hadn't been helping with the vampires because they searched the guests for silver.

She saw some people coming down the stairs and recognized several of the waitstaff in street clothes. Security must have escorted them to the changing room, let them change, and brought them back down here. As horrible as everything was, things seemed to be moving smoothly.

When the room was about halfway cleared out, Jen and her father approached. Everyone was near the exit, so this side of the hall was empty and calm. Neither paid her any attention as they stood at a table near the dance floor, maybe five feet away, backs to her. Jen's dad was grasping her arm in a vise grip, finger digging in. He leaned in close to her ear but spoke clearly. "Do you know what your roots are, girl?"

Jen jerked but couldn't get her arm to release. "I don't know what you're talking about." She yanked her arm, but he held tight. Hissing, she said, "Let me go."

Her dad's gaze took in the room and all the people milling about. "I know we've spoken about this ... I had to have told you. Our history is rich and powerful. Your ancestors were vampire hunters, girl, not blood-sucker fuckers. I can't believe you chose to come here and socialize with the bloodsuckers and bring me! Why haven't you told me about this?"

Another yank of her arm and another flail. Her face reddened as her ire rose. "Tell you what? When? Why? We never talk. Why would I tell you anything? These people have shown me more consideration and support than you ever did. Why would I follow you in your hate? Hating a group because my ancestors historically did is ridiculous!"

Jen's dad began turning as red as his daughter and his nose flared. Shoulders bunching to his ears, he turned away, releasing her arm, and leaving an angry red bruise behind.

Jen's eyes widened. "No!" she screamed. The few people nearby turned to see what the commotion was about. "You *will* hear me out. I'm not done talking!"

Her dad slowly rotated back, and his eyes narrowed. "Our ancestry isn't ridiculous, girl."

Jen practically growled. "You've never told me anything about our history, our past, our family. Vampire hunters! That's the most asinine crap I've ever heard. If we have a history of such stupidity, I'm *glad* to be the one to turn it around and start a new trend of inclusion and acceptance."

He lifted his hand to slap her, but she swung her free hand up in a block, and with the arm he had held, she shot it out, slamming the heel of her hand into his chest. It wasn't a hard hit, but he staggered back a couple of feet.

He glared at her. "You're no daughter of mine, Jennifer Clark. Don't bother returning to my house." He spun and stormed off. Pushing his way to the head of the line, he forced his way out of the hall. Two security guards stopped him to check him over and he seethed, but no one was leaving without being checked.

Jen turned, searching the faces of the people left. Spotting Rowan and Lucas coming down the stairs, she walked over to them. Casey wanted to say something to her, but still had no energy. She continued to focus on her friend, trying to hear what she said to the vampires. Maybe she was worried her dad was part of the attack or knew the group who brought in the poison.

As empty as the hall was, it was easy to hear Jen's voice as she spoke when she was halfway between Casey and the two leaders. "Hey, Rowan, any idea where Casey's gotten to?"

Scrunching up her face in confusion, Casey watched as the two vampire heads looked between Jen and Casey and back before walking to Jen. They spoke quietly to her, too low for Casey to hear, before making their way to her. The two stood facing out towards the room, back to Casey.

Rowan was the first to speak. "Casey, dear, do you know you have a vision shield on right now?"

She stopped breathing for a second. Working up as much of her energy she could, she forced the word out. "What?"

Lucas nodded slowly. "You made your desire for the day to end real."

Exhaustion seeping into her bones, she gazed at the back of their heads. "How can you two see me?"

A chuckle fell from Lucas. "We're old, dear. We see with more than our eyes. Can you stand?"

She groaned. "I don't know."

Rowan turned and, leaning down, lifted her to her feet. Before she could react, she was in her room in Cambia House. He helped her to her bed. "Sleep, vampling."

She stood, arms hugging herself. "Thank you, Rowan."

His gaze softened. "Will you be okay?"

She stared up at him, not knowing what answer to give. Being alone terrified her, but who could she get to stay with her? Stepping back, she watched as he considered her before misting away.

She got out of her dress and stockings and slipped into a t-shirt before crawling into bed. So much had happened.

Hopefully tomorrow would bring answers. Thinking through the food, she couldn't imagine who could've poisoned the vampires.

Just before she fell asleep, Rowan returned in sweats instead of his suit. "Care for company tonight?" He climbed into the bed behind her. With a sigh, she relaxed into his hard chest and minty scent, feeling the demons finally held at bay.

Chapter 20

The next morning, Casey woke up with her nose pushed into Rowan's chest, their legs twined together, and his arms wrapped around her. She breathed in his spicy mint scent and her body relaxed. For the first time in days, her demons were gone, so she rested her cheek against the solidness of his body and shut her eyes to revel in the peace she felt.

She must've fallen asleep again, because Rowan's arms tightening around her woke her up. He kissed the top of her head as she stretched. "Morning sunshine."

Rolling to her back, she looked up at him and smiled. "Morning." Her eyes focused on the dragon hanging in the rafters above her. "That may be the best sleep I've had since ... um. I slept really well, thanks."

He lifted up on his elbow. "Good. You seemed ready to give up last night. Better now?"

She nodded. "Yeah. Lots of questions, but better."

He quirked a smile. "Can they wait until after breakfast?"

A growl from her stomach answered for her. She climbed out of bed and headed to the bathroom to clean up. When she got back to her room, it was empty. Still tired from the night before, she grabbed a pair of jean shorts and a clean shirt before heading down to the cafeteria. She piled up a big plate with pancakes, scrambled eggs, and sausage, and found a table. Once she placed the food down, she headed back for a large mug of coffee.

As she ate, she realized she'd barely eaten yesterday. Most of the day she'd focused on graduation and the party ... *no wonder I was so drained from the small amount of magic.* She'd made good progress on her plate when Rowan joined her, sporting jeans and a Lost Boys t-shirt. The irony was not lost on her. The plate he set down was stacked almost as full as hers. She let him have a few bites before she couldn't hold back. "Did you figure anything out last night?"

Taking a sip of coffee, he gave her a smile. "I'm shocked you waited that long. The moon milk had a combination of silver, lavender, and turmeric."

Casey thought about it, but it didn't click. "I understand about the silver, but not the rest."

Rowan put down his fork. "There are stories of lavender and turmeric creating a poison in vampires. The lavender brings on a long sleep, slowing the system from being able to heal itself, and the turmeric is a type of poison. The thing is, we heal too fast for these two herbs to do anything in normal circumstances. It has to be mixed with the silver for it to act as a poison. Only a vampire would know that."

Her food stopped halfway to her mouth. "Are you telling me a vampire is part of this hate group, this H.O.A.P. group?"

"That's the working theory. But there were no vampires at the venue before the party began."

Casey began to bounce. "Right, because I tried the moon milk about an hour before the party began, and I didn't get sick, not at all. So, someone got in there after me."

Rowan nodded as he took a few more bites. "The kitchen had the moon milk stored in the extra walk-in refrigerators. They are accessible from the hallway and not monitored. Five people passed through the hall for security checks after your walk-through."

"One of them was Ginger. You don't think it was her, do you?" Casey leaned back, her breakfast forgotten. *I know Ginger and I have had our differences and she's shown her dislike for vampires, but not this ... she wouldn't do this.*

Licking his lips, Rowan lowered his fork. "She is one of the five. We need to interview them all, but, with Ginger, I'm worried about something more. I agree with you. I don't think she'd do something that would potentially kill you. I want you to check out her mind, see if anyone has gone in and done anything."

Casey bit her lip and nodded, the idea of someone messing with her friend's mind ... again, made her feel nauseous. "Yeah, okay. When?"

Jen slipped in next to her. "When what? What are we doing? Can I come? Where did you go last night?" She picked up her fork and pointed at Casey. "And you should have *seen* me with my dad, the ass. I put him in his place."

Casey chuckled. "I heard. Good job. So, you're not seeing him again this visit?"

Jen took a sip of her juice. "I hope not. He wasn't going to leave until tomorrow, but if he thinks we're doing anything else, he'd better change his attitude on a lot of things. Vampire hunters, Case, my ancestry is vampire hunters."

Rowan snorted. "So is mine. My sisters married into it. It doesn't have to define you."

Jen smiled up at him. "Cool, we have something in common."

Grabbing her hand, he smiled back. "So we do. We also share a lack of other family members, Miss Clark. But with a line of vampire hunters, I think I prefer the family I've built."

She gazed across the room. "Yeah ..." Her voice trailed off for a moment. "Yeah!" she said with authority. "I like the family you built here better too."

He grabbed up his fork and took another bite of food, finishing off his breakfast. "Excellent. So, when you go off to get your job in some far-off corner of the state, you'll return here to your family for holidays and summer break? You won't forget about us?" His face was serious, but his mouth twitched a bit as he teased her.

Jen, however, was having none of it. "Oh, you'll never get rid of me. I've staked out my room, and it's mine."

Once breakfast was done, Casey and Rowan went back to the party venue. Cots had been brought in for the sick.

All the vampire heads had agreed they wanted to keep everyone together while they tried to figure out what had happened. Grandpa, Hildegard, and the other witches were there as well. Together, the seven witches approached the remaining vampires who were down with the silver/poison combination.

The three that Casey had helped the night before were still sick in cots as well. They hadn't woken up. The silver had done its job, giving the other herbs time to integrate into the vampires' systems. They would heal, but not quickly.

Hildegard eyed them all. "My magic is still sticky. The silver was removed by Parker, but a residual must have been left behind. I think if the six of you each take two vampires, we can see how you each feel for the remaining three."

As coven leader, she began directing their efforts. Each removal was as nauseating and head-splitting as the night before. Casey's first patient was Jaxon. Casey hadn't even realized he was down the night before. She did a full probe of his body, found what she could, and pulled it all out. They were each wearing a white glove and when the silver was out, the glove was removed so the silver could be studied. They also wanted to compare what was removed from each vampire.

Once Jaxon's silver filled her hand, his breathing smoothed out. She rested her bare hand on his forehead.

His body burned, but she hoped it would heal. One of the human helpers came around and removed her glove and handed her a new one. Moving away from Jaxon, she slipped it on as Hildegard pointed to the next cot.

She headed to a vampire she didn't know. He had light brown curls that framed his face. She felt he'd be heartbreakingly beautiful if he were awake. Lucas stood near the head of the cot, concern wafting off him. "He is my third, Jacque. Please be kind to him."

Casey gave him a somber smile. Closing her eyes and placing her hand palm up on the vampire's chest, she focused on the silver in his body. There was more, so much more. She gathered it up, nearly doubling over with the nausea, as her head slit open. She felt the silver land in her hand as her forehead rested on the prone vampire's bicep.

A hand on her shoulder began to rub, as other hands removed the glove. "Thank you, child. You did well." Lucas's voice was as soothing as his hands. "Can you do another, or do you need to stop?"

With a moan, she lifted her head. "I can do one more, if you need me to."

Hildegard came over. "Up to you, Fräulein Strega. Your grandfather is the strongest conjurer here. Tilly is good as well, as is Zen. You are strong as well. You would be in the top four here. You can choose to do a third or sit the third out."

Sitting up, she looked at the leader. "I can do it." Standing, she moved to Cyran. He lay on his back. His head was warm and his breathing rough. Collapsing on the chair next to him, she lay her cheek on his body. She slid the glove onto her hand and cradled it in her lap. Tears burned across Casey's nose and face as the pain in her head increased. Taking a deep breath, she searched. There wasn't a lot of silver, but she made sure to find every bit of it, pulling it out and dumping it in the gloved palm.

Once done, her body shook with pain and fatigue. She thought her head would break if anyone touched her. Every muscle in her body spasmed. Not moving, she tried to relax, to release the tension flowing through her body.

A sound of wings and her dragon landed next to her on Cyran's chest. Zoryda rubbed her nose on Casey's cheek, it felt like a soothing waterfall washed through her body. The pounding in her head was there, but suddenly she felt like the pain was manageable.

One of the human helpers came over and she lifted her hand so that they could collect the glove. A moment of worry that the secret of her familiar would be discovered was replaced by amusement when she realized she was the only one who knew Zoryda had come. Her brilliant Zoryda had a vision shield on. Almost giddy from everything that had happened, she started to giggle.

Chapter 21

Returning to Cambia House, Casey knew she needed blood. It had been a rough few days, and she'd used a lot of her magic. After pushing herself so hard, she needed to sleep and build back her reserves. She'd been dropped off so others could watch over the healing vampires and start the interviews.

Heading up the stairs, she stopped at a door across the hall from her room. She knocked, hoping there would be an answer. She didn't want to be alone. She waited. After a minute, she dropped her arm. She fisted her hands then tapped her fist on her leg. She was about to give up and go to her room when the door finally opened.

Riley stood there with her black hair spiked out in all directions, black eyes devouring Casey, and a black tank top on, barely concealing anything. With a smirk, her eyes narrowed. "How much time do we have?"

Casey smiled back. "I have a meeting after breakfast tomorrow morning."

Stepping back, Riley let her into her room. "You look awful, by the way. Should we call someone in for a quick feed before we start? Will I be enough?"

A small smile played over Casey's mouth as she navigated over the mounds of black clothes. She sat on the edge of the bed. "You'll be enough."

"Good," Riley said. "Then lie back and let's begin."

Casey's eyebrow rose. "Anyone tell you you're very bossy?"

Slinking over in just a back tank top and skimpy black panties, a line of skin showing, Riley smiled. "You're in my room. My rules. Now, it seems to me, you're wearing too much. Take off the extra clothes."

Cocking her head to the side, Casey watched Riley approach. Bantering with this vixen was always a balm to her soul. "Which clothes, exactly, are the extra ones? I mean, are some allowed?"

Riley stopped half-way to the bed atop a mountain of clothes, queen of her domain. Hands on her hips, Riley considered her. "That all depends on what you have on under that." She waved her hand up and down. "I can't judge you on what I don't know, now can I?"

Casey leaned back on her hands and narrowed her eyes. "So, what you're saying is you want to know what's under my t-shirt and shorts?"

Shrugging, Riley's eyebrows mirrored the movement. "That would be a start."

Casey kicked off her shoes, then, sitting back up, stripped off her shirt. Knowing what the plans were for the day, she'd thrown on a shirt without a bra. Riley's smile at seeing Casey half naked was worth the reveal. Biting her lower lip, she started to unbutton and slip off her shorts, but Riley shook her head.

Moving to Casey, she placed her hands on Casey's shoulders and leaned down to whisper in her ear, "Time to lie down, lovely."

With a chill running through her, she rotated and stretched out on Riley's bed. Riley climbed up, straddling Casey's hips. She bent and kissed her, bringing Casey to the here and now, letting her release all the hell of the past week. Casey grasped Riley's waist and rubbed up her sides, under her shirt, until her thumbs could trace the vixen's breasts.

Riley moaned, deepening the kiss, her tongue tasting every inch of Casey's mouth. She rocked where she perched, her hands cradling Casey's face.

Casey continued to play, letting her hands explore as the woman above her squirmed.

Pulling back, Riley grabbed Casey's wrists out from under her clothes. "I would like you to hold onto the headboard and leave your hands there. Is that going to be okay?"

Biting her lower lip, she thought about it. She wasn't sure what Riley knew, but someone had told her to be gentle. The question and the ability to say 'no' was enough to allow Casey to pull her hands away, stretch out, and grasp the bars of the headboard. This was a common position for the two of them. She smiled up at her partner. "Anything else?"

Practically purring, Riley said, "I'm going to put my wrist on your mouth, then my mouth is going to go to other places. You do your thing, while I do mine. Leave your hands where they are. I'm not going to blindfold you, but please keep your eyes shut, love."

Closing her eyes, she felt the warmth of an arm placed across her mouth. Her body tensed for a moment, but the scent of Riley all around her brought joy and pleasure, erasing the pain of the week before. She rubbed her mouth over the skin, loving the sensations it started in her body. A small flutter of anticipation flowed from her mouth to her core and her muscles tightened. Mimicking her motions, Riley rubbed her closed mouth over one of Casey's nipples.

She licked her lips before opening her mouth and felt the same motion on her breast. A thrill shot through her as the feeling intensified. Her teeth descended, sharp and ready to break skin. Biting down, she knew part of the vampire physiology released pleasure into their donors, their victims, it was how vampires survived. She and Riley moaned in pleasure almost at the same time.

Blood flowed into her mouth. At first, her need was great enough that it was taken without much perception on her part, but then it began—her need, her thrill. Heat and waves of desire, from the blood, from the sucking and scraping of teeth on her nipple from Riley. It grew. A pool of electric power in her core.

The blood infused her system, becoming hers, igniting her lust, healing her soul. Her need for blood satiated, the last drops slid down her throat like liquid fire. She whimpered, her breathing became rough, and then Riley sucked harder, and her hand pinched Casey's other nipple. Casey screamed, liquid pleasure firing through her.

Licking the arm still in her mouth before it moved away, she felt her shorts slide away.

Riley moved back up her body. She stared down at the dark head that stopped at the halfway point. Dark eyes gazed back. "Did I tell you you could open those lovely eyes of yours? Do you want a punishment?"

Snapping her eyes shut, she lay back down and shook her head. There was a weird healing in coming to Riley today and in their type of play. Their bed-play was always a bit rougher, but safe, something they both enjoyed. Riley's mouth was suddenly on Casey's core, and all Casey could do was feel. Riley licked while her fingers probed deep inside. All thought left her as she focused on the talented tongue dancing and lapping, causing a new heat to grow in her center.

Breathing hard, Casey's body arched up as Riley's fingers and tongue continued. Her tongue playing over her clit and her fingers plunging in and out, their onslaught finding a rhythm that built a heat in Casey's gut that quickly exploded with her climax, like lightning throughout her body. Casey cried out, then went boneless, satiated from her release. Riley crawled up until she was lying next to and half on top of Casey, tucking in.

Casey brought her arm around so Riley's head rested in the crook of her arm. Kissing her head she asked, "What about you, love?"

"Next time. You looked like hell when you showed up on my doorstep. I figured you needed a quick release, and someone to cuddle with. I'm glad you chose me."

Chapter 22

Tangled in her drenched blankets, Casey woke in a panic, heart beating fast, and barely able to breathe. Uncertain what about the bad dream had caused her fear, she sat up, peeled the sheets from her body and, shaking, crawled from the bed. Hands trembling, she collected a clean t-shirt, panties, and skirt, and headed to the bathroom to shower.

She turned on the water to high heat and let it sluice away the nightmare that had plagued her sleep. Despite the heat, she shivered, remembering the silver collar and the emptiness she'd felt being trapped by Jude. She stood under the flow until her body relaxed. Once she stopped shaking and her breathing calmed, she turned off the water, dried off, and dressed. Trudging to her room, she did her hair and makeup and put on shoes before heading down and slipping out the front door, unnoticed.

It was early for vampires, so she wasn't surprised her Sunday had been solitary. Part of her wished for some contact—with her night terrors, human contact would've been nice—but a bigger part wanted to get out and meet up with Grandpa before he left. She worried that if she ran into someone, she'd be asked questions. Vampires could smell emotions and she wasn't sure if the fear from the night before still clung to her.

She walked the block and a half to where she'd parked her car before she realized she had her purse, but no keys. Leaning against the side of Chameleon, head down on her crossed arms, she willed herself not to cry. Why did things have to be so difficult?

Frustration coursing through her body, she took a steadying breath and pushed away, ready to hike back home, when she turned to see a black sedan parked in the road behind her. Against her will, her body tensed. There were very few people she wanted to see in her current state. Squinting, she bent down and looked in the lowered window to see Rowan in the driver's seat.

He smiled at her and asked, "Need a lift?"

She glared at him because she knew how much he didn't like her car and snapped, "No, I just need my keys."

She was about to conjure them from her room despite how tired she still felt, but he interrupted her by clearing his throat. "Will you let me drive you anyway? You look tired."

At the concern in his voice, she lost her ire. She opened the passenger door and slid in. "I'll have no way to get around on my own."

His head tilted as he pulled out and headed to the witches' house. "Would you mind if I joined you for breakfast with Parker? I haven't had any time to talk with him. If you want to spend time with him alone, I'll understand."

The spicy mint scent that filled the car put her at ease for the first time since she woke up, and she leaned back with her eyes closed to consider the question. *I want time with my grandpa, but it isn't like I have secrets. And with Hildegard there, I probably won't be completely alone with him anyway.* She licked her lips and shrugged. "It's fine. I'll have time this summer to go out and visit. Skyler's test is next week. If nothing else, I'll just head out early."

She opened her eyes in time to see a beautiful smile spread across his face as he made the final turn onto the street with the witches' home. After he parked, they got out and followed the path through the garden to the front door of the old farmhouse. Casey knocked and Tilly answered, a cheerful smile on her face. "Come in, come in. Rowan, we didn't expect you, but of course you are welcome."

They entered into a large foyer, ahead of them a dining room. To the right were stairs that led to the upper level. There was a dedicated room for her on the second level so she could stay at the house on nights she spelled late. In reality, she had two homes.

To the left was a formal living room and a separate office that had been converted to a meeting room. Through the dining room was a huge eat-in kitchen, the heart of the house.

The kitchen had a walk-in pantry and on the other side of it was a den that had been converted to a spells room. Casey and Rowan walked through the kitchen and out to the backyard to sit in the garden. They found Grandpa sitting on the patio set sipping coffee. After they sat, Tilly brought them each a mug of coffee and a bagel.

Grandpa smiled at them. "Morning, honey child, Mr. Cambia. I didn't know the average vampire would be up this early."

Rowan sipped his coffee. "I try not to be the average vampire, Mr. Daana."

Cringing, her grandpa said, "How about this: I'll call you Rowan, you call me Parker. It's too early for formalities."

"It's a deal," Rowan said with a laugh.

"So, honey child, talk to me."

Casey sipped her coffee and let her environment soak in. *I am surrounded by family and loved ones.* "This week has been rough. You managed to extract silver from five vampires, Grandpa, and walked away fine. Three knocked me out ... why? What is wrong with me?"

Rowan's brows came together in concern as he stared at her.

Grandpa reached across and took her hand. "Child, you know there's nothing wrong with you. I'm the top conjurer. It shouldn't surprise you that I'm good at ... well, conjuration. But, more than that, you're a witch and a vampire. You have silver and poison attacking you from two sides."

She bit her lip and thought about what he said. It made sense. At the start of a headache, she rubbed her fingers into her forehead with her free hand and tried to dispel her misgivings.

Under the table, Rowan's hand rested on her thigh. Her grandpa's eyebrows came together in worry. "What is it, honey child? You look tired. Did you sleep last night?"

She shook her head and gazed into his eyes, trying to figure things out. "Yes and no, and I'm not sure why. I went to bed and woke up a tangled mess. I had nightmares, but I don't remember them."

Next to her, Rowan made a sound of disapproval. "Did you sleep in Riley's room?"

With a big sigh, Casey's shoulders dropped, and she took her hand back from Grandpa to get a bite of her bagel. "No. I moved to my room."

Rowan's hand tightened on her leg. "So, you slept alone?"

Nodding, she smelled the frustration flowing from him, covering the scent of the lilac trees lining the backyard.

Grandpa leaned forward, narrowed his eyes towards Rowan, and rested his elbows on the table. "Why does this annoy you?"

Shifting his focus to her grandpa, Rowan said, "She hasn't been sleeping well since Jude abducted her." He turned back to Casey, his pale green eyes softening with concern. "I thought you were with Riley last night. It helps when you aren't alone."

"Child, I know you're strong, and I love you, but don't take this lightly." Casey turned from Rowan to see the worry in her grandpa's expression. "You work at helping everyone around you, let the people around you help you too."

The door opened and Hildegard walked out holding a tray of cheese, meats, and crackers. Sitting down, she narrowed her eyes at Rowan. "Vampire." Turning to Casey, dismissing Rowan, she continued, "Fräulein Strega, are you ready for testing? Have you decided what challenges you'll be presenting to Skyler?"

Casey's heart began to pound in her chest at the question. Between school, graduation, and Jude, she hadn't had two seconds to think about it, and didn't want to discuss it now.

Gods, why is she bringing this up today? I have two weeks, and in a couple of days, I'll have plenty of time to focus on Skyler and her test. But today? Today there is too much going on. We still have to figure out how to help the unconscious vampires and what to do about Jude and Candy.

Her body starting to tense, Casey opened her mouth to answer when Rowan moved his hand to her arm and turned to Hildegard with a bright smile. "How are you feeling Mrs. Schulz? Have you recovered from your silver-poisoning?"

Slowly shifting her focus to Rowan, Hildegard pursed her lips. "I'm fine, Mr. Cambia. I woke up this morning at full strength. I dare say I could even compete with our young Fräulein Strega in mental magic."

Bowing his head in her direction, Rowan assembled a cheese and salami sandwich and handed it to Casey. "Well, that's wonderful. Our vampires are still struggling with the herbs that were added to the moon milk with the silver, I am hoping we can figure out how to get them healed and back to full health."

With a raised brow, Hildegard said, "Maybe we should mix some of the herbs up for the meeting scheduled for your leaders here later this week? No? In case any get out of line."

Chapter 23

Casey worked Monday morning in the kitchen, making breakfast for the house and prepping lunch. She prepared alone, letting Monica sleep in. She decided on hashbrowns, a casserole with potatoes, sausage, cheese, and bacon, a fruit plate, and, of course, a selection of hot and cold cereals.

She was on her second mug of coffee as vampires and blood donors made their way down to eat. These mornings when she was alone in the kitchen, she could lose herself in the game, forgetting time and worries. As the plates got low, she filled them. Someone wanted something other than what she'd prepared; she made it. Drinks, food, sweets, savory—it was all a dance, and it cleansed her soul to perform it.

The flow of people slowed, and she started to clear the platters. Others came in to clean, and she realized she could retreat upstairs to shower and rest. She grabbed a plate of food and sat at the small table in the back of the kitchen to quickly eat before heading up to get ready for the day. After working through the morning, she neither looked nor felt ready for socialization.

Near her last bite, Rowan sauntered in. With a quick survey of the room, he spotted her and came over to the small kitchen table to sit down across from her. Swallowing and taking a sip of coffee, she gazed at him. "I didn't expect to see you in here. Have you ever even *been* in the kitchen, sir?" She smiled up at him in challenge.

He laughed. "I told you I could make an excellent bread. Again, I'll make it for you some day, just not today. Our meeting with the other heads will be at one, just after lunch. The final time was just agreed on. We're meeting at the witches' house, as Hildegard mentioned yesterday. We figure that's the most neutral location we can use, and the witches agreed. We'll use their meeting room."

Still amazed that the vampires trusted the witches to host such an important meeting and that the witches agreed to the use of the home, Casey shook her head in wonder. "Are we eating with the witches or here?"

Rowan leaned back and crossed his arms over his chest. "I thought I would take you out, but we can decide once you've showered and are ready to go."

Checking her watch, she saw it was just after ten. "Sounds good to me. Thanks." She leapt up, nervous and excited about the upcoming meeting. She put her plate in the sink, finished her coffee, then put her mug in the sink, too.

She headed out to the stairs, running up them. Once she got to her room, she did a quick search of her closet, but nothing jumped out at her. Grabbing a robe, she crossed to the bathroom and stepped into the shower to wash off the morning grease from working in the kitchen.

She spent a few extra minutes letting the hot water flow over her, relaxing her muscles, and trying to let the previous week melt off her. It didn't fully work, but each day was better than the last. Getting out of the shower, she dried off and fluffed out her curls, spraying them to keep the curls set.

Back in her room, she decided on a pale blue sleeveless jumper with a white shirt. She strapped on a wide white belt with a circle belt buckle. The end of the belt hung almost two inches down her leg. She liked the look. Blue eyeshadow and a pink lipstick and she was ready to go.

Lost in her closet, trying to find a purse, she heard her door open and shut. Jen's voice filled the room. "Oh, my gods! I got two callbacks for interviews, Case. They're for later this week, Thursday and Friday. I'm so excited."

Careful not to fall on her butt, Casey backed out of the closet with a black bag. She threw her arms around her friend. "That's amazing, Jen. How far away? Will you need to book a hotel?"

"They're both close enough that I could stay here." Jen was smiling so wide that Casey was afraid she'd hurt herself. "But I need to go shopping for interview outfits. Can we go out tomorrow or Wednesday?"

Bouncing with excitement, Casey rubbed her hands together, thinking over her schedule. "Of course! Let's plan on tomorrow."

Jen pulled back. "You look great. When are you and Rowan heading out to your meeting?"

Casey's face scrunched up as she checked her watch. "Soon? Now? He said we'd go out for lunch and that the meeting is at one. We want to be the first there since it's at the Witch House."

Jen leapt back. "Casey! It's almost eleven. If you two are including lunch before the meeting and planning on arriving early, you have to go." She pushed Casey out, kicking her out of her own room.

"Jen, I know I have to go. Check me out, I'm ready. Calm down."

The two of them turned for the stairs, laughing as they reached the front foyer. Turning to the front room, they saw Rowan in an off-white linen suit. His shirt matched his eyes perfectly and his tie was an off-white with a black stripe. He moved to the two of them, holding his hand out for Casey's as he reached them. "Shall we go?"

Casey gave Jen a quick hug then took Rowan's hand. He led her out to his red Porsche. Sliding in, feeling her outfit wasn't nearly nice enough for his ride, they departed. "Where are we going?"

"I thought we'd try out a seafood restaurant, if that would be acceptable."

Watching the city fly by, she shrugged. "Sounds good." The city gave way to the country, and the car revved up before taking off. Casey felt like they were flying. A few minutes later, they arrived at a small restaurant on a cliff overlooking the ocean.

Inside, the waitress led them to a small private table next to a wall of windows. They sat opposite one another. Looking out the windows, Casey watched the water, and seagulls flying and diving to catch their own lunch.

Rowan ordered the salmon and Casey asked for orange roughie. As they waited, Rowan leaned back, steepling his fingers. "Do you think you're ready for today's meeting?"

Rowan had ordered white wine to pair with their fish. Taking a sip, Casey leaned back. "I don't know what to expect, so I hope so. I'm worried that the heads will look past Jude's misdeeds since he's so much older than me, you know, not really punish him. I think he's been manipulating a lot of people."

Nodding, Rowan swirled the wine in his glass, watching it as the liquid spun and settled. He seemed satisfied, though she didn't know what he was evaluating. "I can only hope your fears are unfounded, but it *is* difficult because Jude is her second."

"What about Candy?" Casey insisted. In all their discussions, the other vampire had always been ignored.

Narrowing his eyes, he took a bite of his lunch while considering her question. "I don't know any vampire named Candy. I spoke with Lucas and Cynthia; they've never heard of Candy either. Velvet may have created her recently, but I don't know. Jude may have created her and never told Velvet. It seems Jude has been running roughshod over our rules more and more the last few years."

Biting her lip, she gazed into his pale green eyes. "So, if we find Candy, she won't get into trouble?"

Tapping a finger on the table, Rowan's brows dipped as he thought. "Do you think she was an instigator, or just went along for the ride, so to speak?"

Casey paused to contemplate his question. "Honestly, I think Jude was the lead and she was following his instructions."

Finishing off his meal, he wiped his mouth with his napkin. "Would you be upset if only Jude were punished?"

Casey looked down at her plate and realized she had about a third of the fish left. Belly full, she took another bite and placed the knife and fork down in an X to signal she was done. "No, not really. As long as Jude gets punished, I think I'll be able to sleep better at night."

Finishing his wine, Rowan signaled the waiter for the bill. "Very good. I just wanted to make sure I knew where you stood on everything. I don't want to end today's meeting with you feeling disappointed."

A bit shocked that he took her opinion that much into consideration, she gazed up at him. "Thank you."

Taking her hand, he led her back to his car and opened her door for her, then slid behind the wheel. Rowan swung the car around and headed to the witches' house.

Approaching the old farmhouse, Casey let the huge garden on the side that circled around to the back center her. The cobblestone walkway that led through the shrubs to the wide plank steps had been weeded since she and Rowan had visited the day before. The porch that wrapped around the house had been cleared of clutter, the chairs, tables, and benches lined up neatly. They passed it all on the way to the double doors and knocked.

Damion answered, wearing black jeans and a black button-down shirt. With a small smile, he nodded at them. "Welcome home, Casey. Rowan, safe passage again for the day."

Rowan nodded back. "I thank you for your offer to host our talks." Out of nowhere, he pulled a bottle of wine. "I offer you a gift of thanks."

Damion took the bottle. Reading the label, his brow shot up. "Truly, thanks, man." With a smile, he backed up to let them pass. "We've set up the meeting room for your gathering. There are finger-foods on the table and drinks on the buffet."

Casey gave him a quick hug. "Thanks, Damion. You've all made this much simpler." She led the way into the room and looked around, making sure everything felt right. The setup was perfect. Turning back to Damion, she asked, "Where are the others?"

The lean witch leaned on the door jamb and watched as they sized everything up. "Hildegard, Parker, and Tilly are having tea in the backyard. Sadie and Zen are upstairs, in case anything is needed."

There was a knock on the door and Damion straightened to play butler. A minute later, Lucas walked in. "I never thought I'd be invited into the witches' house again. It has been too long." He walked around, touching and investigating everything. His face softened as if something in him healed.

Turning to Damion, he asked. "Are there stories, histories, and magics behind these items? Do you know them?" He pointed to several of the objects around the room.

Damion just smiled. "You can talk to Hildegard after the meeting, as long as you're here and so is she."

Lucas's eyes widened, then twinkled in excitement. "She's here? That would be excellent!"

Damion and Casey snorted at the same time at his enthusiasm. Before he could ask about their reaction, there was another knock at the door. Damion quickly slipped off and returned with Cynthia.

Like the others, Cynthia did a quick circuit of the room, cataloging everything. In her case, it felt more like her information would end up in a complete report. She moved to the table, grabbed some of the appetizers, and popped them in her mouth, then went over to the buffet and poured herself a glass of vodka on the rocks. Turning to the room, she smiled. "Anyone else?"

Rowan turned to the other two heads. "Do we need to have a plan amongst us three?"

Lucas walked to the buffet and poured a glass of scotch on the rocks. "Probably, but we don't have much time. Jude has played free and easy for too long; he needs to be punished. None of us will disagree." He shrugged. "What more do we need to say?"

Cynthia threw back her first drink and poured a second. "I'd like to agree to the punishment." There was a knock on the door. "But too much has happened with the drugging of our vampires. Probably a distraction by their damn house to prevent us from planning anything else." She held up a hand before Rowan or Lucas could argue. "I know it was too well planned for them to have arranged it so quickly, but hell, it was convenient to stop us from getting together yesterday to figure this out."

Casey wondered why Rowan hadn't invited Lucas and Cynthia to lunch and arranged for their talk to happen sooner. Cynthia was right, it would've been nice for the four of them to all be on the same page before Velvet and her crew's arrival.

As she stood there wondering, the footsteps of several people caught her attention. Rowan handed her a glass of something, and she was just about to take a sip when Damion escorted Jude and Candy into the room.

Chapter 24

Dread washed through Casey as she watched Jude and Candy walk through the door. She clasped Rowan's hand, shooting glances between the new arrivals and the leaders she trusted. Her heart dropped into her stomach. She began to shake.

The three leaders smiled at the newcomers ... *What is going on? Am I going crazy?* Rowan stepped forward, hand extended, ready to welcome them. Baffled, she searched the faces of the other vampire heads, and momentarily forgot how to breathe as she tried to figure out why they seemed perfectly at ease with the two new additions slithering into the room.

Obviously misunderstanding her anxiety spike, Rowan gave her hand a quick squeeze, rubbed her arm, and his voice filled the room. "Thank you, Damion. If you'd be so kind as to close the door, we'll get this meeting started."

Casey stood frozen, confused. Hearing ice clinking, she saw the drink Rowan handed her shaking in her hand, the ice beating against the side of the glass. Rowan's hand moved to the small of her back, guiding her to a seat. Her feet moved instinctively, though she wasn't sure how she didn't end up on her face. Before she sat, she guzzled the drink. It burned on the way down. She wasn't sure what it'd been, but the fire woke her up.

She sat between Rowan and Cynthia. Chills surged down her arms as she tried to figure out what was going on. *Rowan doesn't know Candy ... Candy is in the room ... it can't be ... there is no way ...* Rowan placed a warm hand on hers as he faced the others at the long oak table. "Velvet, I don't believe you've had the chance to meet Casey."

It felt like a bucket of cold water had been dumped over her head. Hands shaking, she looked up at Rowan's face to make sure she knew exactly where he was staring. *Maybe someone misted in when I wasn't watching? Nope, right at Candy.* Then she gazed back at Candy and Jude. Candy had the grace to be blushing, while Jude, the ass, smirked.

After a moment to let her mind adjust to the idea that Candy was Velvet, Casey slowly blinked, then licked her lips and managed to find words. "Oh, we've met." It was like a tunnel had formed around her vision and the only beings left in the room were her, Jude, and Candy … er, Velvet.

A squeeze on her hand let her know despite her vision, she wasn't really alone. "Where did you meet? How do you know Velvet?"

Jude's slick voice slid out, oily and secure. "She didn't know it was Velvet, now did she? Kind of dumb, this new vampling of yours. She's fun to fuck, though. Not sure why the prophecy chose her. Maybe it was just because she's good on her back."

Raising an eyebrow, her heart racing, Casey licked her lips. "At least one of us was. You've had years to perfect the art, but I guess relying on your little suggestions has made you lazy."

Jude half-rose. "Why you little piece of ..."

Velvet's smooth voice stopped him. "Jude, stop. You're in enough trouble as it is. No reason to make things worse, my second."

Sitting down, he glared at Casey, as if she were the reason he was in this situation and not his own actions. She tried to maintain a blank face as if his presence meant nothing to her. Inside, her emotions were a tsunami, but she wouldn't give either of them the satisfaction of knowing they had any effect on her. She felt Rowan moving next to her before his breath flowed across her ear, a sound so low she barely registered the sound. "Candy?" She gave a slight nod before she felt him sit back up.

Cynthia thumped her cup down. "Jude, I have not missed your arrogance. You are *not* god's gift to women. For the record, I believe Casey is correct in her assessment of you."

Lucas chuckled. "Now that we've got the important gossip out of the way, can we move on? Last week Tuesday, Jude took Casey and kept her strapped down, taking advantage of her, in the hopes of getting her pregnant or ... impregnating Velvet, as I am guessing from the reactions and whispers around me ... to fulfill the prophecy, until she escaped. The fact that you knew about this, Velvet, puts an unfortunate spin on the entire affair."

Cynthia placed her hands on the table. "I don't know that we need to bring Velvet into this, Lucas. Let's focus on the main issue."

Curious about Cynthia's leniency, Casey closed her eyes. She let her awareness flow out around the room. She could taste the manipulative energies flowing from Jude and Velvet. It was a pond filling the room and they were the center. Jude sent out suggestive pulses, like fish in the pond.

When one hit one of the vampires, they were absorbed in, like a subtle hint. Nothing was directly sent; they were all general suggestions.

But this was the witches' domain, chosen for neutrality. With a push of will, Casey triggered a cleansing spell that was built into every room in the house. The pond, the fish, it all was washed away, and a power zap was sent to the creators of the spell. A reminder that no magic was to be done without permission. Opening her eyes, she saw the two vampires jerk while the other three rubbed their heads to clear them.

With a sigh, Casey crossed her arms over her chest. "As a reminder, we are having the meeting here because *we* can stop magic, even your vampy magic. Do it again, and I'll call in Hildegard, let her have her way with you."

Velvet's elegant eyebrow rose. "You knew what we were doing?"

Casey's brow rose in disbelief. "I've known almost from the start. Once I figured it out, there was no hiding it. It was whether or not I could stop you. Today, I can stop you easily. If you try again, I may be able to reverse it as well, give you a taste of your own medicine. It actually sounds a bit fun." Raising a brow, and smiling excitedly, Casey leaned in, "Shall we give it a try?"

Velvet leaned back and crossed her legs. "I've always liked you, Casey. Last Thursday, I didn't realize what Jude was doing. He said you two were back together and playing ... you'd finally decided you wanted to have some candy. So, I came in to play." She stood to refill her glass with a random bottle of alcohol.

"I don't believe you. What excuse did he give for the silver collar he had placed around my neck?"

Jude's smirk grew. "Too young to even use her senses. If she did, she would know that Velvet was telling the truth. But again, so dumb. You must have chosen her for her cute body, Rowan. Oh, wait, you *didn't* choose her, did you? One of Lucas's vampires did. Why isn't she one of his? Why did you decide to keep her? You could've let her die."

Rowan began to chuckle, Cynthia joining him. Grabbing Casey's hand, Rowan gave it a squeeze. "You are a character, Jude. Casey stopping your manipulations was nice, though unnecessary. Your house's tricks haven't worked on me in years, youngling. Not even yours, Velvet; you are still too young. There isn't a vampire around that can manipulate Lucas. Thinking you can is just cute. As for Cynthia ... she was playing with you. Seeing Casey take you two down, at under four years a vampire, brilliant. How terrified you must be that she is stronger than you and better than you ... and at such a young age."

He stood and circled the table, gazing at each of the items hanging on the wall. When he got to Jude, he placed his hands on the younger vampire's shoulders. "Now, we are here to discuss your punishment for taking my vampire, tying her down, and raping her. You bound her in silver so she couldn't escape. You will stop trying to change the subject, confuse the topic, or in any way put Casey down, or I *will* kill you here and now. Do I make myself understood, vampling?"

Lucas huffed. "Velvet, if you want to keep your second, might I suggest keeping him quiet? You can control him, can't you?"

A low sound came from Velvet as Rowan made his way to the buffet to pour a glass of wine. After he took a sip, he poured a second one and placed it in front of Casey before he sat. Finally, Velvet, whose face was set in cold fury, said, "Jude will stay silent for the remainder of this meeting. I will talk with him after the decision is made about the proper way to handle himself at these proceedings in the future."

Cynthia slid her chair back. "So, now that we've gotten all the introductions out of the way and are all caught up on what happened, what will be the punishment?"

Rowan put down his glass. "I would be happy with him being placed in a silver cuff for three years. One for each day Casey was captive and raped."

Cynthia nodded. "That sounds better than death. But where would the silver be placed to not be easily removed? A bracelet or necklace, he can go anywhere and remove it."

Velvet tilted her head. "He won't. He'll accept any punishment we give. I raise my vampires to behave. But if you're worried, we can add a compulsion that he can't remove the silver himself."

Casey had a hard time not reacting. She couldn't stop herself from jumping in. "What ability will he have without his magic? Do you really trust him?"

Cynthia faced her. "What do you mean, child?"

Casey wasn't sure how much Cynthia knew. "Even with silver, each family should retain some inherent aspect of their ability, something that has nothing to do with their magic."

Velvet smiled beatifically. "What she means is, even with a silver collar on, she could shift to a male presentation and hold it. We haven't played around, but I'm guessing my family will still be able to do basic manipulation. As for your families," she waved towards Lucas and Cynthia, "you can figure that out yourselves."

Jude raised his hand. With a smile, Lucas waved at him. Jude nodded in acknowledgment. "If I have to wear silver, can it be a cock ring or attached to my balls? I'd rather not advertise my punishment."

Lucas snorted and nodded. "I see no problem with that."

Chapter 25

Damion led the vampires to the front door as Casey slipped out back to see the coven leaders. Again, she found them at the garden table, this time drinking tea and enjoying the day. She headed over and hugged her grandpa before falling into one of the open seats.

Smiling at her, he asked, "How did it go?"

Hildegard sniffed, her thick German accent filling the garden. "I felt you pull on the cleansing charms. They didn't behave." Her statement was absolute.

Relaxing back, letting all her guards down, she gave a quick rundown of the meeting. "It went well in the end, but I still feel dirty about the whole affair."

Jude may have received a punishment, but somehow, Casey felt it wouldn't be as bad for him as everyone thought. She knew Velvet didn't control him the way the other heads ran their houses. He was too much of a force in that family. In the end, Casey felt she still needed to be wary of him and his people, because she knew he had them.

The main coven leader gazed over, looking down at her, even though Casey won out in height. "You should spend more of your time living here. I spoke with the witches; they need five for their minor circle. Two days a month isn't enough. Damion and Tilly have agreed to provide blood if that's the issue. You need to split your time with the vampires better, at least ten days a month here."

Dumbfounded, Casey stared into the garden letting the leader's words sink in. Witches offering blood? Shaking her head, she licked her lips. She thought about what it meant to be a blood donor and wondered if Damion and Tilly knew what they were signing up for. *Would any of my regulars want to come with me?* "Okay, yeah. Now that school's done, I'll work on my schedule. You're right, I need to make sure my training is good in both my lines."

Picking up her teacup and pausing until it began to steam, Hildegard gave a single nod. "Make sure you get a copy of your schedule to me. I care about all my witches." The demanding voice didn't carry any of her caring, but her demeanor spoke volumes about what would happen if Casey didn't send an updated schedule with more of her time at the witch's house.

Giving Grandpa one more hug, Casey reluctantly got ready to leave. "I need to go; I'm guessing more than just Rowan is waiting for me up front. I know that Lucas wanted to talk to you, Hildegard, if you have time for him."

She gave a half-shrug. "The elder vampire is interesting."

Knowing she'd gotten as much as she would from Hildegard, and not really wanting to get more, Casey followed the path through the garden around the side of the house. Summer was just around the corner and the spring flowers made her step light, filling her nose with the light scents of the outdoors. Winding her way to the front of the house, she found she'd been right: Rowan, Lucas, and Cynthia all waited for her.

Lucas faced her, giving her a smile. "Can we start up our lessons on the book on Wednesdays? I'm hoping we can get you on a more vampire schedule. Maybe we can meet at one a.m.? Despite Jude's bravado, your mind is great, and we need to continue."

Casey's face scrunched up before she smiled. Everyone was trying to adjust her schedule. Debating the middle of the night meeting time, she gazed up at the cloud-dotted sky.

The sun tended to hurt her eyes and gave her a bit of a headache.

College had kept her in the habit of keeping typical human hours because that was what she felt was expected of her. But now what? School was over. She could stay up later, sleep in later, and try to avoid being outside during the brightest part of the day. Maybe she could learn to sleep from nine in the morning to five in the afternoon. She'd have to give up all day power shopping, but then she could avoid the sun, for the most part.

Finally, laughing at her own thoughts, she nodded. "One in the morning sounds like the perfect time to learn obscure languages with you, Lucas, but, before you leave, you should know Hildegard is sitting in the back, under the very bright sun, willing to spend the afternoon talking with you."

With a bow, he spun on his heel, and retraced Casey's path to the back of the house.

Cynthia watched him practically skip down the path with a smile. "You've made his decade, child. He's been seeking the witches for some time now, and you've brought them back to us."

Lucas was out of sight as Casey turned back to the other two. "Have you all really been looking for that long?"

The older head vampire continued to gaze off. "He has. His past is filled with the combining of vampires and witches. That is his origin. It was over two hundred years ago when witches went into hiding. There were a few that stayed in contact with us, but it only took a generation or so for them to die off. The young vampires, like Jude and even Velvet, don't know about the way in which our peoples used to work together."

Thinking about Lucas and the life he'd lived, Casey couldn't even imagine what all he'd seen. "Even with our scent?"

She nodded. "Even with the scent. Your kind has always been able to figure out how to hide it when needed."

Casey bit her lip, thinking. "Were there many like me in the past?"

Cynthia finally focused on her. "There were ... a few. Most witches wanted to keep the lines separate, but there were a few witches that wanted to become vampires. Not many around here. More in other cities, and in Europe."

Bringing her thoughts back to today, Casey asked, "What do you think will happen with Jude? What will stop him from just removing the silver?"

Rowan placed a hand on her shoulder. The connection brought a sense of peace. "He asked for a ring around his privates. This isn't uncommon. The silver is made with a compulsion that he won't remove it. The bracelets we wore had the same things built in, it's why we didn't try to tear through them on that cliff. Silver is a weak metal when you come down to it. There is also a core of tungsten, one of the toughest metals out there."

Casey rubbed her temples. "How does this ring go on and off?"

Cynthia chuckled. "Full of questions, aren't you? Like your bracelet, with a small lock and key; very small, very intimate procedure. He'll be essentially mortal for three whole years. You know this punishment is practically nothing to him. Neither he nor Velvet fought the punishment or the length. Rowan, you should've started at ten years."

Casey's jaw dropped, but the two old vamps smiled at the thought. Rowan's hand rubbed down her arm until he grasped her hand. "Well, I think social hour is done. We should be heading back home, unless there is more gossip you'd like to share?"

"You two head out. We have the first of the interviews tonight to determine who poisoned the moon milk. I can't wait to learn more about this H-O-A-P organization, what did they call themselves? Hope?" Cynthia shook her head.

They were all walking towards the Porsche. They'd reached the door, but before Casey could reach the handle,

Rowan had the door open for her. Staring back at Cynthia, she asked, "When are your interviews?"

"Oh, in a few hours. But I'll see you around. Good luck in your job search, and kudos again for graduating."

Cynthia shut the door before she could say another word. Rowan slid in next to her. "We have a few hours. Do you want to head home, or did you want to do something first?"

She gazed out the window. "I wouldn't mind going somewhere to unwind, slough off the last hour of stress. I can't believe I ever thought Jude was anything but awful."

"We could head over to the trails, do some hiking. Or just go to the park and find a quiet place to sit."

Relaxing into the seat, she eyed his outfit. "I'm fine with either, but you don't look dressed for a hike."

His mouth quirked up. "I always have a spare outfit, not to mention going home to change doesn't take more than a breath of time."

Rolling her eyes, she said, "Cheater."

He laughed. "Let's hike. I wouldn't mind moving my muscles."

The drive to the hiking trails zoomed by, and, instead of changing by the trunk, he misted out and back in a matter of minutes. He was back to his college persona, jeans and a t-shirt. She smiled. "You're a chameleon. You look so different like this."

His brow rose. "Bad?"

She shook her head. "No, not at all. I don't think you have looking bad in your DNA."

He gave her a flat look at the compliment then took her arm to lead her to the trail. They took their time on their walk, though they kept up a steady pace. They continuously chose the steepest trails until they finally got to the lookout point. There hadn't been other people along the way, and they moved as fast as they could. By the end, they were both breathing hard. He watched her as she sucked in air and gazed down at the city. "Care to sit and enjoy the view?"

Nodding, she dropped to a cross-legged position, happy for the break. He took a slower path to sitting next to her, his legs out and crossed, leaning back on his arms. She looked up to watch the clouds and the play of the leaves in the wind. The breeze was a balm to her warm body. "Do you ever try to find shapes in the clouds?" She almost fell over as she leaned back.

His arm shot out. "You could just lie down, you know. It may be safer."

She laughed. "The ground is too hard on my head."

He sighed. "Then use my leg. This all seems rather silly, doesn't it? Just enjoy the clouds. And yes, everyone enjoys the clouds, don't they?"

Spinning on her butt, she placed her head on his thigh and gazed up.

"So, why no partner? I only ever see you alone."

Rowan's head dropped back to gaze up at the sky as he sighed. "Back to this topic, are we? Lots of reasons. At first, when I was establishing the house, I didn't know who was a friend and who was a double agent."

Her focus shifted from the clouds to him. "That happens?"

He chuckled. "It does ... even now. I just got into the habit of keeping my own company ... I guess."

Casey smiled. "Ah, so self-service."

Shaking his head, he blew out some air. "No, not that, but I filled my needs outside of the house. Places where people didn't know I was a vampire."

Bending her knees, she watched the leaves shimmy in the wind. "That's sad. You deserve more than that. How long has it been since you've had more?"

He dropped down so he was lying flat on the ground and rested his hand on her shoulder. She wasn't sure if she'd pushed too far in her questions, so she relaxed and enjoyed the moment of peace. His voice came out low. "Would my chest be more comfortable for you?"

She rolled her head to look up at him. His head was resting on his forearm. "Probably for me, not sure about you." But she moved so they were resting next to each other, her head in the crook of his arm. She had to admit it was a much nicer position.

His arm curled in around her. "What about you? Do you see yourself settling with one person? You seem content with the life you're building."

She paused. "I don't know. I always imagined myself finding my one true love, getting married, having kids. It's funny, I usually was more drawn to girls, yet my future always included marriage and kids."

He laughed. "I get it. It's one of the reasons I was willing to enter the life of a blood donor. Back then, liking the same gender was frowned on even more than it is now. I knew my family would've set me up with some match to help grow the family's wealth or prestige." He shivered. "There are never really words to describe the gift this family gave me. I prefer my body like this. The female form never really fit. And I've always preferred the company of women. I would've been miserable if I'd not become a blood slave and eventually a vampire."

She wrapped her arm across his chest. "Did anyone in your family know you? Anyone at all?"

In a voice barely over a whisper he said, "No."

Chapter 26

They walked into Cambia House to a whirlwind of action. People ran around setting up tables, an array of food and drinks in the back of the front sitting room available to anyone. Casey rubbed her forehead before gazing up at Rowan. "What am I forgetting?"

His mouth pinched together. "Too much is going on this week. The interviews are in two hours. This is Kailey's celebratory party. Thursday, she becomes one of us."

Casey's hand slammed against her forehead. "Gods above, how could I forget?"

Jen ran up. "Finally, you two are back. Casey, you got a call from someone at the police station. An Officer Shade.

He left a message and said you could call any time before seven."

A shudder ran up and down her back followed by a splash of excitement. Before she could speak, a sword of premonition scraped down her spine, followed by shivers. The intensity of the warning made her pause. She'd have to think about what the message was about. There were too many things happening in her life to pinpoint just one. Licking her lips, she took a calming breath as she felt Rowan's hand rub down her back in response to her speeding heart. "Which phone is the message by?"

Jen smelled worried. "It's in the study room you always use. No one's in there now. Why don't you go call? The celebration dinner starts in about twenty minutes. Hopefully, you'll be here for the start." Then she ran off to help with the party set up.

Casey continued to stand frozen. At first, the thought of the call thrilled her. Officer Caleb Shade, the name on the application she sent in last month to the local juvenile detention to work as a counselor, led the department she'd wanted to get into since she heard about it. They had an opening and she thought working with teens would fit perfectly with her personality and temperament. But the premonition ...

A pressure on her lower back made her realize Rowan still stood by her side. *Had he been talking to her?* Tipping her head back, she tried to play back anything he may have said, but nothing came to her. "I'm sorry, what?"

He smiled down at her. "Do you want company? You seem ... tense."

She leaned into him, breathing in his spicy mint scent, letting her body relax. "That isn't necessary. I'll be fine. Thanks for the offer." Straightening up, Casey made her way back to the study rooms, and found the message waiting for her.

The tension of the day threatened to overtake her as she dropped her head into her hands and closed her eyes. With a sigh, she slipped into her mental glass bubble and sat cross legged on a cushion on the floor as she tried to figure out what had caused the premonition. She thought about Officer Shade, but nothing happened. She thought about the phone call ... nothing. She couldn't seem to trigger the feeling of the knife on her spine again. Like flipping through the pages of a book, she let the events of the day flash through her mind, but nothing from lunch with Rowan to the meeting at Witch House caused a twinge.

She scrunched up her face in frustration as she pulled herself out of her bubble. It was time to make this call so she could return to the party. She found the number on the pad of paper and dialed. The phone rang and rang and rang. She hung up. Standing, she shook out her hands. Circling the table, she found a pad of paper and pencil and returned to the phone. She tried the number again. As it rang, she started to doodle, mind adrift.

After the third attempt, someone with a gruff voice answered. "Yeah."

Snapped from her near-trance, she dropped the pencil and gazed at the picture on the far wall. It depicted a field of flowers and trees. It always made her think of the vampires in the house, bringing color to their home. Taking a calming breath, she said, "Can I speak with Officer Shade?"

The voice snapped out, "Speaking."

She picked up the pencil and continued to doodle with her extra energy, though she didn't really focus on what she drew. "Hi, my name is Casey Strega. I got a call from you today?"

"Why, yes, I received an application from you for the position of counselor at the juvenile detention center. It looks like you just graduated college and had decent grades."

Nodding, though he couldn't see her, she said, "Thank you, sir."

He cleared his throat. "Because of the nature of the job and the kids in lock up, I have to ask, we have to have people who can handle the potential of working with witches and vampires. Will that bother you? Will it be an issue for you?"

She wasn't sure where he was going to go with his question. Her shoulders relaxed. "No, sir. That won't be a problem."

He let out his breath as if he'd been holding it. "Very good. Next Monday? Four?"

As the conversation came to an end, she gazed at the paper she'd been doodling on. She'd drawn a capital **M** and the number four. "That sounds perfect, sir. I'll see you then."

With a grunt, he hung up the phone.

Her muscles slackened and she slumped in the chair. A tiny thrill shot through her at the thought of getting an interview. She took a few breaths, letting her head drop onto her crossed arms. Sitting up, she knew she had to get back to the party—it was starting soon, and she wanted to change into a dress.

As she saw her doodle, she froze. She hadn't been paying attention as she drew, and her heart pounded as she gazed at the image she'd created. A field of flowers with a butterfly. In the middle of the field was a tiny house with a capital **S**, which could be a snake. A snake in a house ... betrayal.

A shiver ran up her spine and her body shook. How could the officer bring betrayal to her house? Standing quickly, she left the pad on the table, not ready to process the image. Casey took the back stairs up to her room, wanting to avoid people for a few more minutes. She changed into a pale pink skirt and white button-down sleeveless shirt. Though she wanted to take a shower, she knew there wasn't time.

Once dressed, she saw a flower Cyran had given her the previous week in a vase on her desk. She sat down on the side of the bed. She and Rowan should've stopped at the event center to visit the sick today. Cyran wasn't here to celebrate: neither were Jaxon or Jess. Was the removal of the silver enough for them to heal? Would the silver band be enough to hold Jude? Who else was going to betray her and the family? Should she tell Rowan? Slouching with a sigh, she tried to gather herself. Finally, she stood to head out.

The hallway tingled with quiet; it was so empty. Everyone was downstairs celebrating with Kailey. Heading to the stairs, Casey descended slowly, watching the others buzzing around. She felt like she moved in slow motion.

At the bottom, Jen collected her, wrapping her in a half-hug, dragging her into the dining room and to a table. Kailey plopped down across from them, and Casey snapped out of her hazy place. "I would expect you to be with Rowan, or the important people."

Kailey smiled. "I want to be next to my friends. Where have you been all day?"

Plates were being handed out by a few blood donors who were on duty. "Can we not talk about it? Today is the kind of day I'd like to forget. Tell me about your day. Or, better yet, what will you do with your last days before you become a vampire?"

Kailey smiled. "I'm spending the next few days sitting in the high sun. I know you can go in the sun, but not in the sun sun, like, middle of the day. I'm going to bake! Maybe I'll get a sunburn, just cuz."

Jen laughed. "That sounds perfect. I have two interviews this week, so I'm preparing."

Kailey's eyes got very wide. "You do? Really? Two interviews? I hadn't heard. That's amazing."

Jen reached across the table and lightly tapped her shoulder in a friendly slap. "Fine, okay. Maybe I've told you that already today."

Kailey's eyes rolled. "You think? Maybe a few times?"

Riley slid in next to Kailey. "What did I miss? Wait, don't tell me. Was it about Jen's interview? Or am I spoiling the surprise? No one here knew, right?"

One of Jen's tomatoes flew through the air and would've hit Riley if she hadn't caught it. They all laughed. After dinner, they moved to the front room. It had been transformed. All the furniture had been moved, and lights had been strung. Music played and they all got to dance. It wasn't quite the same as going out to the bars, but there was alcohol to be had, and they all had fun.

As the night progressed, people came and went, and Casey debated calling it. She'd woken early and was tired, but she wanted to support Kailey. She headed out to find some water when the front door opened. Turning to see who was coming in, she froze as she came face to face with Cyran.

Chapter 27

They stood gazing at each other until he took two steps and swept her into a hug. He buried his nose in her neck and sniffed and she felt the muscles in his arms and back relax as they embraced. He whispered, "How did you know I was coming home tonight?"

Her head shook a bit, but in his embrace, it wasn't much. "I didn't. I was just heading up to bed. Long day."

He froze in her arms. "Can I join you?"

She didn't know how to answer. She really just wanted and needed sleep. But she didn't want to hurt him after everything he'd been through. Resting her head on his shoulder, she debated an answer. Before she could think up the words he said, "Just sleep. I ... I'd prefer to have you in my arms ... not be alone."

Relaxing, she knew she'd sleep better with someone with her. She nodded. She pulled away and grabbed his hand, leading him up to her room. At the top of the first set of stairs, he tugged to bring her to his rooms. There she saw he had a bigger room, bigger bed, nicer accommodations. It only made sense; he was a more senior vampire in the house.

Once his door closed, he pulled her close and dipped his head for a kiss. It felt like coming home, and she realized how much she'd missed him, worried about him. His body shook, so she pulled away, tracing her finger across his forehead, searching his face, his eyes for answers. "You need more rest. Why did they let you leave?"

He smirked. "They didn't. I just left. I was tired of being there and decided home sounded much better."

Her eyes widened. "Do they know where you are?"

Kicking off his shoes and stripping, he shrugged. "It won't be hard to figure it out."

She huffed and followed him to his bed. He tossed her one of his t-shirts, and she stripped out of her clothes and put it on. When she was done, he was already in bed on his back. She crawled in, tucking herself in against his chest.

He sighed in contentment. "This will be much more healing than staying where I was." He kissed her forehead. "Tell me about today. You had that meeting with all the heads. Did you ever figure out who Candy was?"

She groaned and told him about her day. His laugh both irritated and amused her. Being fooled about the head of a family for so long irked her and was embarrassing, but then again, how could she have known? Then she told him about her call with Officer Shade and her premonition. He was the security of the house or would be when he was back on his feet ... he needed to know.

His arm tightened around her. "So, someone in the house, or attached to your interview, will betray you?"

She slumped into him, taking solace from his strength. "I guess. Premonitions are hard to interpret. I can talk to my grandpa about it tomorrow. He usually knows more about these things than I do."

"I'm glad you told me; it helps me to keep you safe. I'll send someone to drive you to the interview and pick you up. That should help protect you and keep me from worrying about you. As for the possible betrayer in the house, I'll speak with Rowan in the morning."

She smiled. "Good. I'm shopping tomorrow with Jen to get both of us interview outfits."

He paused. "Wait. Jen has an interview?"

The next morning Casey woke up in a strange bed with arms wrapped around her. Every muscle in her body locked up and she couldn't breathe until she remembered Cyran. Once she did, she rolled until she faced him. He was awake, watching her.

Relaxed, she smiled. "Morning, sexy."

He groaned and bent to kiss her. "Morning, yourself. I wish I felt even a bit better. I could really get used to waking up with you in my bed."

Her brow shot up. His words were a bit more than she was ready to hear. Trying to figure out why, her stomach growled. "Breakfast?"

Slumping down, he said, "I need a shower first."

"Me, too. Then I'm off with Jen." She checked the clock. Eight-thirty. "We said we'd leave by nine." Shifting up onto her arm, she leaned over for another kiss. "Good luck today, Cyran. I'll see you tonight."

She grabbed her clothes and headed down the stairs to her room. She threw all the dirty clothes into the hamper and ran to the shower then found a clean outfit. Down in the cafeteria, she selected a bagel and coffee and joined Jen already eating. "Heya, you beat me down here."

Jen set down her coffee and smiled mischievously up at Casey. "I bet; I saw you disappear with Cyran. Did you get any sleep?"

She held her coffee in both hands to pull in the heat, then took a sip before answering. "Nothing but. He's still healing. He wanted company, and I was tired."

"Fair enough. So, shopping today?"

"I need something, too."

Jen's jaw dropped. "Wait, what?"

Smiling, Casey sipped her coffee. "That's what the officer was calling me about. I submitted an application a few weeks ago. I have an interview next Monday."

She squealed. Casey flinched and covered her ears.

Quickly finishing breakfast, they took the Chameleon to the local mall. In the first store they visited, they found a section of jeans, shirts, dresses, and skirts. Nothing that would work for an interview. They walked the store for what felt like hours and couldn't find anything that would work.

Frustration wrapped around her like a cape and Casey stomped around the store. Jen eventually grabbed Casey's arm. "Relax, hon. That's why we came to the mall. We'll just go to another store. There are plenty of options here."

Feeling a bit like a bull in a China shop, Casey let Jen pull her out. They headed to the next shop. On the way, they saw Ginger. Casey pulled Jen to a stop as a boulder dropped to her gut ... she didn't want a scene today. The stress of shopping was more than enough. She knew Ginger had to have seen them; they were walking right towards her. *Well, one of us has to be the bigger person.*

As they got close, Casey waved. "Hi, Ginger."

Ginger's eyes narrowed. "Hi." Her voice came out flat and clipped.

With a harrumph, Jen growled, "Really? Four years of friendship and you're just going to throw it away? Fine, whatever. We need to find interview outfits and don't have time for this anyway."

Ginger crossed her arms across her chest, hip thrust out. "Both of you have interviews?"

Sighing, Casey slipped her hands into her pockets. "We do. We have today to get outfits. Now, unless you plan on helping us, we need to find a store with ... something. The first store had nothing. And I hate this."

Demeanor softening, Ginger asked, "Us fighting, or shopping?"

Snorting, Casey shook her head. "Yes!"

Mouth twitching, Ginger looked them both up and down. Then she reached out and, spinning, grabbed one of each of their wrists. "You two are hopeless. This way." She led them through the crowded halls and around a few turns. Eventually they entered a store.

The dragging didn't end there. She walked them right up to a rack. Reaching in, she grabbed suits, brown and navy-blue. She handed the brown one to Jen, and the blue to Casey. "Go." She waved her hands in a sweeping manner. "Try them on."

Casey stood frozen. "Did you even check sizes?"

Ginger's brow rose. "I said, try them on."

Taking the suit, she went to one of the small changing rooms to try it on. It had a skirt and a jacket. She was about to tuck in her t-shirt, when an off-white button-down flew over the door. Just like old times. "Thanks, Ginger."

Casey piled on all the clothes. Looking at herself in the mirror, she was surprised how easy Ginger made shopping. Stepping out, she saw Jen looked as well put-together as she did. She also seemed confused about the whole process.

Ginger checked them out. "Good. I have two more for you both to try on."

Baffled, Casey's hands flew out to the side. "What? Why?"

Shoulders dropping, she got *the* look. "You'll have more than one interview. Then, when you get the job, you'll need to wear clothes, like, all the days. With different shirts you can wear the same base, but you need more than one, dearie."

She slapped her forehead then took the clothes. "Oh."

An hour later, she and Jen had four suits and a half-dozen shirts. They were sitting in the food court with Ginger. They'd taken enough time that it was mid-afternoon, and the room was mostly empty. A few families were scattered around, eating their various foods, but in general, Casey felt like they could eat and speak in private.

Eating Chinese food, Ginger asked, "Did you hear a restaurant was hit again last night with that same silver poisoning that downed the vampires at your graduation party?"

Confused, Casey grabbed her soda to wash down the steak sandwich she'd bought, but Jen got the question out first. "What are you talking about?"

Ginger placed her fork down. "There's an Italian restaurant downtown. It's a popular twenty-four-hour place. At about three in the morning, three vampires keeled over dead. They were all young. None were strong enough to survive for any witches to be found, even if any of the patrons knew to find any."

The food in Casey's stomach turned to cement. "What? Do all the heads know?"

Ginger's head bobbed. "Yeah. They were called right away. I think a hotline's going to be established with the witches, if they'll agree. That is, until the perpetrators can be found."

Casey bit her lip. "I hate to ask, but ... I know you've always been against vampires. Is this something you're really against?"

She looked slapped. "In the end, they're people Casey. It hurt me that you lied. And yes, I don't like vampires or witches, but I don't want them killed. I just ... I don't know what I want." The scent of confusion bubbled from her, more than Casey expected.

Clasping her fists, she had one more question to ask. "Would you come in for an interview? One with me? Rowan wants to clear you from any suspicion for any of this."

Her face closed up and her shoulders started to hunch. "Why would you need to interview *me*? Why would *I* be a suspect?"

Closing her eyes to try to remain calm, Casey tried to relax all her muscles. She didn't need to start a new fight. "On Saturday, when I ran into you, I had just tried the moon milk. It wasn't drugged yet. Anyone who was at the party venue at the time I was there or after is being interviewed, that's it."

The tension didn't release. "Do you think I did this, Casey?"

She shook her head. "No, I don't. Neither do Rowan or the other vampire heads. None of us think you would do something that could kill me, or others. I think you don't like what I am, but not enough to kill. But that doesn't mean you aren't a suspect. We just need to eliminate you from the pool of suspects."

Her mouth twitched. "I guess I should be mollified that they want *you* to interview me, not one of the older master vampires that can really get in and read my mind, play around in there. You're such a newbie. I guess that means you all really don't suspect me."

Casey bit her tongue. She was being asked because she was the best at getting into a person's mind and reading the information without doing harm. She had the skills of both the witch and the vampire. But if Ginger's belief could save their friendship, she wasn't going to stroke her own ego.

Jen snorted. "Yeah, good thing it's *only* Casey playing in your brain. The only person who is a witch *and* a vampire. A mind witch at that. Then again, if she weren't a mind witch, her skills wouldn't be good enough and she could melt your brain."

Ginger's eyes widened and fear started to roll off her. "Really? A vampire can melt a brain? Or is that a witch skill?"

Jen laughed. "I'm just teasing you."

Casey finished her soda. "So, can we meet for the interview tonight? Tomorrow?"

Searching her purse, Ginger found a pocket calendar. "I can meet with you at the party venue Wednesday night, say, six?"

Casey nodded in agreement.

As they packed up to go, Ginger asked, "Have you tried the new restaurant that opened up across from campus? I'm trying it out tonight. I've heard it's great."

With that, it felt like their friendship was back on track.

Chapter 28

Once all her new clothes were organized, Casey returned to the crowded front sitting room. She found Cyran sitting with Sydney at a small desk near the front window. Sydney was the third most powerful vampire in the house and helped with house security. She radiated power, but visually was so different than Cyran. She was one of the shortest vampires Casey knew, and her light brown hair, cut in a bob, made her look like a teacher, in comparison to Cyran's tall lean form, dark hair, and dark eyes. But when the two security officers sparred, everyone watched ... and bet on who would win.

Casey didn't want to disturb them, so she turned to one of the couches on the opposite side of the room. Halfway there a soft, melodic voice carried across the room, cutting through the chatter of the other people talking. "Casey, care to join us?"

Checking over her shoulder, she realized it was Sydney inviting her to their chat. With a shrug, she grabbed a chair, and pulled it behind her. "I figured you two were catching up from the weekend. How can I help?"

Sydney gave her a smile. "A few things actually." Her accent was a bit English, though she'd lived here long enough that most of her slang was American. "Cyran was filling me in on the premonition you had. I felt you should know. We need to line up the interview with Ginger. The big three want us to ask you to arrange with the witches a way to call one of you in if there's another hit, like at your party."

Casey sighed. "Or the restaurant last night."

The two security officers gazed at her. Nodding, Sydney confirmed her suspicion. "Or like last night. The vampires were from Cynthia's house. They died so quickly that even if they'd had a way to contact a witch, I don't think anyone could've been saved. We're going to put in a system where there's always an older vamp, someone who can hopefully mist, heading out with the younger ones. We would love it if there were a place on the witch's grounds we could mist to for a quick heal, if healing is even possible."

Staring back and forth between them, Casey bit her lip, trying to form her thoughts. "I will talk to them tomorrow. I'll be going over there for lunch. As for Ginger, I'll be interviewing her tomorrow as well, at the party venue, at six."

Cyran smiled. "You seem to have all your ducks in a row. Any other big plans for tomorrow?"

"Only training with Lucas. He wants to meet at one in the morning. He feels I'm too set on human normal hours."

Both vampires snickered at her. Sydney took some notes down then gazed at Casey with her pale brown eyes. "That's all very good. One of us should go with you to the interview. I'd like someone to trail you to witch house as well, but I'm guessing you'd rather not have a babysitter. Any chance you won't try to slip anyone we assign you?"

She leaned back and considered Sydney. "Is this all because of my premonition? Are you two planning on keeping me on full watch until it's figured out?"

Her eyes sparkled as she nodded. "That's our plan. How often do you get a warning that one of your wards is in danger?"

"I haven't felt anything today. I think I'll be fine."

Cyran reached over and grabbed her hand. "Will you humor us?"

Trying to keep a flat face, she shrugged. "Fine. Do I get to choose my partner in crime tomorrow, or do I have to suck it up and take whomever you assign?"

His thumb stroked her hand. "That depends. What are you doing for dinner tonight?"

Shifting her eyes to Sydney, then back to Cyran, she said, "Well, truth be told, Ginger told me about a restaurant that opened up across from campus. I was curious. I thought Kailey might want to check it out with me." She narrowed her eyes and quirked a smile at him. "Why do you ask?"

He licked his lips. "Well. In the spirit of keeping you safe," his brows shifted up and down suggestively, "I could tag along. Security you know."

Considering him, her head tilted a bit. "Well, I haven't actually invited Kailey yet. It was just an idea I had."

He nodded. "So, what your say—"

Sydney snorted. "Gods above, get a room you two, go to dinner, do something. You're awful. Any way you do it, I'm out. Have fun tonight. I've wondered about the food though. Let me know how it is, Cyran." She stood and stalked off.

Smiling wide, he leaned over the table and gently kissed her. "When do you want to leave?"

"I don't remember saying I'd go to dinner with you." Her brow rose in defiance.

"Oh, is that the case? So, you're leaving me with the order to bring back the report on this restaurant and no one to go with?"

She sighed dramatically. "Well, if you put it that way, what choice do I have?"

His mouth curled up. "A pity date? I'll take it!"

Two hours later, they walked into the new restaurant. It was a human establishment, so there was no jumping ahead in line this time. Once they had a table, Casey quickly decided on what she wanted and could take in the other people and decorations. It was an American joint, with flags and farm equipment decorating the walls. It looked somehow high-end despite the stirrups and chaps.

When the waiter came around Casey got the ribeye and a potato, plain with butter and sour cream, hold the special seasoning. Cyran got the porterhouse with garlic mashed potatoes.

Cyran put out his hands, and Casey placed hers in them. She smiled at him. "How are you feeling? Should you be out and about so soon? Shouldn't you still be in bed?"

He waggled his brows. "Are you offering to play bed nurse?"

She leaned back and started to pull her hands away. He held on tight. She sighed. "What's gotten into you?" *I really like him, but how serious does he think this is?* "I know that you've always dated around ... almost as much as my reputation. Don't you have a line of possible nurses?"

He shrugged. "I was wondering. ...you're smart, Casey, and beautiful. And a vampire of my age eventually slows down."

"Your age? How old are you?"

His fingers began to massage her hands. "Not as old as Rowan. I'm from Egypt, where he's from Italy. I did come to this country with him, though. I was one of the few who left Ashby to join Rowan in the new country."

She forgot to breathe as she gazed into his dark eyes. "How did you end up with Ashby?"

His face scrunched up. "It isn't a pretty story. None of us have nice stories. My family was originally from the land that is now Poland. We were slaves in Egypt. I was stolen from my family when I was young. I kept getting traded. I ran one day and was found by one of Ashby's people. I was still young, and Rowan asked if I could be his man servant. He'd never had one before. The idea amused Ashby, so he agreed."

The food came and they released their hands and began eating. The food was good. After a few bites, Cyran stared up at her. "Do you want to know something funny?"

She nodded. "Always."

"When I first started dressing Rowan, it was like he didn't even know how to work men's clothing. I don't know how to explain it. He'd never had someone help him, but he was also confused by them. You know what I mean?"

She froze mid-bite, not knowing what to say. Then she forced a bite of the steak that practically melted on her tongue like butter. "Not really. What do you mean?"

His mouth scrunched up, then he relaxed. "I think, like me, he came from poverty. Then when he was changed, he suddenly was being presented as a rich man. He had no idea how the wealthy dressed. When I showed up, Ashby gave Rowan all these rich man's clothes, and me to dress him because otherwise Rowan would've run around naked."

Casey relaxed and laughed. Rowan was right that no one from his past actually knew anything about his history. It was strange to have so many people, family, and be so alone. It made her sad for him.

Taking a sip of the wine Cyran had ordered, she decided to let Rowan worry about himself. "How long were you working for him before you were changed?"

Like Rowan had before, Cyran swirled his wine. She really had to figure out the reason why. "I reached the house when I was eleven. Ashby refused to change anyone before the age of twenty-two. Rowan kept me until I was sixteen, then I became a blood donor for the house. At the time, Rowan was against the move, but I was curious. Living in his rooms, I didn't know much of what the family could do."

Interest piqued, she leaned in. "Like, their ability to shift sexes?"

Placing his glass down, he blushed. "It sounds crazy, doesn't it? Rowan was private back then too. I lived in his room, and he kept me away from everything. I knew about the coupling, but ... let's just say, I had an awakening when my position shifted."

Her hand flew to cover her mouth to hold back a snort just as voices in the restaurant shifted to screaming.

Chapter 29

Whipping her head around, Casey saw people falling around the room. She leapt up and ran to the first one, a young vampire who, crumpled to the floor, was already dead. Across the room, Cyran yelled to her, "Over here."

The path was blocked. The patrons of the restaurant had pushed out their chairs, standing, gaping at the commotion. Casey tried to navigate her way around quietly, slipping around people as best she could, but there were so many people, and they didn't know where to look. Pushing and shoving, she finally made it to Cyran.

He was kneeling by a vampire who was on his back but not dead. Hands shaking, she grabbed a white cloth napkin from the floor next to the man, closed her eyes, and focused on him. There was silver in him, a lot of silver. More than what had been in the vampires at her party. Gasping, she concentrated on collecting every bit of it and moving it to the hand with the napkin. What had been dust a few nights before felt like sand now.

She slumped, fell over onto the prone man, and gasped for air. Her head pounded in agony. A shiver ran up and down her body and her vision began to waver. Cyran took the napkin and, making a ball with the silver in the middle, put it in his pocket. "Can you do more?"

Shaking, she forced herself to her feet. "I hurt, but they're dying. I'll do more."

Cyran put an arm around her and led her to another downed vampire. Trembling, she searched for a napkin, then Cyran handed her one. Again, she closed her eyes. This time the level of silver was almost as low as at her party. The extraction was more bearable. By the end, sweat poured down her back and Cyran had a second napkin in his pocket.

Casey rested her head on the cold floor, needing a few seconds. Finally, hands helped her up. She was surprised when, instead of Cyran, she looked into the pale green eyes of Rowan. Collapsing into his embrace, she let him hold her as her body shook. Tears burned her cheeks, but she managed to get out, "I can do one more."

He leaned down, lips near her ears, and whispered, "No need. I brought your grandpa. He'll finish up. He assures me he is stronger at pulling silver from people than anyone else, especially his silly granddaughter. Now, Cyran has to stay to run security. I'm going to take you home. Can you stand on your own?"

She nodded, but when he moved away her legs began to crumple under her. With a small chuckle, he caught her. "Ah, by yes, you mean no." Then her world misted, and they were standing in a room she didn't recognize. It was large with light wood walls. The furniture was a darker cherrywood and all matched. There was a huge bed with light, soft looking linens.

After gazing around the room, she looked up at him. "You need blood, and most of the donors are out barhopping with Kailey. The ones here have been used and are not on rotation. Bad planning, except no one expected the need tonight. I don't know if taking my blood will lead to anything, but your room is too small and public."

Her heart started beating faster as he led her to the bed and set her down. She sat on the edge and gazed up at his beauty, not believing the turn of events that had happened. "Will you be taking any of my blood?"

His mouth quirked. "Maybe."

Something about that word vibrated through her body in a shot of excitement. Shutting her eyes, she licked her lips. Despite her wanting this, a secret she hadn't wanted to even admit to herself, she had to know ... "Is this something you want? You've been avoiding the people in this house, Rowan." Opening her eyes, she stared directly into his, trying to see the truth. "Because, if this isn't something you want ... I can wait. But if it is ..." she knew he could hear the pounding of her heart. Her hands started to shake. She bit her lip, but knew she wanted to be honest. It was time he stopped holding himself apart from every vampire in his house. She took a breath. "But if it is something you want ... so do I."

His eyes softened as he used a finger to lift her chin. Bending, he softly kissed her. Then he pulled back and unbuttoned his shirt and pulled it off, revealing a well-muscled chest. Sitting next to her, he removed his shoes, then hers. Helping her to stand, he unzipped her dress, and with a quick motion, she was standing in only her black silk panties.

He turned her to him, slipping his warm hands around her back and bent to kiss her again, this time licking across her lips, asking to be invited in. When she opened slightly, he deepened his kiss, bringing his spicy mint with him. She reached up, wrapping her arms around his neck, letting her fingers play in his soft, silky hair.

Continuing the kiss, he bent and lifted her, placing her gently on the bed. He backed away for a second, and she heard his pants fall to the floor before he stretched out next to her and partially on top of her. "We're going to do this the old-fashioned way. From the neck ... together."

His bed was large and soft. It felt like she was lying on one of the clouds they'd been watching the other day. "At the same time?"

He smirked. "Trust me." He lay on top of her, then rolled, so she was on top of him. She quickly spread her legs to straddle him. She leaned down and nuzzled his neck, intoxicated by his scent. Her teeth descended, and, opening her mouth, she bit down. The slow trickle of blood that filled her mouth began as a balm, healing her, helping fill the needs of her body. After the night she'd had, her body was desperate.

By the fourth pull, the blood became electric. She felt a zing from her tongue to her center, hot, and pulsing, and she moaned, almost collapsing with need. Then she felt a bite on her neck and the pull of her blood, and her world exploded. She didn't know where she began and Rowan ended. The sizzle and heat of the blood seared her, and her eyes rolled back as her body began to shake.

Her body crashed in fireworks, then the world went black for a second, and she was lying next to Rowan, his smile the first thing she saw. "You okay? The first time you share blood like that can be intense. It's why it isn't done with new vamps."

"More." Her voice was wispy as she panted through sensations she could never have imagined.

He leaned down and kissed her. "How about we do things the other way? Save more of that for another day."

Her eyes widened and she smiled. "We can do this again?"

He shrugged. "We'll see."

Pushing him back, she began to kiss down his well-sculpted body until she got to his cock, standing thick and proud. Grabbing it, she guided the end into her mouth and slowly determined how far she could go before she had to back up. His noises as he tried to maintain control became a challenge. She would win when he lost.

His groans intensified as his body tightened, then he sat up and grabbed her and tossed her on the bed next to him. Rolling half on her, he kissed her again, his hands roaming her body. Pulling away, he sighed. "I've wanted to ..." He shook his head and leaned down, taking her nipple into his mouth.

She arched up, the sensation of his mouth, hot and wet, with his hand on her other nipple, rubbing and pinching, sent tiny pulses of pleasure through her. Her breath got rough as she pushed up into him. His hand moved lower, dipping under the waistband of her panties, and found her center of sensation. He began to play there as his mouth continued where it was. Electricity zinged between the two spots, and her head fell back with a moan.

Then he moved down, sliding off her panties. His mouth replaced his hand, and his fingers began probing in her. At first he shifted from pressure to teasing her nerve center with his teeth, but then he bit down. The initial pain made her scream, but then his tongue began to flick, and her world narrowed down to one spot.

She groaned as the feelings grew. His sucking and skillful knowledge of her body brought on a tsunami of sensations. She squirmed with the onslaught. Then the pressure of his finger in her got more insistent and the ocean of desire grew. Her body bowed off the bed and incomprehensible sounds came from her.

Right before she crashed, his teeth disengaged, and he moved up her body, slamming into her. He filled her, almost too much. She wrapped her legs around him, giving him a bit more space as he found a rhythm, pounding in and out. His eyes sparkled down as they watched her move closer and closer to orgasm. It didn't take long before her world was taken over by explosions. He grunted and collapsed on top of her. She wrapped her arms and legs around him, keeping him from rolling away.

After a minute, he pushed himself up. "I'm guessing there's a more comfortable way for us to sleep." Rolling off her, he wrapped her in his arms, and she quickly fell asleep.

Chapter 30

She woke late the next morning in her own bed and wondered if she'd dreamt the night before. If she had, it had been a great dream. Her thoughts shifted to her grandpa and how he fared after last night at the restaurant. She knew that much at least had been real.

With a groan, she pushed herself up and stretched, realizing she'd slept really well the night before. After dragging herself from bed, she made it to the bathroom, then took a quick shower. Back in her room, she dressed in a black skirt, black tights with a garter belt, and a green button-down top. A jean jacket and boots completed the outfit.

When she got to the stairs, she ran into Rowan in a gray linen suit. He reached out a hand and placed it on the small of her back. He leaned down to quickly kiss her. "If you don't mind, I'll be your escort for the day. Cyran needs to stay around the house, and I'll need to be present at the interview with Ginger later anyway."

Her heart beat fast and all she could do was nod. At the bottom of the stairs, he looked between the door and the kitchen. "Hungry?"

Nodding, she finally managed to say, "Very."

He led her out of the house and to his red Porsche. Once again, he got the door for her before sliding behind the wheel himself. Moving into traffic, she asked, "Where are we headed?"

"A small diner I know of. It's near campus."

Her stomach growled as she thought she knew of the place he meant. It was an old favorite of hers and Ginger. They'd go for lunch when they couldn't stomach college food. As they pulled into a spot, she was happy to see she was correct.

Once inside, the waitress recognized her and pointed to her favorite booth. "Your usual, dearie?"

Casey nodded as Rowan waved off a menu. "I'll have what she's having."

Laughing, Casey shook her head. "Very daring. You know you're risking a lot trusting a college student's order."

His eyes danced. "I'll take my chances."

After the coffee was brought, she opened one of the small creamer containers and added it and a splash of sugar. Leaning back, she took a sip and said quietly, "You kissed me on the stairs." Her heart beat faster as she awaited his response.

"Is that not allowed?"

"When I woke up in my own room ... well, I thought you were giving me a signal that you either regretted what happened or wanted to keep it on the down low."

He lifted his coffee to take a sip. Grimacing, he added a bit of sugar then took another sip. The spoiled master vampire was obviously not used to diner coffee. "I shifted you to your own bed when my phone started ringing at six in the morning. I didn't think you should have to wake up that early ... that's all."

She stared at him, a bit nervous about his answer. "What does that mean ... I mean, for us, in the house. I know you've always been private. I just want to respect you and your boundaries."

He opened his mouth to answer when the food arrived. Two plates with blueberry Belgian waffles, two sides of hash browns covered in fried eggs, two plates of bacon, and two sides of sourdough toast. A small plate with syrup, butter, and jelly was placed between them.

Rowan closed his mouth, then opened it again. "Is this what you always order ... just for yourself?"

A smile nearly broke her face in half. She nodded. "Trust me, you won't want to give up any of it." They spent the next few minutes eating. Everything was as good as she remembered. It had been a few months since she'd been to the diner, and she missed it. Halfway through, she thought she might explode.

She watched Rowan for a few minutes, eating as proper as you could with a diner bounty in front of you. He'd tried everything and was working on the hashbrowns, one of the best items on the menu. She sipped her coffee as he concentrated on the food.

He finally noticed her gaze and paused. "Done already?"

"Nope, just taking a break, enjoying the view." A small smile played across her face, and her cheeks heated.

His brow shot up. "Well, I guess I can take a small break, see if what I've eaten will settle. Maybe answer your question, now that *it's* had time to settle."

She froze, watching him intently. "Okay. A good settle?"

He placed his fork down. "You know I've avoided all the house intrigue. Last night was a big shift for me, but I trust you. I would like to play this out. I know you are freer with yourself, and as a vampire, especially in our house, I won't ask you to change your ways while we are together, but I would request that if we've made plans, I'm your first priority."

A lightness filled her as she sat with him. "I can agree to that. As long as we can add one more item to our agreement."

His eyes narrowed. "What's that?"

"I want to see your natural form."

He froze. "Let me think about it. I usually switch back every week or so for a bit, but I do it in private."

She felt a longing she couldn't explain. Casey knew what she asked wasn't reasonable, but she'd felt a pull towards Rowan for a while, something she'd ignored, outside of asking anything she could think of every time they ended up together. He settled something in her, made her feel whole and complete, something more than just a master with one of his vamplings. Even if he said no, the fact he trusted her with any part of his inner self thrilled her.

"It isn't like I don't know. You're so ..." She ducked her head and blushed. Biting her lip, she decided to just go for it. "Okay, you're so handsome, I can't imagine how beautiful you'd be."

"Like I said, I'll think about it. But now we need to finish up and get to your other family home."

When they made it to Witch House, Tilly told them everyone was around back in the garden enjoying the beautiful weather. Casey drooped. "Can you ask my grandpa to meet us in the living room?"

Tilly's brow furrowed. "Is it secret?"

Casey sighed. "No, I've just had way too much sun lately. It's been giving me headaches. I would prefer to stay out of it, if possible. The garden is lovely, but I need shade right now."

Her eyes widened. "Oh! Especially with the extra silver extractions happening."

"Yeah, and there weren't any blood donors at the house last night. Not human at least ..." Tilly began to look worried. "I'm fine, I just want to stay indoors." She moved to a couch and sat. Rowan sat next to her.

Tilly headed out the back door and returned with the others who filled in. Hildegard sat in a high-backed rocking

290

chair and looked down her nose at Rowan. "Ah, the vampire house head. To what do we owe your attendance today?"

Casey put a hand on his arm, letting the group know she wanted him there, and then sat forward. "I got a premonition yesterday. When I got home, Jen told me I had a call from an Officer Shade. He was who my application for a job went to. After she mentioned the call, I felt the ..."

Grandpa interrupted her. "I feel it, child. You're in danger."

"When I went to make the call, I couldn't recreate the feeling. But I did create a doodle."

Both Hildegard and Grandpa leaned forward. "Did you bring it, Fräulein Strega?"

Slumping down, she shook her head. "I didn't, but I can either recreate it or describe it. It was pretty simple."

With a flat face, Hildegard shrugged. "Go ahead."

She nodded. "It was a field of flowers with a butterfly and a small house. There was a capital S in the center of the house."

All the witches sucked in air at the quick rundown of the doodle. Damion was the first to speak. "Betrayal in your house. You must be the butterfly, unless ... you said there is a new vampire being created ... it could be that one. Either way, I see why you have an escort."

Rubbing her hands, Casey watched Grandpa. "How do you feel after last night? How many did you help? I helped two and one of them had a huge load of silver."

Her grandpa's mouth scrunched up in serious thought. He didn't look as tired as she felt. "I cleared out four of them. It was serious business. Afterwards, Cyran and I searched the kitchen. There was a seasoning used on the baked potatoes, the chicken, and some of the other veggies that had the tri-fold mix dumped in it. There had been vampires in earlier who were fine, so they think only the one bottle was tampered with."

Casey's hands started to shake, and Rowan grabbed one, rubbing it with his warmth to calm her. "If you hadn't been there last night, there would've been more deaths. You and Cyran saved those people. Calling in your grandpa saved more. You did well ..." It sounded like he wanted to say more but wasn't sure if he was ready.

He turned to Hildegard. "Your people saved us last night. Can we set up a system where we bring you in or bring our sick to you until we get this figured out?"

She turned to Damion. "Yes. We've spoken, and those of us living at the house are willing to step up to help. We'll work with you to find a way to help save the sick."

They spent the next few hours working through the logistics of how the vampires and witches would work together to keep everyone safe.

Chapter 31

Walking into the party venue, there were cots set up in rows. Casey circled the sick vamps, quickly sensing to see if she felt any silver. It wasn't that she didn't trust that it had all been extracted, but just in case.

Jaxon was sitting at one end arguing. His voice cut through everyone else's. "I've been here since Saturday. I've been awake and moving around since Tuesday ... when can I head home?"

He stood, hands clenched. "Cyran and Jacque have already misted away. Just because I'm younger and can't mist, why am I being punished?"

The vampire in charge stood firm, but his eyes kept looking down at the paperwork. "I can't release you without the approval of your head of house."

Rowan cleared his throat. "I think it's fine for him to head home."

The two turned to them as one. Jaxon yelled, "Rowan!" then ran over to give him a hug.

Rowan smiled down at Casey. "If you'll give me a minute." He misted away with his vampire, reappearing a few seconds later.

"Sir, that isn't how this works. We have procedures in place, and they don't involve you coming in and stealing my patients away," the vampire in charge sputtered.

Rowan's brow rose. "You understand, this is my building, my cots, and my procedures. If you have an issue, file a complaint, and when it hits my desk, I'll file it away where I believe it belongs."

The man's face turned more and more red with every word spoken. By the end, he spun on his heel and returned to the vampires sick enough they weren't complaining about being stuck in a party venue turned infirmary.

Mouth twitching, Casey looked up at Rowan. "Is this how you make new friends, sir?"

"We have a half-hour before Ginger arrives. Care to walk with me?" He reached down and twined his fingers in hers.

There was a mischievous edge in his voice she wasn't sure she trusted, but she nodded. He led her up the stairs and past a private room with a reserved sign for six o'clock. At the back of the hallway stood another private door which he opened with a key. Inside was a large desk and chair. He shut the door and she turned, checking out the wooden bookcases filled with books that lined the walls and the file cabinets made of the same dark wood.

Her investigation ended with her facing him. "Is this your office?"

He placed his hands on either side of her face and dropped his head down to hers. "I find, now that I've given in, I keep wanting to touch you. I know Miss Rotta will be here soon, and we only have minutes, but I ... gods, I need to feel you."

Tipping her head back, she kissed him, letting him feel her need as well.

Rowan stroked his hands down her body and lifted her up. She wrapped her legs around his waist. He made a sound of approval when he felt her stocking only went halfway up her thighs, and she knew her panties wouldn't be much of an obstacle. Focused on their kiss, and his taste, she was shocked when the back of her legs hit the cold desk, and a squeal escaped her.

One of his hands slipped between their bodies, under her skirt, to find her clit. Gently playing with her, he began to build her body up to a steady hum. His finger slid lower, sliding in her, and he groaned. He pulled back. "You are so hot and wet. You make it hard to take things slow."

Her breathing was rough as she reached down and unzipped his pants. He was hard and ready for her. "Why take it slow?"

His breathing came fast. He lifted her up and slid her down onto him. He was thick and stretched her out, and her breathing was choppy as he filled her. For a second, she tightened her legs and arms and just felt him fully in her, enjoying the sensation. Then she let him place her back on the desk and loosened her legs. He found a pace that worked for them both.

It was hard and fast, and soon her head fell back as she lost herself in the eruption of feelings. He gently laid her down, unbuttoned a few of her shirt's buttons, and used his mouth to play with a breast. Arching up, she began to climax again as he continued to pump into her. Just as she screamed out a second time, vision darkening, he too made a sound of pleasure, dropping down on top of her, breathing hard to catch his breath.

They stayed there for several minutes before, with a sound of protest, he moved away from her. The meeting would start soon, and they had to get put together. Her clothes were easier to fix, and she continued to sit on his desk watching him make himself presentable. Right before they had to leave, he came over for one last kiss. "I like the garter belt, by the way."

She laughed and leapt down. "I couldn't guess." She did one last check of her outfit before they headed back out to the reserved room to wait for Ginger.

The interview room, normally a conference room for the leaders of the city, had a large rectangular oak table down the center. The walls were painted a light blue, and there were paintings on the two long walls of scenery. Casey sat in a chair on one of the long sides, and Rowan took a chair at the head of the table, facing the door. Ginger came in a couple of minutes after them.

She stopped when she noticed Rowan. "I thought I was being interviewed by Casey?"

Rowan leaned back and folded his long fingers in front of him. "I'm here as security. She's young in the house, and with the threat to the vampires, all younger vampires must be accompanied by an older escort."

Her brow furrowed. "Aren't you a bit important to be playing nursemaid to a newbie vamp, sir?"

His smile didn't reach his eyes. "I guess I am, but I've been at all the other interviews, so I was curious how this one would turn out. Does my presence bother you, Miss Rotta?"

Plastering on a fake smile and taking a seat across from Casey, Ginger shook her head. "Of course not, Mr. Cambia. I'm just surprised to find you here." She turned to Casey, pointedly ignoring Rowan. "So, how are we going to do this?"

Casey smiled at her friend. "Hi, Ginge. I've missed you. So, I'm going to do this a bit differently than most interviews. If you are okay with it, I'm going to use some of my witch magic and check out some of your memories. See what you did when you were here last Saturday. That will be the easiest way to clear you of the deed."

Ginger's eyes widened and her arms moved as if she were wringing her hands in her lap, but her head moved up and down slightly. "Okay, Case, I'm going to trust you. Do we ... I dunno, need to be touching?"

Shaking her head, Casey placed a hand on the table. "It isn't necessary, but it can be soothing. It's up to you if you want to hold my hand."

Her eyes darted from Casey's face to her hand and back up, as if her hand were a snake that would bite her. She seemed to stop breathing for a few seconds before she slowly brought one hand up from under the table. The hand was fisted as she brought it up to her mouth, then shot it out to the center of the table. At the last minute, her fingers extended, landing on top of Casey's.

Gently, Casey wrapped her thumb over Ginger's fingers. "Just relax and close your eyes."

Following her own advice, Casey moved into Ginger's mind. It opened up like a child's playground, free for anyone's use. She was careful, not wanting to harm her friend or leave any emotional evidence or her passage. When she got to the center of the memories, she was shocked to see a field of boxes, like cubicles in an office building, each box a different color. Some were clear, some blue, some red, and some a golden yellow, like a sunshiny day.

This is not normal ...

Floating over the boxes, Casey saw images, people, and tableaux within them. She went into the first corner one. It was clear.

I really like this new girl, but she seems so uptight. A night in the bar should really help. I can't believe she finally agreed. "Come on Casey, sit here, I'll go grab us some Margaritas ... you do drink, don't you?"

She rolled her eyes at me, like the question was so ridiculous. All the girl did was go to class and study; it really was a fair question. "Of course, I'll drink, I'm not that uptight, Ginger. I'm at the bar with you, aren't I?"

Heading up to the bar. The bartender is hot! He has dark curly hair and midnight blue eyes. I wonder if he's single. "What will you have, gorgeous?"

Yummy, he's a flirt! "Two margaritas for me and my friend over there at the table." He looked over my shoulder at Casey and froze.

Eyes narrowing, he asked, "What do you think about the new vampire and witch legislation going down?"

Not this again. Why don't people just let others live their lives? It's so frustrating! "I believe that everyone should be able to live their lives. Why? What do you think?"

Thrown from the memory, Casey found herself floating above the field of boxes. Since when was Ginger pro-vampire and witch? She'd always been against them; at least, as long as they'd been talking about them. The next box was red. Casey slid inside.

The scene continued, but this time Jude was staring into Ginger's eyes and holding her hands. Two margaritas stood on the bar next to her, ready to go.

Jude's voice droned, mesmerizing. "You do not like vampires or witches. You think they are bad for the world. You want to try to date me, so you won't point me out to your friend or introduce us yet. Repeat my commands, Ginger Rotta."

I did.

The memory ended.

Dread flowed through Casey. She moved towards the middle of the boxes and flew into another box, a blue one.

Again, Jude's handsome face and voice dominated my view. "Convince your friend she needs to work with you at your job. You make good money; she'd make good money there as well. You should both make good money there and you'd be spending more time together. Repeat my commands, Ginger Rotta."

I did.

The memory ended.

Finding a blue box next to a golden yellow one, she descended into it. Ginger was sitting in the back room of the bar with Jude and Velvet.

"Velvet, love, her friend is the newest vampire that was made last weekend. She doesn't even know the friend is a vamp ... or a witch."

Velvet smiled down at me. She was so pretty. I didn't even like girls, but good god, she was lovely. "Did you program her to not like vamps and witches?"

"I did. Don't want her siding with her friend over me in the end."

Velvet's hand rested on my knee; it was as soft as I thought it'd be. "Excellent. I'm heading out, so I have plausible deniability here, love." Velvet stood, her outfit pulling tight against her body in interesting ways. Smiling a goodbye, she kissed his cheek before giving me a small smile. Was I jealous that she got to kiss him or that she didn't kiss me?

Jude caught my chin and tilted my face towards his. Having claimed my attention he said, "Ginger, you will make sure Casey meets me tomorrow night. Tell her how jealous you are of her to have made such a catch. Now, you will forget this meeting; you never had it, you never met Velvet. Go."

Casey was getting the hang of the colors. Clear were Ginger's real memories, untouched. Red were small commands she was told to forget. Blue memories were things too big to simply forget, so those memories were replaced by the fake golden yellow ones.

She slipped into a golden yellow box and watched as Ginger sat at the bar with Jude and ordered drinks. The fake memory to replace the forgotten one. Floating higher, every blue box had a golden yellow one right next to it.

Moving near to the end, she dropped into a blue box.

Jude walked into my office. "Hiya, sexy lady."

"What do you want, Jude? I'm busy."

His smile, as charming as always, stretched across his face, and I melted. Suddenly, I wanted to do anything he asked. He always could make me agree to almost anything ... I think? Why does he confuse me so much?

Grabbing my hand, he kissed the back. "Well, love, I have this vial. I know you won't remember any of this, but I'll let you know it's a rather nasty business. I want to get the attention of some important people. Since I know you're running the security check at tonight's venue, I'd like you to dump this in these little cups I requested made on the governor's behalf."

I looked at a tiny cup he held up. "What is it?"

His smile widened. "It's called moon milk, love. You just add a bit of the powder to each, and I'll be happy as a clam."

The memory ended. Casey had seen enough, though she wanted to go through and clean up all of Jude's ugly business. Between his work and what had been done at her waitstaff job, Ginger's brain was a wreck.

As Casey sat back, she realized tears slid down her face. Looking between Rowan and Ginger she shrugged. The relief at knowing who had poisoned the moon milk warred with who the culprit was. "It was her, but it wasn't."

It took a while to explain, but in the end, Ginger asked to be brought to the witch house. When they got there, all the witches met her in the living room. Casey did a quick rundown of what happened.

Ginger stared at Hildegard. "I want my mind back. I need the best to fix me. Who's the best?"

As one, everyone stared at Casey.

Chapter 32

Casey sat in the study room waiting for Lucas. Her day had been long, and she was tired. Ginger was staying at Witch House until her memories could be fixed, it would be a long process if the process was completed without harming her.

Seeing the early memories where Ginger fought to defend witches and vampires confused Casey and gave her hope. *I wonder if the person we find under all Jude's manipulations is the same person I've been friends with all these years. Her mind needs to be free, but I hope the process doesn't make her hate me once again.*

Five minutes before Lucas was scheduled to arrive, Casey got up and headed to the front door to meet him. The front room was full of housemates playing cards and watching TV. She didn't have to wait long before he arrived. Looking her up and down his face scrunched in concern. "Are you okay, child?"

She led him back to the study room. He had the feel of her grandpa, though he looked to be in his late twenties. "It's just been a long day. I'm sure Rowan will fill you and Cynthia in on what happened with Ginger, if he hasn't already."

He nodded. "We've been told. It's a lot to have to learn about your friend. She's been messed with for nearly four years. That's a lot of clean up. I know you're the best, but will Hildegard help?"

Casey nodded. "Yeah. I'm busy here. She and I will work together until Ginger's mind is hers again. It means that she and my grandpa will be staying a few extra weeks."

They sat at the table she'd claimed for studying over the last few years. Sometimes Jen would join her, but she loved the feel of the room and always used it. If she was going to continue lessons, this is where she felt like she'd have the most success.

Lucas checked out the decorations. "You know, we don't often visit each other's homes, especially the heads. I may have visited here once, but it was years ago. This room was definitely not decorated like this then."

Waggling her brows, she had to ask. "Was there even electricity back then?"

His mouth dropped open. "Scoundrel of a witch!"

She laughed. "Can I grab you something to eat or drink?"

His eyes went up and he said, "Tea, if you don't mind." She was about to get up when he continued. "Witch fashion, if you don't mind?"

"If you end up covered in hot water, don't say I didn't warn you." Closing her eyes, she gathered the cups, hot water, and tea bags. There weren't free floating tea leaves here, like at home, but she'd do with what they had. With a push of will she brought two cups of hot tea to the table. Over the years she'd gotten better, and the tea came with the cups, thankfully.

When she opened her eyes, Lucas was staring intently at something to Casey's right. Following his line of sight, she realized he was studying her doodle. Biting her lip, she tried to cover it up, but it was too late.

He reached across the table and grabbed the pad. "What's this?"

She slumped. "It's a doodle. I drew it while on a phone call."

"Do you know all of the symbolism, historically, that is?"

Casey straightened. "The snake in the house is someone who will betray me or the house. I assumed I was the butterfly because I'm of two forms ... or maybe Kailey since she is changing tomorrow. Then the flowers ... in symbology, weren't vampires symbolically shown as flowers because flowers always reappear in the same place as if they've always been there and will always be there?"

He was nodding. "You have that close enough. The flower was the vampire. Symbolically, the witch was represented by birds. There, but not as common. Butterflies were transition."

She gazed at the image. "The big issue is the snake in the house. Who is the betrayer? Who should be worried? Is it me, since I got the premonition? Is it someone else in the house? Or is it the house in general?"

His face dropped. "Or, child, is it the vampires in general."

A shiver ran down her spine, not a premonition, just a chill at his words. How big of a betrayal was coming?

"Both Cyran here and my grandpa with the witches are looking into this. No one is taking it lightly."

It was time to move onto her lesson. Lucas placed his hand in hers and she invited him into her glass bubble. They sat at a table, not unlike the one they sat at in the real world.

Rubbing his hand over the imagined wood, he laughed. "Now I see where you modeled this table from."

She took down a book from the shelf and brought it to him. He studied the cover. "This isn't the book with the prophecy."

"No, that one's old. I thought we'd start with me just learning the language. Once I know it, we can move up to that one. I won't read it without you, don't worry."

He gave her some side eye, but chuckled. "Fair enough."

They spent the next few hours learning the basics of the language. Then Lucas searched her library, finding books he wanted to read. "If I make a pile, will they be here when I return?"

She waved a hand and a small empty bookcase appeared. "Are you planning on spending that much time in my head?"

After the books were sorted, he looked at the books, then up at her. "It's really easy to forget that's where we are. I figure, eventually you'll have work, and I'll be able to read while monitoring your work. This is good."

She laughed. "Okay, but we're done for tonight, right?"

He nodded, and she pulled them out.

She led him to the door, and decided she needed to get some blood. Checking the main floor of the house, everything was quiet and empty. It was four-thirty in the morning, she didn't expect the house to be this quiet. Heading up the stairs, she still only felt the peace and quiet of the house, no sound or movement. Rubbing her eyes, she thought she may be able to sleep through the blood lust.

She got to the point between her room and the bathroom and decided a bath sounded amazing. Closing her eyes, she thought about whether she needed anything in her room but decided grabbing a towel from the closet was enough. The house was so quiet, it felt like no one was around.

Entering the bathroom, she hung the towel on the bar and turned on the hot water. Her hands were shaking with her need for blood. The bath would help until she found one of the donors. In the cupboard there were some bath salts, smelling them, one smelled like mint, feeing her muscles relax at the smell, she spilled some in. She turned off the water and stepped in.

Sinking into the warm water, she breathed deeply as her body shook. The minty smell infused her mind and body as she tried to stop her need for blood, just for a few hours.

She closed her eyes and let her body lie suspended in the warm water.

Why was her need for blood this strong? Thinking back, she realized her last fix was with Rowan ... not good enough. She'd been so busy; she'd forgotten that had only been a stop gap. She needed human blood, a donor. How could she forget?

Her mind flitted over the day, coming up with a plan on how she'd help Ginger. She knew she'd have help, but she wanted to make sure she was there for her friend as well. There was also Jen's interview in a few hours. Jen had to be told about Ginger and hearing it from a friend was important.

Then there was Lucas and her languages. She wondered if Rowan knew any of the old tongue or was interested in learning as well.

She took a breath and debated getting out of the tub, but her legs still twitched. She was about to give up and head back to her room when a hand covered her mouth, and a needle was pushed into her arm.

Chapter 33

Casey woke up and groaned. She recognized instantly where she was, the chains around her arms and legs, and when she moved her neck, she could feel the collar. The cramping in her belly told her that silver didn't put a damper on the need for blood. Anger flooded through her. *Damn it! I'm going to kill him!*

She closed her eyes and was about to reach out to her dragon, when a soft voice spoke up. "Jude, love, she's awake. How long do we have to wait?" The voice was familiar, but Casey refused to thrash around on the bed to seek it out and confirm who it was. She also worried to much motion would cause more of her muscles to seize, so she tried to lie still and relax.

Footsteps came from the other room. As they approached, Casey thought of all the things she'd planned to do if she weren't here. She wouldn't let Jude and his pet know they had affected her at all. If she were back home, she'd wake up and have breakfast with Jen. Help her get ready for her interview, maybe even drive her out, practicing questions as they went, singing songs loudly from the radio. During the afternoon she had planned to spend a few hours with Ginger, starting to unravel the damage done to her mind. And then it was all Kailey.

First it was a small last dinner as a human, then she'd be taken up to her room with Cyran and Rowan. According to them, she'd need to sleep for the night to let her body adjust to the new blood, but in the morning they'd all celebrate the new vampire in the house. She didn't want to miss any of it. It would be her first time witnessing the transition and being aware of it.

Well, her morning was ruined, maybe she could still help Ginger and be there for Kailey. If these two would leave her alone, she could call in her dragon and escape. She just needed a few answers first. How had they gotten her and why now? Wasn't Jude leashed?

His footsteps ended with him standing over her. His hand reached down and petted her from forehead to chin. "Oh my, kitten, it's so nice for you to agree to return ... but you're so hungry. How did you get to such a state? I would never treat you as poorly as you're treating yourself. I can feed you some blood, would you like that?"

Despite trying to ignore his words, the pain of the cramping of her stomach and the twitching of her muscles were too pronounced for her to hide. His hand moved to rest on her stomach. "Do you know what will happen if you don't get blood soon? You won't die, but the pain ... it's how we used to torture our enemy vampires. Leave them long enough and you can break the hardest soul to your bidding."

Her body wanted to double over in pain, but the restraints were so tight they held her spread in an X position. He began to trace a circle around her belly and the twinges of pain followed his motion, radiating out to her legs and arms. She began to whimper.

He looked away from her. "Do you see this? It's really rather simple in the end. She isn't broken, but if we leave her for a few days, the pain will grow, and she'll do anything we want. A week ... a month, she'd be ours. If every few days we fed her a bit of blood, giving her a reprieve from the pain, eventually she'd only remember us as her saviors, not her punishers. That's the trick, pain and pleasure."

Releasing her jaw, Casey bit out. "Is this because of the silver they put on you? Are you trying to get back at me?"

His laughter filled the room like bells. The backs of his fingers tracing up her body, tracing pain instead of pleasure. When he got to her breast the sensations changed, the breast didn't have muscle to cramp, and he started to stroke. He looked over his shoulder as Casey's eyes widened, her body shooting of conflicting signals. "You see this, love. She's dumbfounded. Her body is in knots."

Leaning down he placed a gentle kiss on Casey's mouth before she could turn away. "The ring was a simple enough obstacle. The metal they put over the silver couldn't be cut, but it could be shattered. I'll let you figure out how I managed that while maintaining all my parts. My family's ability to manipulate allows for a stable of servants, some not even dear old Velvet know about."

"You removed it?"

His head shook in disappointment. "Are you always this slow?"

"And Velvet doesn't know?" Realizing she was repeating herself, Casey tried to stop asking questions, but the pain made it hard to focus. It had taken him only a couple of days to get out of his silver and somehow plan this. And he was using her as an instruction lesson for someone else, whoever helped to kidnap her, she was sure of it.

He slapped her face. The motion caused all her muscles to cramp, and she couldn't hold back the scream of pain. His voice went hard. "Now Casey. Despite how much I'd love to begin to break you, I've made a promise to my partner, and you're going to help me fulfill it."

Eyes blurry, her unfocused gaze fell to the side table and the stylized lamp sitting on it. Every inch of her body hurt, and now he wanted her to help him. Gods above, what could she do?

His voice came at her again like a whip. "Shall I slap you again, or are you going to agree?"

Arms trembling, she rolled her head to face him. "What do you want me to do? I can't even breathe without pain, Jude."

He leaned down and forced her into a deep kiss, she started to pull away, seal her mouth, but he rubbed up her side, then squeezed her breast, the sensations of pain and then pleasure caused her to gasp and then freeze in confusion. He pulled away when he was done, satisfied. "I want you to take my partner's blood. She deserves it. Do you know what she's done, kitten? She's spent the last few years spying for me. All her acting skills were used to pretend to be someone she wasn't. She even pretended to be your friend. I have it on good authority, it was all an act."

A tear escaped Casey's eye, flowing down towards her ear. *He's lying ... none of it's true!* "No, you played with her mind, it wasn't her, it was you."

"Not this one, kitten. She loves to play. She brought me so many secrets. Now, before you lot can make her one of yours, she wants to be one of mine. I could take her blood, but honestly, I don't much like the flavor of the stuff. So, you'll drink her dry and I'll give her mine. Then, my kittycat, we'll play."

There is no way she's the traitor ... it's all lies.

"What are you going to do, just throw her on me to bite? Let her have her way with me? Then have lunch and call it a morning?"

"Oh no, kitten, once you drain her, and she takes from me, she'll sleep as the transition happens, at least for a few hours. And it's early afternoon."

Casey's heart dropped; how long had she been strapped to this bed? "It's what? I thought it was morning."

Jude's mouth quirked. "No kitten, the drug we gave you knocked you out for almost ten hours. I'm going to go grab a table and we're going to eat our dinner. Well, you'll eat afterwards, a liquid diet for you tonight. Then, after the blood, you and I will play."

The voice from across the room spoke up again, soft, indiscernible. "I don't get to join in?"

Jude's focus snapped to her. "Not this time, darling, you'll be passed out."

Her voice lowered. "How about before?"

The pieces were falling into place, and anger started to boil in Casey's gut again, burning away her confusion. "I thought you said she didn't like me, or any of us from Cambia house. If that's the case," She raised her voice, aiming it at the other person in the room. "Why do you want to play?"

Jude's brow rose in warning, and the other player's voice didn't join in the conversation again. After staring over at the woman who was still human to make sure she didn't have any more comments, Jude plastered on a smile, and faced Casey. "Why kitten, you look good enough to eat, tied down to the bed, how could she not want to play." He stood. "I'll be right back with the table and chairs for our dinner. Wouldn't want you to feel lonely without us." There was a rustle of fabric as he left the room.

"You don't have to do this. There are other ways." Casey gazed at the ceiling, the embers of frustration and hate starting to build. The only answer she got was the pain from the cramping of her body.

Jude returned with a small table. He left and came back with two chairs. He finally returned with two plates of Chinese food. The smell caused more pain as Casey realized how hungry she was ... food, blood, anything and everything.

Jude sat in the chair facing the door. "Will you join me, darling?"

Casey heard the woman stand, but it wasn't until she sat that she knew who the snake in the house was ... who would betray them all.

Jude leaned over and kissed her cheek. "Enjoy your last meal as a human, Kailey."

Chapter 34

As the two ate, Casey closed her eyes trying to ride the waves of pain that flowed through her body. Her muscles twitched and her stomach cramped. The smell of the food reminded her she hadn't eaten in hours. Hunger became a new pain, an icing on top of everything else.

She tried to stay silent, but her breathing was rough, and now and then she realized she moaned with the throbbing in her muscles and head. She became aware of the silence in the room. Turning to stare, she saw Jude stand and clear the dishes away. Kailey continued to watch her mutely.

The betrayal hurt, but the pain of her muscles overwhelmed everything else. She couldn't figure out her thoughts on Kailey yet ... maybe ever. The hurt was just one more pain within her body.

Once the room was cleared of the plates and table, Jude stood over Casey and smiled down. "I assume we won't have any issues with you, kitten. You're so blood starved; I can't imagine you fighting this. There really isn't a reason to fight either, she'll be made a vampire one way or another, giving you the blood is a gift to end your suffering."

Her lip twitched in a sneer. "And to make me amiable for whatever you want to do?"

"You're tied down, what does that matter?"

There wasn't much she could argue on that point, so she stayed silent. Moving hurt, thinking hurt, she just wanted to get the next few minutes over with. He wasn't wrong that she'd do almost anything for blood.

His hand reached out behind him. "Kailey, love, climb up onto Casey so she can have access to your neck. It will hurt her, but in the end she'll be happy."

Kailey cut her eyes to Jude, then down at Casey. "Can I play a bit first? She's just lying there, all open and available."

Jude wrapped an arm around her. "No, love, every touch is pain to her. We really aren't trying for torture at this point. Once we're done turning you and she's full of your blood, then you can have free reign of her body. She'll be our plaything until one of you is pregnant with the prophecy child."

The hope in Kailey's eyes made Casey queasy and she was glad she hadn't eaten. The brown-haired beauty crawled up onto the tall bed and straddled her. Her weight felt like a blanket of knives cutting through her. She gulped in air at the sudden shock of pain. "You know Casey, I've wanted to tell you the truth for years. You're a fun fuck, but beyond that, I'm so over you. Having you tied down as a play toy where I'm in control? This is going to be so much fun."

She reached down and pinched Casey's nipples and Casey bucked up with a grunt of surprise. Then Kailey slowly draped herself down until her neck was near Casey's mouth. Casey's mouth began to water, and her teeth descended, pushing into her lower lip. A groan of need escaped her, and she felt her eyes roll back in anticipation.

Trying not to tear out the throat floating above her face, killing Kailey wouldn't get her the blood she needed, and Casey wasn't a killer. Casey opened her mouth, and, shifting up slightly to a flurry of tiny shards of pain throughout her body, she bit down. Every muscle in Kailey's body turned liquid as she draped herself fully on top of Casey. Her blood flowed over Casey's tongue like ambrosia. Closing her eyes, Casey felt the tightening in her muscles alleviated with the increase of blood. It took longer than ever for the feeling to shift from healing to pleasure, but eventually the tingling in her body morphed to desire.

An electricity of pleasure began as the blood dripped from Kailey's neck, and she recognized the scent of vanilla and cinnamon. Breathing deeply, Casey shivered, and she felt her toes curl. Drawing deeply from the woman who she once thought was her friend, her skin began to tingle and her heart beat faster. Above her Kailey began to gyrate, rubbing her body suggestively on Casey.

Unable to move much more than her mouth, Casey tried to move Kailey's neck away, but the woman pushed her neck down, forcing more blood into Casey's mouth. She continued to drink deeply. She felt intoxicated by the blood, shivers ran up and down her body, and a moan escaped her despite her attempts to stay quiet. She felt a hand slide up her inner thigh, and her eyes snapped open to see Jude standing there with a knowing smile as he began to play in her most intimate area.

His fingers began to rub her clit and she bucked up, knocking Kailey's neck more securely onto her teeth. More blood filled her mouth, a gush she had to swallow quickly, going both to her head and to a pool of sensation growing in her center, making her hot and lightheaded at once. Jude continued and as her breath got choppy. The more blood infused her system, the closer she got to breaking. Her body wanted more; it was so close to orgasm. Instinctively, she pulled more and more blood into her mouth. Kailey held on tighter, breathing suggestively in her ear, making her body vibrate more.

Jude's playing got rougher, and he slipped two fingers into her. Her vision began to darken as Kailey started to make panting sounds, she sounded close herself. Then one more push, and Jude put Casey over the top, she exploded with her teeth still in Kailey, blood filling her mouth.

Moving fast, Jude pulled Kailey from her, tearing her skin from Casey's teeth. Casey managed to swallow the last of the blood. She wanted more, needed more. Gods above, she didn't want Jude, but ... more. She was drunk on the blood, floating in a euphoric haze of orgasm, but it wasn't enough. She had to ... remember. Was she alone? Where were the others?

Shaking her head, oh gods, it finally didn't hurt, she tried to see where Jude and Kailey were. She heard them in the living room. Closing her eyes, she reached for her dragon. "Zoryda, come to me, invisible, I need help."

It didn't take long for her dragon to pop into the room. The dragon flew to the silver collar and with a magic all her own and removed it. She wrapped her tail around Casey's wrist and Casey misted to the one person she wanted ... needed ... right then.

She landed in Rowan's room, on his bed, naked. As soon as she landed, she rolled up to a sitting position, then fell back down grabbing her head, groaning, her body still sensitive. She heard footsteps running from another room. Were there more than one room up here?

From around the corner came the most beautiful woman Casey had ever seen. She was tall with strawberry blond hair. Her pale green eyes took her in before racing to her. She dropped down on her knees and grabbed her hands. "Casey, are you okay?"

Her voice. Casey looked into her eyes. "You're so beautiful. I'm sorry for ... I just didn't know where to go. He made me ... I need ... gods ... I need ... you."

With her soft hands, the woman ... no Rowan, pushed back Casey's hair and then he leaned in and kissed her. Casey melted into the kiss, falling back down on the bed as he, the original version, took off his rob, and joined her in bed. "What happened to you Casey?"

"I can't ... I need, oh gods, so much blood, so much desire ... and for you, gods you're beautiful, and your scent." His scent of spicy mint was making Casey's head spin; she wasn't sure which way was up. Pushing at Rowan's shoulders to get him on his back, she straddled him and kissed him deeply. Casey's pool of want and need boiled in her core, too hot to ignore.

She began kissing down Rowan's neck towards his chest. It wasn't large—bigger than hers, but not by much. Casey took one breast into her mouth and the other in her hand. Her teeth scrapped along the tip and Rowan arched into her mouth, intensifying the sensations. Her tongue flicked across his hardening nipple then she sucked in, nibbling. She almost swooned at Rowan's groan. After a few minutes of play, she continued down, enjoying the hard plains of his abs.

When she got to Rowan's apex, the scent of his need for her perfumed the air. Rowan already breathed heavily. Casey opened him up, licking and teasing. She thrust one, and then two fingers in Rowan. He was so wet. His need matched Casey's. Then Casey gazed up his nearly perfect body. Casey's breath was choppy. She was nearly ready to explode herself. "Can I do to you what you did to me?"

With a gruff voice Rowan said, "Yes."

Casey licked and sucked a few more times, then, centering herself over Rowan's clit, she brought her teeth down, and bit. A bit of blood filled her mouth and she thought she would come right there. It was almost overwhelmed her. Her tongue flashed out teasing as she heard sounds of pleasure coming from Rowan, music to her ears. She continued to suck and lick, earning more bits of blood, and pumped her fingers into Rowan.

It didn't take long for Rowan to buck up, screaming his release, Casey wasn't far behind. Disengaging her teeth, Casey crawled up and curled onto her side. Rowan wrapped his arms around her. "Did you get enough of a release?"

She was suddenly tired. Curling in tighter she mumbled a small agreement. But before she could fall asleep, she forced herself up. "It was Jude. Oh gods, what came over us? I have to take you there. He has Kailey ... no, they both took me."

At those words Rowan's face fell into a frown. "Are you awake enough, strong enough, to do more? You look ready to collapse."

Casey's body felt like a dead weight. "I ... I don't know. But I have to take you to him."

Rowan sat up. Kissing her forehead, he held her hands. "Can you just show me where? Give me a visual?"

Trembling with fatigue, Casey nodded. Closing her eyes, she reached out to Rowan and gave him an image of Jude's place. When she opened her eyes, he was male again. A sound of disappointment escaped her.

He leaned down and kissed her. "I know, maybe another time, but I need to work, and no one knows her." He moved through a door and a minute later returned wearing slacks and a button down. "Stay here, sleep. I'm going to gather Cyran and see what we can do." And then he disappeared.

Her stomach growled, but she didn't have any clothes. She decided she'd head down to her room, right after she tested out his pillows.

Chapter 35

She floated in a field of mint, safe and relaxed. Arms tightened around her, and she let her head fall back. Cracking open her eyes, she smiled up. "I could eat you up."

Rowan chuckled. "You're insatiable, dear heart."

"Not this time ... I was being literal. I haven't eaten ... gods, what day is it? Since before Lucas came for my lesson. I think I really could take a nibble at this point." The memories circled through her head, but, curled into Rowan, she felt safe.

His chuckle turned into a laugh. "Do you want a shower first? I grabbed some of your clothes before returning last night."

She rested her head against his warm chest. "It's so far away. Can't we eat first?"

He stiffened. "There's a shower in the other room. A private one. Currently you smell of me, Jude, and Kailey. I'd prefer not to have every vampire in the house smell that mixture on you ... it's ..."

When his pause went on, she pulled back to gaze into his face. It was closed down tight. *Maybe he isn't quite ready for people to know we're together.* She reached out and placed a hand on his cheek. "We can shower."

He nodded and, shifting to sit, gathered her in his arms. She swatted at his chest. "I can walk on my own!"

A low grumble came from his chest as he kissed the top of her head and loosened his grip. She got to her feet then followed him as he led the way to his private bathroom.

The room was tiled in white with black trim. When they walked in, they faced a vanity and mirror that took up most of the wall. Casey noticed how tired and thin she looked. *No wonder he didn't think I could walk.* To the right was a toilet and tub, to the left a walk-in shower big enough for two.

He turned to her. "Do you need to use the ..." he trailed off waving at the commode. At her nod, he walked out. "I'm going to grab some towels."

He returned when she was washing her hands. He put the towels on the counter next to her and got the shower started. Once the water was warm, they both got in. The warm water felt wonderful, sluicing away the pain of Jude's place. She detangled her hair to make sure it was wet before she reached for the shampoo. Stopping her, he rotated her away, and began washing her hair. "Have you read much on vampires and their relationships?"

The feel of him massaging her scalp made her want to purr. She tried to focus on his words, but it wasn't easy. "Um, not much. I ... oh gods that feels good." At his nonverbal cues, she leaned her head back, and he rested his hands on her shoulders, continuing to rub.

He grabbed soap and began to lather her back. "It's important you learn. Do you have any books up here?" He tapped her head.

His minty scent started to infuse the room as he rubbed her back from her neck down. He made sure to hit everywhere, and though he concentrated on private areas, it was a clinical cleaning, not sexual at all. Shaking her head to clear it, she thought about her mental library. "I ... yeah, I think I do. There's a lot in there."

He was kneeling, washing her legs. "Turn." She did and he began to clean her front. "You're driving Jen to her interview today?"

Excitement bubbled in her. "I didn't miss it?"

His motions stopped. "You missed the first, but not the second ..." He bit his lip as if he wanted to say more but stopped himself.

Her joy dampened, but only slightly. "Then yes, I want to take her."

He'd moved up to the apex of her legs and was making sure to get her clean. Again, it wasn't sexual, but slightly embarrassing. She made a squawking sound. His eyes shifted up to her face. "I just want to get their scents gone. I'm sorry. I can stop. Do you want to clean yourself?"

Biting her lip, she gazed into his pale green eyes. There was something so sexy about having him clean her, she couldn't explain it. She just shook her head, placing her hands on the tile walls for support as he continued.

His hands moved up her body, covering her in clouds of spicy mint. "I'd like you to find one of your books and read it. Then, when Sydney takes you over to Ginger later, ask Sydney questions."

Now that he was standing, she dropped her arms. Raising a brow teasingly, she asked, "Should I tell her about the shower and you cleaning me?"

He started to quickly wash himself, letting her rinse off. His voice was flat. "Yes. It will help her to know what to tell you. Though, she'll probably already know."

She froze in her motions. "Why can't you tell me?"

His breathing rough enough she could hear it, he shivered. "It's not about me, it's about us. I want you to learn, to know, to decide. If I tell you, you may choose to please me. I can't have that." He cupped her face in his hands and kissed her gently.

Their shower ended shortly after that, and they both dried off in the thick, soft towels. Casey found a yellow skirt, white button-down shirt, and jean jacket waiting for her, along with panties, no bra. Shrugging into her clothes, she found Rowan in a light gray suit. They headed down to breakfast together. Anyone seeing them would absolutely know they'd spent the night together. Every inch of her smelled of him.

When they got to the hallway outside the cafeteria, the vampires in the hall turned and stared at them with wide eyes, whispering. Casey was beginning to feel self-conscious. She saw Jen, and, pulling away, ran to her friend. "Let's get food and head out. I want to drive you to your interview."

Jen gaped at her. "You're back! No one knew where you were yesterday. What happened, everything okay?"

Nodding fast, Casey pulled her towards the food. "I'll explain everything, I promise. I just ... I really need food right now."

They grabbed plates and Casey started piling eggs, sausage, and toast on hers. Needing more, she grabbed a bowl for oatmeal and piled it high with nuts and berries, then placed it all on a table. On her last trip, she secured liquid ambrosia: coffee. She shook hard enough she worried she wouldn't be able to get the food to her mouth, but, ignoring the stares, she ate.

After a few bites, her body settled down, and she finally took a calming breath. Checking out the others at the table, she realized Rowan, Cyran, Jen, and Sydney, had all joined her. With a sheepish smile she put down her fork. She faced Jen. "I was taken again. I haven't eaten since the last time you saw me. I'm just really hungry."

Jen froze. "Who took you? Are you okay? Did they take Kailey, too?"

Continuing to eat, Casey looked at Cyran, the head of security. His eyes were sad as he watched her eat. Guilt stabbed her gut knowing he wanted more from her than she could give. She didn't understand what was happening between her and Rowan, but she couldn't give Cyran the depth of a relationship he desired.

He nodded at her and took over the story. "We didn't find anyone in the room where you were held captive, Casey. They'd both misted away. We can only assume once Jude realized you'd escaped, he took her somewhere safe."

Jen sucked in air. "Is Kailey safe? Is she a prisoner like Casey was? Can we mount a rescue for her?"

A mewling sound left Casey as Kailey's deception punched her in the stomach once again. Hunger still driving her, she continued to eat. Cyran's focus shifted to her momentarily before he continued. "We believe she's been working for Jude since the beginning. She was probably the one who drugged Casey and carried her out Wednesday night." He watched her eat. "We need your confirmation for the next part."

She sighed, draining her coffee, before sitting back. She'd eaten about half her food, and still felt empty. "She never wanted to become one of Rowan's vampires, she wanted to become one of Jude's ... not even Velvets. I think he's trying to start his own house. He said he couldn't cut off the ring, but smash it? Shatter it? I'm not sure. He said he has a host of servants that not even Velvet knows about."

A fist hit the table and dishes rattled. Jerking in her seat, she found Cyran's face was contorted in rage. "I knew he agreed to his punishment too easily from your stories. He's gone. We're going to have to set up a meeting and set trackers on him." His face softened as he peered into Casey's eyes as if trying to see into her soul. "Did he *do* anything to you this time?"

There was an uprise of protests from the group saying she didn't have to answer, but Casey held up her hands. "Wait, listen, stop, please." She finally got through. The previous evening didn't make her happy, but these people were her family, and they wanted to keep her safe. "I was blood starved. I had gotten low, and Rowan had helped me, after pulling silver out at the restaurant. The next day was busy ... and it had slipped my mind because I hadn't felt the pull. By that evening, after my lesson, I realized it had been too long, but the house felt empty ..."

Sydney's face fell. "Holy shit, girl. How much pain were you in?"

Casey huffed out a laugh, the memory still close to her skin. "Enough that it kept me safe from most things they may have done. Their immediate plan was to turn Kailey. Jude doesn't like the taste of blood, and I needed blood, they used me for her transformation. I didn't want to, but I couldn't stop myself. Once he took her away, I called in Zoryda and misted to Rowan. You know the rest."

Everyone at the table seemed to drop in tension when they realized she hadn't included him forcing himself on her ... everyone except Jen. "That bitch! She's been playing us for years."

Rowan put a hand on her arm. "Miss Clark, you have an interview. Miss Strega." He reached in a pocket and dropped a set of keys on the table. "I'd prefer if you take one of the house cars. Your car is a death-trap."

Casey's mouth dropped. "But ..."

Jen's eyes danced as she snatched up the keys. "Thanks! We'd love to."

Glaring at her friend, she mumbled, "Traitor."

Rowan's brow twitched minutely at their play. "When you two return, give the keys to Sydney who will then take you to Witch House for your meeting with Ginger."

Jen looked back and forth between Rowan and Casey. "Can I join? I haven't seen Ginger in such a long time."

Casey shrugged.

Watching them, Rowan's mouth pursed. "There are sensitive matters Casey needs to discuss with Sydney. Maybe next time."

Knowing exactly what he meant, Casey sighed at her friend. Jen shrugged back. "I'm going to go change. I'll meet you by the door in twenty?"

Looking down at her plate, she still had food to eat. Casey smiled as her friend ran off, and she dug in. "Sounds good."

A half-hour later they were driving in a dark gray Mercury Cougar, Madonna playing on the tape deck, and they both sang along. As Jen drove, Casey slipped into her glass bubble and found a book on vampire relationships and mating practices and got down to studying. She had a feeling she'd missed a lot of signals and bits in the previous days of conversation.

Chapter 36

Several hours later, they pulled up in front of Cambia House. Jen said the interview had gone great, and they'd celebrated with ice cream cones on the way home. They sat in the car and ate while waiting for Sydney to figure out they were home.

Jen reached over and turned off the music. "Are you going to tell me why you're so pensive?"

Casey tried to catch a drip of chocolate mint chip before it reached her fingers as she considered the question. "You saw me come down with Rowan this morning. I don't know if it means more than a one-night thing ... or one-week thing.

It's why he's sending me off with Sydney this afternoon, so she can explain everything to me."

Jen took a bite off the top of her butter pecan ice cream. "Is there more? Are you still thinking about yesterday with Jude and Kailey?"

"No. I mean, yes, but no. I need time to contemplate that. I'll want to take a longer hike with you in ... maybe in a week ... or a year. I mean, it sucked, but I survived. I'm letting Cyran and his security deal with the outcome of that right now ... focusing on other matters. Right now, I'm thinking about the Rowan thing ... you see, I have all these books in my mental library. I was trying to figure out what I could about vampires and their dating rules. Dumb, right?"

"Nah, it makes sense. It's cute. Did you find anything out?"

She slumped, taking a few more bites of her sugary treat. Too many clashing thoughts swirled in her mind to sort out yet. "Maybe. I think I want to work things out with Sydney before I come to any conclusions, for good *or* ill."

Jen nodded. "That's fair. If you're confused and she can help, you should get things worked out first."

As they finished up their cones, Sydney wandered out. Jen popped out of the car and let Sydney take her place. Before Sydney turned on the car, she asked, "Can we talk for a few minutes first?"

Casey bit her lip and nodded, her voice flat. "Yeah, sure, fine. That'd be great."

Sydney laughed. "You sound so excited. Let me start with this: how much do you know about vampire dating?"

Letting out a rush of air, Casey popped the last of her cone in her mouth while she thought about how she wanted to answer. She rotated in her seat to face the older vamp. "In most cases, vampires don't really date. They are free creatures. The blood they need makes them vulnerable to the people who donate. Dating a single person becomes difficult when so many of us are promiscuous."

She licked off her fingers, delaying before she plunged into the next bit she'd read. "At times, two vampires connect ... they form a pairing, maybe a bond? If this union is strong, it may transcend the flighty nature of most vampires, and they will almost act like a solidary unit. When blood is needed, they'll bring in a human, and at times have him or her join them, but more often, they send the human away after they've taken what they need."

The information buzzed through her head and her muscles tensed with stress. She shook out her hand to release her tension. She stared up into Sydney's compassionate gaze. "Did I miss something?"

Sydney nodded. "You did, child. But what you missed wouldn't be in books. When a vampire as strong as our

Rowan finds another to join with, it's pretty powerful stuff. He's not going to want to share."

Casey's head snapped up at that. "But he said—"

"I'm sure he said many things and that he believed them, but what his head believes, and what his heart can produce may be two very different things, child." Her warm hand stroked down Casey's arm.

A pounding began in Casey's head. "What are you saying ... slowly please."

"Only this. You've a decision to make. You came down this morning covered in Rowan's scent. He was telling each and every one of us that he is claiming you for his own. He's never done that before. He's never even touched another vampire from his house before. It all comes down to you. You're young, and it's a big question. Are you ready to try and focus on one person? You've been hopping beds as much as any new member of the family. If you take Rowan up on his offer, the two of you will have to figure out what that means for you."

Casey sat there mutely. Her hands clasped in her lap trying to hide her nervous shaking. Closing her eyes, she took a deep breath and relaxed back into her seat. She felt Sydney's hand on her arm, rubbing. "You don't need to decide this minute. And it doesn't have to be a lifelong commitment. The two of you have a bond, it's there for anyone to see. We all noticed it when you first came into the house, but you both seemed to ignore it, so we ignored it, too. I'm not sure what happened in the last few weeks, but it's gotten stronger. My guess is the two of you began to get intimate, share blood, have sex. That will change things, strengthen a bond. I think if you try to ignore it, you'll still be drawn to him and him to you."

Her shoulders sank into the seat as she faced out to watch the world pass by. *What do I want? Am I ready for this? I kept telling Rowan he needed to find someone to trust, and if I'm honest with myself, I hoped it was me, but am I ready to follow through with what I asked for?*

After a few minutes, she turned to Sydney and gave a quick smile to the vampire next to her. Sydney started the car to head to see Ginger. A few blocks from Cambia House, Casey began to feel centered. The confusion of ideas finally took root in her mind for her to figure out later. Pieces of conversations she'd had began to make sense. "Thank you for your information. It helps fill in the gaps and explain things. I think ... well, I have a lot to think about."

They arrived at the farmhouse and took the path through the plants towards the front door. As they walked up, Casey grabbed Sydney's hand. "They want me to move back ten to fifteen days a month. How would that affect ... everything?"

Sydney paused at the bottom of the steps. "My guess, if you two are linked, it wouldn't affect much. Once the pairing is established, much of the jealousy goes down ... eventually. I would suggest, if you decide you are accepting Rowan's offer, you don't move out right away. He'd probably follow you, and I doubt the witches would appreciate him living here."

A laugh bubbled out of her at the thought, and she shook her head, imagining the vampire head living in her small room. With her mind chugging on all her possible futures, she led the way up to the door. She gave a couple of knocks before opening the door and walking in.

She found everyone, the witches and Ginger, sitting in the front room. Sydney nodded. "I can wait in the kitchen. Is there tea or coffee?"

Zen stood. "I'm the weakest at mind magic. I'll help you out in there, find you some cookies as well."

Casey sat on the couch next to Ginger. Her friend looked relaxed. "Hi, Casey. I've been working with Hildegard. She started at the beginning, cleaning up some of my lost memories ... wanna know something funny?"

Bumping shoulders with her friend, she gave her a smile. "Always."

"Growing up, my best friend was a witch. She'd show me all her new skills and I'd help her practice. Jude had to go through and erase her entire existence when we first met. At graduation, my parents had a woman with them who I didn't recognize. She ran up to me squealing in excitement and threw her arms around me in a hug. I just gaped at her and backed away. It was her. We were best friends for our whole lives, and he took her from me to help convince me I didn't like witches or vampires."

Tears flowed down her face as she told her story. Turning slightly, Casey engulfed Ginger in a hug, trying to warm a piece of her soul that had broken over the last four years. Pulling back, she gently tried to wipe away some of the wetness. "We can call her, if you want."

Ginger sniffled, and Casey grabbed the tissue box from the small table in the center of the room. She took one and blew her nose. "We tried. She's moved and I don't know where."

Rubbing her friend's knee, Casey's heart started to break with her. "I'll talk to Cyran, see if his people can find her. Just give me her name. They're good at finding people ... okay?"

Ginger's head bobbed. "Yeah, that'd be great. I just can't believe what he did to me, made me do. Case, I don't know if I want all the memories back. I don't want to remember trying to poison and kill all those vampires. Did I do it at the restaurant, too? Gods, how many crimes did he make me commit over the years?"

Casey turned to look at Hildegard and her grandpa. Their faces were drawn, but hard. A tear flowed down Tilly's cheek. Gazing back at Ginger, Casey placed the box of tissues back on the table. "If we don't free your memories, we can't unravel everything he's done and fix it all. We need to know what he's done, and you're the key."

Body shaking, Ginger nodded. "Okay, Casey. I'll do it for you."

Chapter 37

They worked on cleaning up Ginger's mind well into the middle of the night. After they'd gotten done with as much as they could, Sydney and Casey explained about Jude and what had happened with the second kidnapping. Though she explained about getting caught, she glossed over how she escaped, not wanting to discuss her dragon around Ginger.

Guilt washed through her that she hadn't told her grandpa yet, but the whole affair had happened so quickly that the house hadn't told anyone yet.

By the time the discussion finished, it was too late to drive back. Sydney agreed to sleep on the couch. After Tilly saw a shake in Casey's hand, she offered to give her some blood so that she'd be a bit more stable. After taking a few sips from Tilly's wrist, Casey slipped off to her room for sleep.

The next morning at breakfast, Casey joined Ginger, who looked worn out. She was hugging her coffee like a lifeline. "I remember you telling me Jude was a vampire ... and about yourself."

Casey grabbed a large mug and filled it with coffee. She added some cream and sugar. "I know. I debated releasing that, but decided I had no right hiding anything, even if it'd be easier for me. Sorry about that."

Ginger gazed down into her mug, breathing deeply the aroma of the morning brew. "I was so messed up. I was mad for a real reason—you disappeared on your birthday. But god, until Jude came along, I was such a different person. I mean, not my personality, he didn't change that, but ... some parts of me. He's such an ass. But the scary thing is, I know if he gets close to me, he can do it all again. It terrifies me."

She sat next to her friend. "I know. I think my grandpa and Hildegard are working with the greater coven to find a way to help people like you. I think I could put up wards that he couldn't get through, protect your mind. You'd have to come by and let me reset them every week or so."

Ginger's eyes, moist with frustration and sadness, gazed up at her with a flicker of hope. "Do you really think you could help?"

Shrugging, Casey sipped her coffee. "I don't know. All I can do is try."

Hildegard came in and grabbed a cup of tea before joining them. "Fräulein Strega, next week Saturday is Skyler's test. You seem to have the basics down. I expect you at the barn no later than ten in the morning so we can make sure everything is set up for her arrival at eleven. Do you understand?"

Casey's shoulders slumped, but she nodded. "Yes ma'am. I'll head up on Friday. I'll probably bring a friend or two with me."

The coven leader shrugged. "That's between you and Parker. Now, I want to walk you out to the car, discuss some coven matters." Her eyes darted to Ginger.

Standing, Casey gave Ginger a hug. She looked towards the front door and saw Sydney walking down the path, already near the car. Once she and Hildegard were outside, Casey shut the door but a hand on her arm stopped her before she descended the stairs.

Hildegard gazed around the garden, staring at the flowers and plants. "You were a bit cryptic last night. Am I to understand Zoryda came at your call, even with the silver collar on, and using her own magic, saved you again?"

Casey relaxed at the topic and moved to stand by Hildegard at the rail. "Yes. What grandpa told me about calling to her worked, even with the silver on. She popped in and could use her own magic to release the collar, even while staying invisible. I think this should be added to the training, it was brilliant."

With a gentle rub down her arm, and a pat on the back, Casey found herself alone on the wide porch. The door to the house quietly shut behind her as her coven leader left with the information she needed. With a small smile, she made her way to the car, sliding into the passenger seat.

The key was slid into the ignition, but before Sydney started the car, she placed a hand on Casey's arm. "When we get back, Rowan's going to try to act civil, like he doesn't have a care in the world, but inside he'll be a mess. The choice is yours. He made his claim when he paraded you with his scent. With vampires, this is instinct; don't think he's acting like himself right now. And please, don't take too long to decide."

Casey knew the words came from a place of respect for their head of house. Sydney wasn't trying to pressure her, though it was how it felt. She'd spent some time during the morning thinking about the pros and cons of accepting what

Rowan offered. They'd been dancing around their bond for three years, talking, learning about each other, but never doing anything more. She hadn't really been conscious of it until they'd shared blood, gotten physical. But once they'd crossed that line ... gods, it was hot.

The car stopped sooner than she thought possible. Looking up, she saw they were indeed in front of the house. Getting out, she and Sydney headed in. She was hungry so she walked towards the cafeteria to grab a sandwich. Along the way, she ran into Cyran. "Case, can we talk?"

Her stomach dropping, she nodded, pausing in the hallway between him and the food.

He approached her. "Have you eaten?" She shook her head. "Let's grab something, then head to my office. We can eat in there."

They slipped into the kitchen to grab some sandwiches from the fridge, a couple of sodas, and candy bars. Working in the kitchen did have its privileges, though Monica swatted them out when she saw where Casey dug.

Cyran's office was small and tucked away in the back. He had a huge computer on his desk, buried under a sea of papers. There was a second table to the side with a printer, and a stream of paper led into and out of it in a continuous ribbon of green and white stripes.

Behind his desk was a well-worn brown leather chair. Two smaller metal chairs with padded seats and backs faced the desk. The chairs were in a dated seventies gold-and-brown-striped pattern. She took the far seat and, not wanting to get anything dirty, placed her plate on her lap. Cyran moved a bit of his ocean of papers for her can of soda.

They both began eating before any business. A few bites of ham and cheese, some soda—it wasn't enough, but his face was serious. "Okay, talk to me, Cyran."

He leaned back in his chair. "I have a few things I want to discuss with you."

She placed her sandwich plate on top of the ocean. "I have a request for you as well."

Cyran's brows shot up with his hands palm up, his fingers waggled at her in invitation. She smiled and then filled him in on her evening with Ginger and what she found out. "I know you're really busy, but if you could find her friend ..." she ended with a shrug.

He huffed out a laugh and typed a few things on his keyboard. "You have created more work for me than anyone in this house except our leader ... okay, I'll see what I can do. I guess we can start there. We've been looking into Jen's father's past. It wasn't easy, but it's there. His family goes back to Europe. We traced it as far as a farm couple ... Piero and Livia Chiara." He handed her a slip of paper with that name on it, as well as a town, and a date. "This couple filed as vampire hunters in a town with an established vampire house. They didn't put any family on their paperwork. This was common back then when they didn't want to be associated with possible vampire sympathizers."

Casey's heart beat faster as she took the paper. "You lived back then; do you know the town? Do you know the house?"

A sadness flowed over his face, though he tried to cover it with a smile. "Yes. Their farm was only a few kilometers ... sorry, miles, from Ashby's house where I lived for many years. I didn't know this hateful family, but if they had their way, all of my family would've been killed."

A shiver ran through her body. "Did you face many of these fanatics in the area?"

"More than we liked to talk about. Many of the surrounding farms were filled with them. We had several people in the house who came from the farms ... people like Rowan. Some of their families were okay with the transition, some decided the move brought shame, and it twisted them into something ugly."

She felt the color drain from her face. "You know ... that Rowan came from a farm?"

He looked at her like she was daft. "Of course. I've been with him for years. He told me about his family and how they became vampire hunters."

"Do you know more about them? Who they were?"

He sighed. "Not much. After his sisters left and married those hateful men, we followed them for a bit, but then they moved and changed their names. I never knew their new names. It was almost impossible to track them after that. We didn't have the resources we have now."

Gazing at the names, a lump formed in her throat. "What about—"

"Casey, focus on the here and now. We have other things we need to discuss."

Her eyes shot up, and she realized he was right. She slipped the paper with the names into a pocket and nodded. "Sorry, what next?"

He grabbed a second sheet. "Two things really. First of all, I have a personal question. It isn't appropriate, and you don't have to answer, but ... hell, I don't care." He began to straighten some of the piles of paper on his desk. Finally, he took a long breath. "I like you, Case. I've made that very obvious. Now, so has Rowan. I just ..." His eyes snapped to hers, sad and desperate. "Should I stop? Should I stop flirting with you?"

She froze. This was all happening so fast she didn't know what to say, to do. Her mouth opened to answer, then closed. She licked her lips and tried again. "I ..." She blew out her held breath and tried again. "I don't know. I'm so drawn to him it hurts. But I'm also attracted to you. I need to talk to him before I make any decisions, and you were there the last time I saw him."

He stood and circled the desk, shaking out his fists until his hands were relaxed. "Right. Okay." He got to her chair and leaned down, lifting her chin until they were face to face, then he gently kissed her. Backing up he took a choppy breath. "Right. I'm going after Jude. I'll tell Rowan. My sources tell me he's left the city with Kailey. It's a man hunt. I'll be leaving ... probably Monday, once I figure out who my partner will be." He turned away from her. "Good luck, Casey."

She recognized the dismissal, and it felt like her heart was breaking.

Chapter 38

She left Cyran in his office and decided she wanted some time alone in her room. Heading towards the stairs, she was shocked to run into Cynthia of all people. Vampires from other houses didn't usually visit Cambia house, especially the heads of other houses.

In her stupefaction she blurted out, "What are you doing here?" Freezing, she took a step back and lifted her hands up. "I'm sorry, I mean, hi, and welcome to Cambia House."

Cynthia laughed. "You look like you've had a rough night. We're having a meeting, one I believe you're invited to. It's starting soon, though you don't look ready for it." For the head of the information house of vampires, Cynthia was doing a great job at not being helpful.

She heard a chuckle from behind her and, checking over her shoulder, saw Sydney standing there listening in. She'd changed into a business suit while Casey was meeting with Cyran. She didn't look like something the cat dragged in.

Footsteps on the stairs had them all turning to see Rowan coming down. He spotted them standing there. "Ah, Cynthia, Casey, excellent. The meeting will begin in twenty minutes in one of our study rooms. Sydney, if you could escort our guest. Casey, if you'll join me upstairs, I'll catch you up on what you missed." He turned to head back up and she scrambled to follow.

He headed for her room, for which she was grateful. If she was going to a meeting, she'd like to dress better. Once there, he sat on her bed, and she began looking for something to wear—a black skirt, thigh high stockings, white button-down shirt, black jacket. She could manage to look professional ... thanks to some help from Ginger.

She stripped out of what she was wearing and found a garter belt. Some appreciative noises from her bed reminded her she wasn't alone. "Okay, what is this meeting about?"

A soft chuckle. "Right, I'm not here to enjoy a show. Everyone came to discuss Jude. We need you there as witness to what he said and did."

"Everyone, meaning you, Cynthia, and Lucas?" She shot a glance over her shoulder at him.

He adjusted his cufflinks. "No, everyone includes Velvet this time."

Casey froze. *Am I ready to face her and think about the last few days?* She continued to connect her stockings to her garter belt, shifting her focus from the small clips to Rowan's face. He was intent on her legs and the clips she worked on. A tiny thrill ran through her. Ignoring the need building in her, she took a shaky breath. "Velvet's coming ... here?"

His eyes traced her body, still mostly naked, up to her face, warming her. She licked her lips, trying to focus on the conversation. His eyes were dilated, burning with his own desire. His voice was low and seeped through her pores, making her shiver. "Yes. We need to discuss the fallout of the past few days."

She closed her eyes, breaking the connection. Lowering her face, she gazed at the clips, quickly getting her legwear secure. Turning her back on Rowan, she slipped on her shirt, buttoning it, then her skirt and jacket. Checking out her reflection, she tried to make her hair and face presentable, ignoring anything but her own features. By the time she was done, it was time for them to return to the meeting room.

She spun from the vanity to find him right behind her. He caught her in his arms and pulled her in for a deep kiss. Wrapping her arms around his neck, she melted in before pushing at his shoulders. "We don't have time for this."

His smile was slow. "Will you join me at that new vampire restaurant tonight, Miss Strega? I'd like to take you out on a date."

Still enclosed in his arms, breathing in his scent, her mind filled with him. She licked her lips, and, in a small husky voice she barely recognized, she said, "Yes."

They were walking down the steps when there was a knock on the front door of the house. Casey skipped ahead to answer. Opening it up, she saw Velvet. Behind her was a woman with long auburn hair and blue eyes, a bit taller than Velvet. She looked to be in her late twenties, but most vampires did since that's when most of them were changed. She and Velvet were both wearing black tank dresses that fit like second skins. She instantly felt the manipulative drag from the two and narrowed her eyes. "You'll only be welcome into our house if you turn off the power, ladies. It isn't welcome."

Velvet's mouth slowly turned up in a sensual smile. "Lovely to see you, Casey. Did you have the witches install that same backlash spell here as at their home?"

Still holding the door mostly closed, Casey's face remained blank and impersonal. "I don't need anything external to shock you if you misbehave. Now, will you and ..."

The red head held out her hand. "Gwendolyn, but you can call me Gwen."

Casey debated for a second before taking the woman's hand. If she tried to do anything, she'd knock her out cold, good relations be damned, but Gwen just shook her hand with a nice smile. "Will you and Gwen be behaving ... Velvet?"

Velvet slowly licked her lips. She said, "Why of course ... kitten."

Casey dug her nails into her palm to stay calm and held a blank face. She finally opened the door to allow the two women to enter. As she stepped back, she felt Rowan's arm wrap around her waist in support. "Welcome, Velvet. Gwen, it's been a while since I've seen you. You've slipped up the ranks rather quickly, I see."

Gwen blushed, but then the four of them made their way to the study room. Once there, they took their seats around the table, Casey, Rowan, and Lucas on one side, Velvet, Gwen, and Cynthia on the other.

Rowan stood. "I've asked for some food and drinks to be delivered in about twenty minutes. Until then, I think we need to figure out what to do about Jude."

Velvet bristled. "I don't know why you think this is something everyone needs to be involved in, Rowan. Why do you always think to take control of every situation? You aren't the king of all the vampires."

There were those words again. Back when Casey'd first met Jude, he'd told her that Rowan wanted to rule all the vampires and witches. Over the last few years, she'd learned that wasn't true. Rowan wanted humans to stop fearing what they didn't understand. He wanted the lines between the vampire families to be less deep so that much of the 'us and them' language and feelings would go away. Jude was a monster, but some of his beliefs obviously had come from Velvet.

Lucas laughed. "Why, Velvet, how *did* you become the head of your house? You are barely a hundred and fifty years old, so very young. This is why you have no control over your other master vampires. Rowan has never wanted to be king, nor have I, nor Cynthia. Your limited view of the world is showing ... now, listen, and learn."

She began to bristle, but Cynthia put a hand over her forearm. "Listen to him, he is older than all of us put together, hon. Your house has gotten us here because of your idiocy. Do you want to try to fix it, or make it worse?"

Glaring, Velvet sat back, crossing her arms over her chest.

Rowan's brow rose at her, then he turned to Casey. "Care to explain what happened to you?"

Sitting up straighter, she started when she left her lesson with Lucas and headed up to take a bath. Told about waking up in the room with Kailey and Jude, and how much pain she was in from her blood craving. Then launched into what she knew about Jude and his plans. She didn't give all the play-by-play details, but enough to let them know what had happened.

Velvet's arms uncrossed and she leaned forward as Casey's story went on. When she got to the part about making Kailey a vampire, and Jude having servants, Velvet shot to her feet. "None of that is possible. Jude has a silver ring on. This girl is lying."

Everyone in the room turned to face Velvet. Her chest rose and fell with her deep breaths as if she'd run a marathon. Her glare focused only on Casey.

Next to her, Cynthia's head tilted. "Do you actually believe what you say? Are you that simple?"

With a squawk, Velvet spun. "What do you mean?"

Her finger tapped on the table as she considered the woman standing next to her. "I have spies everywhere. The silver ring had a layer of tungsten metal. That can't be cut."

Velvet whipped a finger at Rowan. "See, I *told* you so!"

Cynthia cleared her throat. "But it can be fractured and removed. From what I understand, he had one of his people, one that you don't know about, use vise grips to fracture the ring. It took him just over twenty-four hours to get free. From there, he seems to have arranged his second capture of Casey. My spies confirmed this after the fact." Cynthia's face darkened. "Velvet, your control over your house leaves something to be desired."

There was a knock on the door and Jen came in with a tray of food and drink. She gazed at the faces around the table until she got to Gwen, then she froze, dropping the tray. "Mom?"

Chapter 39

Casey looked back and forth between Velvet's second and her best friend. There was a bit of a resemblance, but they were close in age, so it wasn't obvious. They could be sisters.

Rowan stood. "Miss Clark, Miss Calvin, it seems the two of you need some privacy. There is another study room down the hall. Why don't you two take some time to talk? The rest of us can continue figuring out what we can do about Jude."

Jen's eyes flicked between Gwen and Casey, her arms were shaking, and her face was pale as a ghost. Her mouth opened and closed a few times. She finally focused on

Rowan. "My mom died, sir, when I was eight. I don't know who this woman is. I'm sorry to interrupt you all. I can't." She spun on her heel and ran.

Gazing up at him, Casey half-stood. "Sir, if it's the same to you, I think I've done all I can here. I'd like to go help my friend."

He'd been watching the empty door, but at her words looked down. "Yes, of course, go after her. If she changes her mind, let us know. Maybe Gwen can stay here for a bit ... be available to her."

She nodded as she headed for the door. Casey saw Jen start up the stairs once she'd cleared the room. Closing the door behind her, she ran. She caught up with Jen at the top of the steps. Her friend was crying and didn't seem to know where to go. She wrapped her arms around her and let Jen cry.

Jen's body shook with emotion. "I thought she was dead." She sniffled, breathing rough, her eyes pressed hard into Casey's shoulder. "For fourteen years, Casey, and now she's sitting there. She looks ... the same." Casey's shoulder was getting warm with the wet tears. "I don't know what to say to her ... she left me ... with *him*!"

Casey thought that may have been the worst part: abandoning her daughter to an uncaring father. She held onto Jen tight as her body shook with sobs. After a few minutes, Jen finally pulled away, her face splotchy and eyes puffy. Casey said, "I know you're hurt, but don't you want answers? It's been fourteen years. There has to be a reason. You told me she was always your best friend, then she died ... but obviously she didn't."

Jen's eyes got wide again, and she smelled scared. "I can't, Casey, what if ... what if ... gods, why did she leave? What if I was too much? What if she had to get away from me? What if it's all my fault?"

Jen's words hurt Casey's heart. "I love you, Jen." Her friend trembled as she cried.

The two stood in the hall, holding on to each other, while Jen cried.

There has to be more to this story. When I met Gwen, she was the first of Velvet's family that didn't seem awful. I don't know what reason she could possibly give for the horrible treatment of my best friend, leaving her with that awful man, but there has to be something there, and something good. Casey tightened her hold, letting Jen know she wasn't alone.

"Jen, you can't be the reason she left. It has to be something more."

Her voice was soft, her face tucked tight into Casey's neck. "But what? Why? If I didn't do something awful, why would she leave me with that monster?"

"You're thinking the worst of all of this and believing it. You're only going to learn the truth from her. Let's go talk to her." Jen's trembling got worse, and her tears fell faster. "I'll stay with you if you want. I won't leave you alone. Then you'll know for sure. If it's what you believe, and I honestly don't think it is, we'll figure it out. I love you like a sister. I'm sure Grandpa will adopt you, okay?"

Jen laughed. "Okay, but I'm really scared. Why did she leave me with him?"

Casey hugged her friend again. "I don't know, but let's go find out."

They made their way back down the stairs and to the empty study room. Closing her eyes, Casey called in a pot of tea and three empty cups. Then she pulled in a plate of cookies. Jen laughed. "Wow, not a drop of tea on me. About time!"

Casey snorted. "Smart ass! I'm going to go ahead and get your mom."

The teacup stopped a few inches from the table, and Jen's attention snapped to Casey. "Gwen. Until there is proof otherwise, that woman is Gwendolyn, not my mom."

She knocked on the closed door across the hall, then poked her head in. The four leaders and Gwen all faced her. The mess was still on the floor, but there was a new tray of food and drinks on the edge of the table. She smiled at

Rowan then faced Gwen. "If you want, you can come with me. I think Jen is ready. She wants me to be in the room, though. She isn't in the best of places."

Velvet shot to her feet again, a sneer on her face. "I refuse to allow that witch to have my second alone in a room. I have no idea what plans she has, what plans any of you have. My answer is an absolute no!"

Gwen, hands shaking, placed one on her leader's arm. "Please, Velvet, that's my daughter. I have to see her ... explain things to her. She thought I was dead. It's been ... years."

"Fourteen years." Casey added helpfully.

Gwen sighed. "Fourteen years. I owe her answers. If she wants her friend there, I can't blame her. This isn't about witches and vampires, it's about a mother and a daughter. I have to go. This may be my only chance."

Velvet glared down at her second. "We can make this happen again, without the witch."

Rowan shook his head. "Maybe the daughter isn't much like the mother, but our Jen is stubborn. I'm not sure what words Casey used to make this happen, but if Gwen walks away now, I doubt she'll have another chance. Whatever story Jen has made up as to *why* her mother abandoned her, and to a pill of a man, I might add, will become lodged in her heart."

Gwen's eyes grew wide. "You've met her father?"

Rowan huffed out a laugh. "Yes, he came to their graduation party, you know the one Jude had poisoned. He was thrilled to learn that your daughter had been consorting with vampires during her years at college."

Her face blanched, and she stood, pushing past Velvet. "I'm going." She faced Casey. "Please take me to my daughter ... I have a lot to tell her."

Leading the way, Casey ignored any more complaints from Velvet as she and Gwen headed out and the door closed behind them. She was pleased that Gwen chose Jen over Velvet. That boded well for the next few minutes. When she snuck a peek at Gwen, she noticed the vampire's face had lost all its color, and she shifted as if nervous.

When they got to the room with Jen, she sat, pale and small looking, in the corner with her tea and a small plate of cookies. Gwen followed Casey in and sat across from Jen, taking a cup and pouring herself a cup of tea. Gwen's hands trembled as she poured.

Casey sat at the head of the table, there but separate. The two watched each other, tense and not speaking. After what felt like hours, but was only a couple of minutes, Casey cleared her throat. "One of you has to start things off before Velvet comes in and insists this time is over."

Gwen pursed her lips together before she nodded. "You look lovely, Jennifer. I had no idea you were living here, or even that you'd gone to college so close. Did you go to college here? Is that how you became a blood donor?"

Jen spit out her tea, coughing. She glared at her mom. "I am *not* a blood donor, which you would know if you knew *anything* about me, Gwen."

Gwen froze and looked to Casey for help. Casey stared at Jen and then back at Gwen. Jen's sadness had morphed into anger, and she seemed ready to throttle the vampire across from her. Biting her lip, she said, "Jen was my roommate my freshman year. When we met, she thought of herself as anti-vampire and witch, mainly from the way she was raised, which was pretty lonely from what I gather. When I was bitten, she stepped up and helped me."

Gwen's brow furrowed. "Helped you? How?"

Jen snapped. "I'm a trainer, Gwen, which you would know if you cared enough to not abandon me. If you knew anything about me. I trained her. First in witch practices, and then vampire skills. I was brought on to help train the new vampires here. I don't let anyone bite me; I work for the house."

Gazing back and forth, Casey realized Jen was about to explode. Her breathing sounded like she'd just run a race.

Placing her hands on the table, she turned to Gwen. "Can you explain to us how it is you're one of Velvet's vampires?"

Gwen nodded a few times before taking a bite of a cookie. "I come from a long line of vampires. Jen, so do you. Most of our family live in other cities, but we have a few here in town as well. That's why Cynthia was glaring, my mother is one of hers."

Jen and Casey stared at each other, bewildered at that news. Her mother was a vampire born from a vampire, and her father was a descendant of vampire hunters, from a line of them, though she didn't know that yet. Her anger was slowly melting away, morphing into curiosity.

Gwen finished her cookie while we let that information settle. When she was done, she took a sip of tea. "When I married your father, I didn't realize what he was. When you were two, about the time more people were discussing vampires and witches publicly, he let it slip that he came from a line of vampire hunters. Normally, I'd've told him my family history and introduced him, but at that point that was not possible ... I freaked. You were so young. I waited until you were older, but eventually I went to Cynthia. She thought because Velvet was new, I might try a new family. None of us expected her to be ... so ... green."

Jen drooped. "But why did you pretend to die? Why didn't you tell me you were alive? Didn't you know I needed you? Did I do something wrong? Was it my fault?"

There it is, Casey thought, *Jen's biggest fear.*

Gwen froze. "No, it wasn't you, sweet pea. It was your dad. If he found out about me or my family, he would have killed me, then you. He'd told me about his uncle who'd killed his daughter after she became a vampire. He was proud of his family's history of fighting what he referred to as the good fight. I had to protect you. The only way to save you was to disappear from your life. You were only eight. If I tried to let you know I was still alive, you would've told your dad, it was too big of a secret. As you got older, I didn't know when to come and tell you. I thought you might be better off without me, especially when I saw Velvet's erratic behavior. I was planning on finding Cynthia after this ordeal and discussing it with her. But then, there you were."

Jen stared into her tea for a few minutes, not moving. "I wish you'd come back for me; he was awful. I don't know how you ever loved him."

"He was good once, or maybe it was all a show to woo me. I don't know. But I'm sorry. If I could go back and do it again, I would ... even with Velvet the way she is, maybe have Cynthia protect you."

Jen sat frozen. "What if I don't want to be a vampire?"

Gwen smiled. "Then don't. I would like for you to meet your grandmother, but that can wait ... I would also like to get to know you better."

Jen suddenly laughed. "Is my great-grandma part of Lucas's family? Because then, with me living here, I'm connected to all the houses." Her eyes got wide, and a bit wild looking.

Gwen smiled. "No, dear, only the two, well, three with you here. That's a pretty amazing feat already."

As the tension dropped and mother and daughter began to connect, Casey realized she wasn't needed anymore. She stood. "I think you two are going to be okay. I'm going to go find the others and see how they are doing. Jen's head bounced. "Yeah, I think things are going good. Thanks, Case, I'll talk to you later tonight."

Leaving the two to talk, Casey headed out and ran into Rowan in the hallway. He reached for her arm and started leading her towards the stairs. "Everything okay in there?"

She laughed. "No, but they're healing. Where are you taking me?"

"To dinner. Did you forget already?"

Tugging on his arm, she directed him towards her room. "I need to change my clothes."

In her room, he sat on her bed while she rummaged through her closet. She grabbed the skirt from earlier off the floor and the paper from the pocket drifted out and fell at her feet. Rowan, seeing it land, picked it up. Brows coming together and head tilting, he asked, "Casey, why do you have my dead's sister's name on a piece of paper in your pocket?"

Chapter 40

Casey backed out of her closet with a fitted suit jacket that went just about as low as her skirt. It had a couple of buttons down the center and a hidden hook at the bottom to keep it shut. There was nothing at the top and the cut went a few inches below her chest, but she was getting used to this style. It was made of two fabrics, hot pink, and a pink and white abstract design. She striped off everything but her garter and stockings and put on the coat dress.

Once dressed, she sat next to Rowan on her bed, who was gazing at the name on the paper Cyran had given her. She'd spent the time getting dressed debating how to approach him on this matter. Grabbing his hand, she leaned into him.

Rowan smiled softly. "Livia. My younger sister. She used to crawl into bed with me when it stormed outside. She was always like my little baby. I think her hating me hurt me the worst. I ran into her once, when she was older ... she recognized me and spit on my face. That was the day I decided I wasn't going to try to be female any longer. It hadn't ever felt right, and that was the final straw. I didn't want anyone to recognize me. It took a long time to relearn how to do everything, but now that other form is so foreign to me. I don't know if I'd know how to move properly like that any longer."

Kissing his cheek, she took the paper back, and slipped it into one of her pockets. Standing, she pulled him up, and faced him. "Do I need to bring a purse?"

He smiled down, then leaned down and placed a gentle kiss on her lips. "No, not tonight. You'll be fine just as you are. Now, no changing the subject. Will you tell me about the paper?"

She took his hand. "Patience. Can we go say goodbye to Jen first? I have one more thing I'd like to tell her, and share with you, before we leave."

His movements became stiff as they headed for the door, but he agreed. They headed to the study room, hoping that Jen would still be there with Gwen. They were in luck as the two women were still talking. As they entered, Gwen looked confused, but Jen's face blossomed into a bright smile. "You look great! Heading out for a date?"

Casey came around to sit next to her friend. "Yes, but there was one more thing I wanted to tell you before this crazy day ended."

Jen froze. "I don't know how much more I can take, Case."

Taking her friend's arm in a squeeze, she gave her a smile. "I know, it's been a lot. But this will hopefully be the last." She watched as Rowan took the seat at the head of the table. Then she turned back to Jen. "I asked Cyran to trace your dad's family back, see if he could trace your family tree."

From the corner of her eye, she saw Rowan's eyes widen.

Gwen harrumphed. "Why would you do such a thing? His family is horrid."

Glaring at the interruption, Casey smiled at her friend. She pulled the paper out of her pocket and placed it on the table next to the plate of cookies. "Here is the crazy part; you dad was correct, this couple *were* vampire hunters, and they lived near the house Rowan and Cyran came from in Italy ..."

Casey stared at Rowan, biting her lip. Rowan gazed back sadly, intent on the names. He cleared his throat. "The girl, she wasn't always horrid. When she was young, she was adventurous, she loved to run and play, ride horses, and avoid all her chores. She was the youngest of five kids and didn't have hate in her heart until her oldest sibling became a vampire, and the rest decided this was wrong."

While Rowan continued to watch the paper, Jen's gaze snapped to his, her mouth dropping open in shock. It took a few tries, before giggles erupted from her. "Are you saying you're my uncle? Like my really great uncle?"

Rowan shook his head. "What I'm saying, Miss Clark, is that you and I, and probably the miscreant Casey, will all need to sit and talk. We are many generations separated, but that name on the paper that Cyran found is indeed your ancestor ... and my youngest sister." He stood, slipping his hands in his pockets. "Now, Miss Strega," his voice was serious, but his eyes danced with mischief, "if you've done enough messing about with Jen's life for the day, can we now head out on our date?"

Jen laughed and threw her arms around Casey's neck. "Holy hell, Case. I went from nothing to this in one day? Gwen wants to introduce me to my grandma tomorrow. I just ... I don't even know anymore ..."

Kissing her friend's cheek, Casey got up and followed Rowan out. He took her hand and led her to his car. He lifted her chin for a quick kiss before opening the door for her. They drove downtown to the new vampire restaurant in silence, each lost in their own thoughts. Like Cyran, Rowan was moved to the front of the line, and granted access right away. No waiting in line for the head of a vampire house. Unlike Cyran, even the humans in line recognized him and the reason for his celebrity.

They were given a private table in the back, and Casey quickly chose the items she wanted from the menu. As they waited, Rowan took her hands, rubbing his thumbs over her palms. A tiny thrill ran through her. "Casey, I spoke with Sydney, and she said she explained things to you. Now that you know more about the theory, I want to make things clear ... I want to date you. On my end, it would be exclusive. When I take blood, it rarely leads to more than filling a need. I can hold back anything physical to be shared with only you."

His mere touch was sparking a need in her. Her breathing came faster, and she licked her lips. "For the last few days, you're all I've thought about ... but I don't know if I can make the same promise about being exclusive. The call of blood ... it still overwhelms me."

The waitress came and delivered their first course. Separating their hands, she felt cold. He took a few bites before continuing. "I know. I wouldn't ask it of you. I also know that you'll be splitting your time with the witches, and I can't be with you there. When you take blood, we both know what will happen. You're a young vampire, a vampling really, and the need is still strong in you."

Despite his words, she felt like a cad. He was talking about being faithful but expecting nothing in return. She knew she was thinking like a human whereas he was approaching this like a vampire, but it still hurt.

Gazing into her eyes, he seemed to read her mind. "I'm asking for your heart and soul, Casey, and your body as often as I can have it. But I am a vampire, and I understand what you are, probably better than you do."

A heat grew in her body as she took slow shallow breaths. She licked her lips, debating her next words to him. Wiping her hands on a napkin, she held her hand out to him, and he gently placed his atop hers. With an invitation to her glass bubble, the two slid into her mind, the privacy of her safe space.

He stood in front of her, hands clasped in hers. Her head was tilted upwards so that she could see his face fully. "I brought you here so that you could see me fully. I am bare, an open book to read. In my private glass bubble, I have no secrets, Rowan." She slid her hands up his arms to his neck and into his hair. "Any question I can answer is yours."

He kissed her; the sensation felt real. "Will you be mine, Casey?"

"Yes."

Chapter 41

It wasn't until they were headed down to the first mezzanine course that Casey thought about her outfit again. When she'd dressed, Rowan requested nothing under the dress but the garter belt and stockings. She wondered, with the shortness of the dress, how many people at the bottom of the stairs could see how naked she was.

As her face deepened in color, she heard Rowan's soft laughter next to her. "Jerk." She mumbled, though she half-laughed herself. The people below were focused on other things.

She was ready for the first blood course this time. She wondered what Rowan would do. Last time Cyran left her while she navigated the blood donors alone. Standing near the center of the suspended platform floor, a stunning woman approached and offered her arm.

Some people took blood from donor's necks, but wrists were much more common.

Casey took her offered wrist, not wanting to request the neck, and brought it to her mouth. As she gazed into the woman's hazel eyes, she bit down, and blood flowed into her mouth, thick and intoxicating.

At the second pull, Rowan's left hand wrapped around Casey's waist and his right slipped into her coat, cupping her breast. He didn't do much more than gently rub his thumb over her nipple, but the combination of the blood, and the tingling of her breast made her body instantly tighten.

A third pull and she licked the wrist clean, releasing the woman. She thanked her, and Rowan returned the pleasantry before she headed off the platform. Casey stood frozen, her muscles buzzing as she held in any reaction that would give away what Rowan was doing to her body.

His mouth reached her ear. "One more, I think."

All she could do was nod as a man walked up. She could barely take in his features; she was so focused on the man behind her. When he got to them, he stood almost equal to Casey in height in her heels. With a quirk of his mouth he asked, "Neck or wrist?"

From behind, Rowan hummed, "Neck, if you don't mind."

The man's dark eyebrow shot up. "Not a common request, but we're here for you, sir. That's fine." He stepped closer and, leaning in, pressed his neck to Casey's mouth. His hands moved to her waist to help with balance.

Her breath shallow, she bit. His blood flowed in, Rowan's hand got more insistent, and then, from behind, he bit her. Her eyes rolled back, and it was only from being sandwiched between the two men that she stayed standing. She knew some of what she felt was being fed back into the man in front of her as waves of pleasure threatened to drown her.

The blood ignited her soul and Rowan was the accelerant, his scent, his teeth, his hands. In just a few gulps, fireworks went off in her mind and the only thing stopping her from screaming out was the gag of a stranger's neck.

Once her thoughts returned to her, she realized she was still attached to the stranger. She quickly disengaged and licked him clean. He smiled down at her and, with a wink said, "Any time you want someone for mezzanine fin, please, request me." Then he turned and headed off the floor.

Rowan's hand slid out from her coat, and he turned her to face him. Tilting up her chin, he kissed her deeply, there, where any vampire or person could see. Sharing blood in a place designed for it was one thing, but he was staking a claim. Then he led her back up to their table.

Once there, he grabbed her around the waist and pulled her onto his lap. Their dessert, a plate with four macaron cookies, already sat in the center of the table. His hand held her hip securely. "I have a challenge for you." His other hand slowly inched up her leg. "You can eat those cookies, love, one at a time." His hand made it to her skirt, which had slid dangerously high when she'd landed on his lap. "But, if I can bring you to climax again before you're done, then I determine the direction of the rest of the night." His hand landed and he began to play.

She jerked at his motions as need and electricity shot through her body. Gulping in air, she reached for one of the cookies, a red one. She took a bite; it melted on her tongue like a sweet cherry. As the sugar dissolved in her mouth, his thumb began tracing up and down her center, dipping in as she went to swallow.

As she leaned forward to grab the yellow cookie, he licked her neck. She paused in her motions, then shook her head. Who did she want to win? Sitting back up, she took a bite—lemon. The tart flavor shocked her brain back into thinking.

His lips came to her ear as he licked a line up her neck. "Open your legs for me, love, just a little."

She hesitated. He began sucking and licking her ear, moaning his delight in her. She relaxed into him at his sounds, and his hand moved her legs apart. With a start, she popped the rest of the cookie in her mouth and tried to get her legs back together, but his hand was where he wanted it.

He began kissing along her jaw as she reached for the brown cookie. Taking a bite, she tasted chocolate. His thumb went back to her clit, and his other hand had moved her jacket back enough that it could fondle her breast. It occurred to her that to anyone watching them, she'd seem practically naked on his lap, and the thought excited her more than she'd expected. The heat in her stirred to a fire. She bit her lip to stop any sounds from escaping.

He'd made it back to her ear, nibbling. "If you make enough noise, everyone will notice us. Just think of the scandal we'll make." Then he pinched both her clit and nipple as his teeth grazed her ear. She arched back against his arm, her vision darkening as a moan escaped her, low and demanding. Her muscles began to clench, and realizing she was losing control, she slapped her hands over her mouth.

With a sound of pleasure, he pushed her over the top, his hands keeping her from sliding to the floor as her body shook with the orgasm. Small squeals escaped her as she tried to hold her breath to stop any noise. He kept plying his pressure on her sensitive areas, seeing how long he could maintain her climax, making sounds of delight in her ear as her body jerked with wave after wave of pleasure.

When she finally slumped over, his hands shifted to holding her. She curled into his embrace, giddy from her wanton display in a public place. Casey searched the other tables and was pretty sure no one had watched, but she wasn't positive. He picked up the last cookie and popped it in his mouth. "Mmm, s'mores. My favorite." He kissed her cheek. "Shall we find our room?"

She whimpered, unable to form words. He stood and pulled her up to standing. Him leading the way, they found the correct door, with the green light above it. Inside there were two blood donors. Rowan gazed at her. "Do you need more blood?"

Thinking about it, she shook her head. "Unless it's part of some plan of yours, no."

He smiled down at her. "Not this time, love." He turned to the two. "You're free to go." The two left, shutting the door behind themselves. Rowan faced Casey. "I'd love to continue to take things slowly, but after the two shows you put on, if I don't get a release soon, I may break."

She laughed. In a few quick motions her dress was off. She started for the garter belt, and he growled. "Leave it." She looked over and saw he'd stripped just as fast, and indeed looked ready for her. He pounced. She landed on her back and wrapped her legs around him. It was fast, deep, and hot; and after the two climaxes he'd given her, she was happy to give him release.

Lying next to him, he pulled her on top of him. "Ride me."

Her eyes widened. "Already? But didn't you just ..."

He smiled. "Well, let's play ... then I want you on top, and then I want ..." His look softened as his voice trailed off.

Unsure of what he wanted in the end, she was happy to let him lead.

Casey gazed down his body and realized he was still somewhat ready for her, but he wasn't budging. She got on her hands and knees and moved so she could take him in her mouth. Her body was near him, so he started stroking what he could reach. She could taste herself on him at first, and he fit fully in her mouth. Sucking him deep and flicking the end of his cock with her tongue, she enjoyed herself, bringing him in and out. He mirrored her motions with his fingers in her. It didn't take long for him to grow too long to fully fit in her mouth, and he hit the back of her throat. His magical fingers had her squirming next to him.

He grabbed her hips and pulled back. "Enough. Ride me woman!"

With a laugh, she threw a leg over his waist and slid his cock in. He was thick and hot and filled her completely. The headboard was made of metal slats, and she grabbed one for leverage and began to roll her hips, riding him. His hands came up to stimulate her bouncing breasts, rough because of her actions, then one of his hands slipped down to her clit.

It barely had to move with her own motions doing all the work. She rubbed against his thumb, pounding herself up and down against his cock. Sweat broke out along her back and hairline. Her body felt electric, every nerve on fire, ready to explode. His sounds of joy were enhancing her joy, his minty scent an intoxicating aroma.

The pool of pleasure in her gut grew and then exploded. Her back arched and she screamed out, head thrown back. She felt Rowan stiffen beneath her as he came with her, and then she collapsed, boneless on top of him, mind blank, unable to control her body. Her head landed on his chest, and she moaned in pleasure, unable to move.

Chapter 42

Monday morning, Casey went for a walk with Jen. They headed for the hiking trails to clear their minds and move their bodies. They'd been moving for a few minutes before Casey turned to her friend. "How was meeting your family?"

Pumping her arms, Jen huffed out a smile. "It was crazy, Case. Gwen and I met her mom ... my grandma, at a restaurant downtown. She and I look so much alike, like, we could almost be twins, it was crazy. She was changed young. I'm going to be visibly older than her soon. Gwen ... mom ... already is. Give it a few years and we'll all be mixed up in our ages ... well, apparent ages."

Laughing, Casey tried to imagine the three out for lunch looking like a group of college students. Anyone listening in would be confused. "Have you thought about the offer to become a vampire? I know you've always been against the idea, but now that you know your history, both sides of it, has anything changed?"

Jen shook her head. "I don't know. I really don't. I know you've adapted, and Jaxon and I *are* happy together. He tells me he'll be happy with me no matter what I choose."

They took a turn and faced one of the larger hills of the hike. Once they got to the top, Casey's heart felt like it wanted to pound out of her chest. "You know ... if you ... do vamp out ... you have several ... options." She tried to catch her breath.

Eyes narrowing, Jen shook her head. "You need to exercise more. That wasn't that bad of a hill. Come on, wimp." She continued on the path. "I spoke with Cynthia about the families. As a teacher, if I follow Gwen, I wouldn't have to worry about feeding. There's enough teen angst in the schools to feed a family of Velvet's kin."

Snorting, Casey caught up with Jen. "That's true, but then you'd be one of Velvet's ... that doesn't seem like a great deal."

She shrugged. "I agree, though, I dunno. Velvet's an idiot. It seems like she'd be pretty easy to work around." They got to the top of the path and started moving down. "Now you. The talk around the house is you're moving up to Rowan's room ... or rooms. Does he really have multiple rooms?"

Their pace quickened with their descent. "He does. A bedroom, walk in closet, bathroom, office, and extra room, which is just used for storage. He said if I moved up to his rooms, that could be my room for whatever I wanted. I could still keep my room on the lower floor for anything I needed, like quick blood fixes."

Jen gaped at her. "I just don't get it. He's going to be faithful to you, but you can sleep around as needed?"

Rubbing her temples, Casey tried to think of how to explain a need to someone who wasn't a vampire, didn't know the feel of blood as it hit the system. Shrugging, she just threw her hands in the air. "Next time you're with Jaxon, let him take your blood. Just once ..."

Smiling, Jen shrugged. "Maybe."

At a quarter to four, Casey walked into the police department for her interview. Sydney had driven her and said she'd wait in the car until the interview was over. Walking in, she gave her name to a woman with her hair in a tight messy bun and an ill-fitting jacket. She had a name tag that read "Assistant." "Have a seat. Officer Shade will be with you in a minute, hon."

The room was lined with orange plastic seats shaped like little cups to fit butts. Casey sat, and the cup fit her perfectly. She wondered how anyone bigger fit into these chairs. It wasn't comfortable. This room was not set to encourage long stays.

Crossing her legs, she placed her purse on her lap and read the posters around the room. "How to avoid rape." Huh. Why was it always the woman's job to avoid rape and not the men's job to not rape? "Suicide prevention line." She could get behind that help. "Runaway helpline, safe, anonymous. Call us first. We'll help you." Again, not bad. She wondered if these were in the schools as well. They hadn't been to hers.

She shut her eyes and rubbed her fingers, trying to dissipate some of the nerves coursing through her body. She really wanted this job. She let her mind wander over her relationship with Rowan. *When had my heart become his? I've loved him longer than I've admitted, but what if I'm too young ... not enough. He always has a way of making me feel whole ... complete. Maybe I do the same to him? By fighting my attraction to him, I'm taking something away from both of them.*

"Miss Strega." She jerked up and saw a man a bit shorter than her with dark, short, straight hair starting halfway back on his head. He wore a pair of dark gray slacks and a white, long sleeve button down with sweat stains in his armpits. A name tag on his shirt read "Shade." A pair of wire-rimmed glasses sat low on nose, and his shoulders drooped, as if he were tired.

Standing quickly, she held out her hand. "That's me."

With a curt shake, he dropped her hand and headed to his office. She followed before the door closed behind him. He sat behind a rectangular desk with a black phone, a pile of papers and a large computer to the side. There was a mug of coffee sitting amongst coffee rings littering the desk. "Do you want coffee?"

Licking her lips, she sat in the one chair facing his domain. "Yes, please."

"Tammy!" he bellowed. "Coffee!"

Trying not to flinch, Casey rubbed one of her ears.

He smiled at her. "Okay, Miss Strega. A few questions. The kids in lock up won't talk with a counselor if they don't feel the person understands them. How will you relate with these youths so that they'll open up to you?"

Clasping her hands, she met his eyes. "I grew up in a small town with friends and a family that never understood me. It wasn't until I moved in with my grandpa between high school and college that I really could open up and train with a coven, sir. I know what it feels like to be in a house, a group, an environment and not feel accepted."

Writing on his clipboard, he nodded. "Have you faced anything like that recently?"

She stared blankly at him; she knew her face had shown up in the papers with Rowan in relation to her graduation and disappearance. There weren't many people in the city, especially on the police force that didn't know she was a vampire. "Sir, I believe you know that, and asking me to disclose what you already know isn't legal. I've given you something you didn't know. I would think you'd be appreciative, not manipulative."

Chuckling, he looked more closely at her. "Very good, Miss Strega. Your school records are good. I've checked into your public records over the last four years since you've joined Cambia House, and you've only done work that has helped the community. You're right that I didn't know you were a witch as well as a vampire. I didn't know that that was possible. Do you want to keep that secret?"

She sighed. "I do, but I've been helping with healing the sick vampires, and only witches can do that. I'm afraid my secret will get out sooner than later. I'm hoping it will be later, but it's good you know before it comes to you on the down low as gossip, assuming I get the job."

His eyes narrowed as he considered her. "I have a slew of questions I'm supposed to ask you, but my job is taking a person's measure in an instant. I like you, Miss Strega. I'm willing to give you a trial run and see how things work out. How about you start next Monday?"

Smiling, she held out her hand and he took it. "Sounds great. Tell me when and where."

"Well, there's the rub. You'll be working two to ten or four to midnight, depending on the day. Can your busy social schedule manage those hours?"

Nodding, she dropped his hand. "I'm a vampire, Officer Shade. That should be just fine."

Chapter 43

Casey was getting used to waking up curled into another body ... however, the body next to hers seemed too soft to be Rowan. Tightening her arms, her hand slid up to feel a nice set of ... oh!

A husky voice came from the person she held. "Morning, lover. I thought you said we didn't have time this morning for play. We'd have to wait until after the testing."

Tightening her arms around Riley, she released her, rolling to her back. Riley rolled over on top of Casey and demanded a deep kiss. Pulling back, she made a sound deep in the back of her throat. "You know, I've been thinking about our talk on the car ride up here. I think staying with you and the witches when you have to move out of Cambia House sounds like fun. I moved in because of you, only makes sense to stick with you to provide blood. I know the witches will provide some as well, but then you have more options."

Sitting up, Casey gazed down at the dark and dangerous woman. "That may work, but right now I need to get ready. I haven't seen Skyler in years ... and testing her won't be fun."

"Oh, it can't be that bad. You survived your testing just fine. Want me to come and wait by the car? That way if you need protection, you have me."

Leaning down for one more kiss, Casey got out of bed to get dressed. She wanted to be a bit less flashy this time. Jeans, light blue button-down shirt, and a jean jacket. Good enough. Riley put on tight black jeans that were ripped in enough places she wasn't sure how they stayed up. A black bra and a net top. Her hair was in a spiked mohawk, and she wore thick black eyeliner and blood red lipstick. Looking at her made Casey hot.

Licking her lips, Casey smiled. "That's subtle."

Riley winked. "Makes you come just looking at me. My job here's done." Then she walked out the door to head to breakfast.

Rubbing her forehead, Casey debated her choice in blood donors this weekend, but finally followed Riley to the kitchen. Her grandpa served sausage, scrambled eggs, and toast. Despite the punk look, often associated with counterculture and disrespect, Riley was being courteous as she ate.

After the meal, they all piled in the car and headed to Hildegard's barn. They arrived just before ten, for once not the last to arrive. Casey took a seat next to her grandpa, and the group discussed what each of them would do. Only Zen and Tilly had come back from the city with her for testing, Casey being better at the mind magic than Damion and Sadie not wanting to test this time around.

At eleven, Skyler walked into the barn in a short miniskirt and green tank top. She looked stylish but tired. She did a quick survey of who would be testing her but seemed to skip right over Casey. Remembering the last few days of studying, Casey could guess the reason Skyler looked tired. Hildegard invited her into the circle to sit in the chair in the center, and the testing began.

Skyler was an earth witch. She could play with fire and water, but she was weak in conjuring and mind magic. The first six challenges flew by, as designed. Any witch who was tripped up by the first few obstacles were in the wrong coven.

As the fire and ice evaluations got harder, Casey watched fascinated. Skyler was asked to perform magic Casey hadn't been asked to do. Make fire dance across the barn without burning the paper on the floor. Make water flow against gravity in an arched design. When she got to the eighth station, Casey had to begin making her way into Skyler's mind.

Technically, Casey was assessor number ten, but mind magic was always slippery. She slid into Skyler's mind and found a brick wall. It appeared to go infinitely in all directions. Hildegard appeared next to her. Pointing to some cracks that would be easy to exploit, Casey signaled she'd go to the right. Hildegard nodded and headed left. Most of her attention stayed with the testing in the real world, but part of her mind flowed out along the expansive wall, noting all the spots she could attack if she really wanted to enter and not be stealthy.

Eventually, Skyler managed to get the ice shards perfectly spherical and rotating in a perfect circle. Casey was impressed. She didn't think she could do that, even with teaching, but she'd talk with Sadie during her time at Witch House. It looked cool ... or cold.

The ninth test was to conjure a plate with two types of cookies ... one plate. Just one. Casey almost lost her connection. Just one plate. Casey had to conjure a plate per tester, thirteen plates ... the evaluations weren't fair! As Skyler's face contorted in concentration, more cracks developed in her mental wall, some large enough to see through. And then, abruptly, there was an end to her protection, no hole needed. Casey slipped in. Once she was through the first boundary, it began growing again. A moment of lost focus was all she'd needed, and Skyler didn't even know.

Skyler's glass bubble, like Casey, held all her most precious memories and secrets. There was no reason to try to enter there. The goal of test ten was to get past her defenses and to touch the outside of the glass bubble. She wasn't a mental magic witch, the goal with her was so much less than Casey's exam.

Moving slowly, in case there were other traps, Casey watched as a plate with a chocolate chip cookie and a sandwich cookie, stamped with the brand name, both obviously store bought, popped into existence in front of Skyler.

Skyler's breathing got choppy as she gazed at Hildegard. "Good, child. Next is the mind magic. Casey's and I will race to touch your glass bubble. The first one gets to choose the first cookie."

Snorting, Casey reached out and touched the bubble. Skyler's eyes bugged out. "How is that possible? Casey's already there. But how? I didn't even ... but how?"

Hildegard glared at Casey. "Child, you have got to stop showing me up!"

Grandpa laughed. "Never! Good work, kiddo."

Pulling out of Skyler's mind, she took the offered plate. She grabbed the chocolate chip cookie and handed the plate over to the coven leader. "Tell Skyler what you saw when you were in there."

Blanching, Casey looked back and forth between the leader and the girl being tested. "Now?"

"Yes, now. This is common amongst everyone here. Everyone has to hear this, listen, and learn."

Biting her lip, Casey nodded. "Okay, you had a wall, but there were cracks in it. If it were an attack, versus something stealthy, I could've slipped in one of those. When you focused on the conjuration, you stopped spreading the wall, and I slipped around the edge, my motions being as fast or faster than you could grow the barrier in general. The more you were concentrating on other magic, the more holes there were. Lastly, once I got around the wall there weren't any other defenses."

Everyone in the circle stared at her. Hildegard grunted. "This I have been trying to tell you. Casey can get to all your centers without any work. You need to practice and get stronger."

Perry, who glared, still seeming to not like her, pointed. "I doubt she could get through my defenses, but if she's so good, why isn't *she* teaching the classes?"

With a smirk, Hildegard nodded. "Excellent question. We will see about getting her on the schedule. As for getting through your paper-thin excuse of a mental wall, you can challenge her at our next meeting, but since she's stronger than I am, I wouldn't suggest it."

That got everyone in the meeting to quiet down. The rest of the testing went quickly. Though Skyler wasn't strong, she passed. A walking stick was presented, and a dove appeared midflight on top of the rowan stick.

After the meeting, Skyler asked Casey if she could talk to her alone. Shrugging, Casey followed her back to Hildegard's house. In a back room, away from any of the public areas, Skyler's mom sat in a room with a toddler running around. The girl had blond hair, and when she looked up at Casey, bright blue eyes.

Skyler picked up the girl. "Casey, it's been three years as of yesterday—her birthday. I want you to meet Kam ... your daughter. I'm tired of being a mom. It's your turn." And with that she handed Casey the girl and both women walked out of the room.

Thank you for reading

Child of Three Halves!

Please Leave a review for this book so others know how much you enjoyed reading it.

Find more information on my books on my website

Acknowledgement

This book wouldn't have been written or become
what it is today without the help of many people. As
always, a special thank you goes out to the most amazing
people I know in the book world: Angela Grimes, Weslee
Imrisek, and Elizabeth Daly.

Once they got done with this story, helping me
make it what you've read, I of course want to thank each
and every one of you. I love to tell stories and because you
read them, I have an excuse to continue to write. Thank
you for giving me all the excuse I need to continue my
favorite side hustle!

About the Author

Harlowe Frost has been a teacher at both the high school and college level. Her parents instilled a love of reading from a young age. She grew up in the queer community. Her favorite genre growing up was fantasy and science fiction, that is, until she discovered urban fantasy and paranormal romance. What she never found in those books was the diversity in background, gender identity, and sexuality she saw in the people around her. She decided if she couldn't find that in what she read, then she would write it herself. This started her writing paranormal romance with a LGBTQ+ background.